THE DAYDREAMER DETECTIVE

MISO COZY MYSTERIES
BOOK 1

STEPH GENNARO

ONIGIRI PRESS

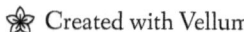 Created with Vellum

THE DAYDREAMER
DETECTIVE

This book is dedicated to miso soup. You're my favorite, miso soup. Don't ever change.

———

CHAPTER
ONE

"You're one of our finest, most industrious, and successful team members. I'm excited to be working with you. In fact, since your performance has been so stellar this past year, we're going to give you a raise."

I did my best to hide the smile on my face and kept my lips cemented in place. It wouldn't do to gloat over my success. But I worked hard for everything I earned, and I did deserve a raise. My heart beat fast as my supervisor grabbed a piece of paper on his desk and handed it across to me.

"Mei Yamagawa, are you paying attention?"

I blinked my eyes a few times, and the world around me came into focus. I was not facing my happy boss. Instead, his face was a frown.

"Yes, I think I'm getting a headache." No need to confess that I was just staring into space and daydreaming again.

My boss's office, warm and stifling, held a heady note of onions, the air inside the room stagnant and reeking of his lunch. I had never spent any time in this room. He always seemed to favor other people on the team over me. Being in here couldn't be good, so my hands were sweating as he looked across his desk to me.

He sighed. "I'm sorry to have to say this, but your performance has been unsatisfactory. Your sales have been low this past year, and other team members have complained that you don't work as hard as they do."

So much for being a successful team member in my dreams.

I opened my mouth to defend myself, but I closed it again, knowing that getting defensive right now was probably not the best idea.

"I'm afraid we're going to have to let you go. New recruits are coming in from colleges, and we need to eliminate our lower performers."

My boss expressed an appropriate amount of shame, his eyes downcast and mouth a frown. He always tried to show the proper respect to everyone on the team, even if they were below him on the pay scale. I guessed I couldn't blame him for my own lack of efficacy, though I didn't see how I was worse than other people I worked with.

"I'm so sorry," I said, bowing my head. "Is there a way you can give me a second chance? I would really like to prove myself."

"Well," he said, pausing, "we did go over your numbers last quarter, and they haven't improved since then. I'm afraid we're all out of options for you."

I bit my lip and figured this was my last chance. "Are there any project manager jobs open? I'm a much better project manager than I am a saleswoman."

Unfortunately, due to the deepening of his frown, that was it for me. "We need salespeople."

"I understand."

How did this happen? I promised myself I would improve over the summer, but the summer just dragged on and on with no new clients. Ugh. Why couldn't I catch a break?

I pinched the bridge of my nose, pushing back the impending

headache. I always got a headache when my blood sugar bottomed out, and I had skipped breakfast this morning to save money.

This was the third job I'd had in the last five years. I had obviously been delusional when I decided to work for a printing company, especially since everyone did their printing online. People with more connections would've done better than me. Managing projects was my skill, not selling them.

Back at my desk, the room was quiet with everybody out to lunch. Lucky me to be fired on a Friday at lunchtime. My stomach grumbled as I packed personal belongings into a box, the photo of my mom and the farm back home went in last, settling on top of my snack collection and books I kept for reading on the train. At least I wouldn't be forced into going out for drinks with everyone tonight. I loved going out, but I had never fit in in this office.

Stepping out into the street, I shielded my eyes from the early fall sun and hoisted the cardboard box onto my hip under my arm.

"Great. What do I do now?" I grumbled under my breath.

I wobbled off down the street, my heels uneven and falling apart, avoiding clumps of people on the sidewalk and searching for the nearest convenience store. This being Tokyo, though, I didn't need to go far.

"Welcome!" The woman at the front register smiled at me as I walked in the door. I smiled back and aimed straight for the ramen aisle. My gaze skipped over the packaged noodles and found my favorite chicken curry ramen in a bowl. I grabbed a bottle of vitamin-infused water and the ramen, paid, and filled up the styrofoam bowl with hot water at the counter by the microwave.

Hauling the box up onto the counter, I sat down, opened the bowl, and breathed in deep. I may not have had much, but at least I could buy myself lunch. I slurped the noodles up and thought about what just happened to me. I was a twenty-six-year-old failure. I had no job. My hair was a mess. My clothes and shoes were at least five years old. And now I had to look for a new job before my bank account dried up completely.

I leaned back in my chair and took a deep breath as the noodles expanded in my stomach. This was a screw up of epic proportions. I thought that doing well in both high school and college meant I would succeed in the big city. Boy was I wrong. I could only go one place now, so I snagged a few painkillers from my purse, chugged them down with some water, and headed out to home.

———

"Why are you home during the day?"

My steps shortened as I reached the front door of my apartment building. The old landlady who owned the place stood outside sorting the trash into several bins, her favorite daily chore. It was also her favorite chore to admonish people for not sorting their trash correctly.

She glanced at the box underneath my arm and sighed. "Did you get fired again?"

Was it possible to be any more embarrassed?

"Well," I said, pausing, "kind of?"

I cringed as the old woman shook her head at me. "I see you, every morning, running to the train station, always late. Maybe if you'd set your alarm earlier, you would have made it into work on time more often."

She was right, of course. I always overslept my alarm. But I hated going to my job, and it didn't make it easier to get up in the morning. Despite hating my job though, I still needed it.

"Yes. You're right. I just lost my job, and I don't know what to do next." I set my box on the sidewalk next to me and rubbed my face. Fatigue and aches from carrying the cardboard box through two trains and up the hill coated every muscle in my body. But if I hoped for sympathy from my landlady, I was mistaken.

"You still owe me two months worth of back rent." She shook her finger at me, and I stepped away from her shame. "Where are you going to find the money to pay me?"

I stammered for a moment, unable to hold back the embarrassment. I totaled up the last paycheck I would get in my head. It would cover a month's rent, but it wasn't enough to get me through the next few months without a job.

I picked up my box. "I promise to give you a check soon." Before she could answer, I swept past her and into the building. I could only take so much shaming in one day.

In my apartment, I dumped my box on my single bed and plopped down on the flimsy mattress. The room I called my apartment was barely livable. The shower and toilet were right next to the refrigerator and the one hotplate I had, and I could touch both walls if I laid on the floor and stretched in each direction. It was the efficiency of efficiencies in Tokyo. And every month, this place set me back a ridiculous amount of yen. Despair flooded over me, so I fell back on the mattress and stared at the ceiling.

With my landlady on my case, I knew I was done for. I was broke, and I didn't have a way for me to make quick money. Other people I knew had skills they could use to freelance, but I didn't. I had graduated with a business degree, and they were all into tech. I made the wrong choice there. On the floor beside my bed sat a pile of overdue bills that I stepped over every day and ignored. The only one I paid regularly was my phone because I couldn't live without the Internet. The Internet kept me sane most days. That and a good book.

I took my phone out of my bag, and I navigated to my bank's app. I had just enough money to pay a few bills and then cancel the services. At least that was something.

My phone rang in my hands, the screen flashing "Mom." My

finger hovered over the answer icon, not sure if I should pick it up. Normally, she left voicemail, and I returned her call after work. And if I answered now, she would know I wasn't in the office. I hesitated long enough that the call went to voicemail, and I set it down on the bed. I took a deep breath and held it, listening to the noise of the street outside and the clink of bottles in the recycling as the landlady continued to sort the trash. My life encompassed a tiny room in the city, no job, and a stack of bills.

The screen on my phone lit up with the notification of a new voicemail. I swiped the screen on and listened to my mother's voice. *"Hi Mei. I was wondering if you wanted to come home this weekend? The fall harvest is starting to come in, and I could use a little help around the house. Let me know if you can make it up on the train. Talk to you soon."*

I shut off the phone and stared at my empty refrigerator across the room. My life had spiraled out of control and I knew my mom would be ashamed of me for failing so miserably. She had spent years farming fourteen hours a day to pay for cram schools, tutors, college, and deposits on my apartments. Going home to her would be the end for me. I cradled my head in my hands and groaned. I needed to figure out what to do quickly before my landlady evicted me, and she would do that in a day or two.

Still, I had no money and no options but one. Fresh air and the dirt of my hometown would do me good.

CHAPTER
TWO

packed as many belongings as I could into my giant rolling bag and booked it to Tokyo Station. If I caught the next train, I could be home by 18:00. The real problem would be navigating the crowds of rush hour with such a large bag. But once I boarded the train, I found a seat near the window for the ninety minute trip home.

Chikata, the town where I grew up, was west of Tokyo. It was a quaint little town that had seen better days. The dilapidated business district and overgrown farm fields made the place feel deserted. Like many of the surrounding farm towns, Chikata was dying out. My neighbors had migrated out of the area to find work in the city, and since they couldn't sell their farms, they left them to turn to dust. I wasn't the only one who left. Everyone my age had abandoned Chikata for Tokyo, but my mother and most of her generation stayed behind. She grew up in this town, and she couldn't leave her friends. I couldn't blame her. Look how well I did in the city.

The train pulled into the station, and I wheeled my bag out onto the platform. Only a few people exited when I did, immediately crossing the tracks and heading towards the cobbled streets of the downtown shopping district. I paused and secured my hair into a quick knot. Had I really lost my job that morning? And what was I doing back at home?

My phone sat silent in my bag, no one checking up on me, and I remembered I forgot to call Mom back. And here I was, showing up on her doorstep, with a bag packed for longer than a weekend. I sighed and loosened my shoulders. She would know I lost my job. She would take one look at me and say, "Mei, what happened?" She could read me like Chiyo reads tea leaves.

I tugged my suitcase through the streets of Chikata, looking in every window along the way. This main part of town was still doing well. A thriving tourist trade kept the local businesses alive since a prominent Buddhist temple was just north of us one more stop on the train or a bus ride up the mountain. The majority of remaining residents lived in the houses and apartments close to the station. The *omiyage* shop that had been open since I was a kid bustled with activity, tourists buying everything from tea to tiny Buddha key chains. I waved to old Minatoru sweeping up the steps outside of his building, and he waved back, bowing, and muttering kind words in my direction. I bowed too, trying to be happy-faced and excited.

Up the street near the corner, where the town divided off with the township buildings on the left and the rest of the business district on the right, a new restaurant beckoned in a stream of people. Huh. When did that open? The building used to be a seamstress shop and kimono repair business back before everyone bought their clothes in the city or online, and now an open, airy, bright eatery with a line of people waiting outside for a seat took up the entire first floor. Young couples, messenger bags slung over their shoulders, talked or texted on their phones while the sound of boisterous conversation leaked out the front door.

"Excuse me," I said, interrupting a cluster of twenty-somethings sitting on a bench outside, "how long has this restaurant been here?"

"About ten months now," a young man responded, nodding his head politely. "The chef was trained in France, and he had another restaurant in Tokyo."

"It's supposed to be delicious," the woman beside him said, huffing. "Not that we would know. We've been waiting for an hour now."

"I see." I stretched up on my toes and tried to peek in through the front window, but all I saw were heads bobbing and eating and a mostly open kitchen near the back. The place was packed. "I'll have to try it out. Sorry to bother you."

I backed away from them, kicking my suitcase out onto the sidewalk next to me. The lantern and light at the front door read "Sawayaka" meaning "fresh or refreshing." Interesting. I had never heard of the place, but I hadn't been home in almost six months. Mom usually picked me up from the station, so I completely missed this place.

At the intersection just past the restaurant, I waited for the light to turn so I could cross, daydreaming about what it would be like to own a restaurant. I imagined myself as a famous chef, conjuring up recipes, and winning Michelin stars while getting married and having a family all at once. Wow. That must be an amazing life to be creative and busy all day. Not that I could ever be a chef. I hadn't cooked anything in years.

Turning to the right, I squinted my eyes into the setting sun. About three blocks from the main intersection a brand-new building took up a whole block that used to be empty space. It looked almost complete, lights on inside, and a green triangle lit-up sign outdoors. A Midori Sankaku grocery store! I couldn't believe they were opening one here. The town's tiny local grocers had always done well without the big chains.

Sirens blared and knocked me straight out of my head. I tripped over my suitcase, falling down hard on my butt at the corner. Ow! I cringed at the pain radiating up my spine as two police cars, blue and white lights blazing and sirens wailing, zipped past me and headed out of town to the outer farming houses.

Towards my neighborhood.

The quiet town of Chikata didn't need a large police force. In fact, I think they only had five cars total. They flew by too quickly to see if I knew anyone inside. Goro, my mom's best friend's son, was a policeman in the town precinct, and I wondered if he worked a desk job or patrolled in the local *koban,* police box.

I increased my pace across the street, my heart beating faster as my legs tried to keep up with my thoughts. The family house was about a kilometer from here, past the school, the town hall, some closed up businesses, and the town's only gas station.

The sun started to set, and the road lost its sidewalk as the land flattened out. Rice fields took over the vista to my left and soy to my right. Damn, I should have called my mom and asked to be picked up, but I was only a ten minute walk from home now.

I switched my suitcase handle around and pulled my phone from my bag, dialing up Mom and hoping she was home.

"*Moshi moshi!* Mei, is that you? Is everything all right?" Mom's breath came in puffs on the other end.

"Hi Mom. I'm fine. I decided to come up for the weekend since you said you needed me. I'm on San-dōri right now walking out to the house. I should be there in ten minutes —"

"I'm coming to get you right now," she said, keys clinking in the background and a door slamming.

"What? Mom, that's not necessary. I'm only ten minutes away, and it's still plenty light outside."

Another door slammed on her end of the phone, and I heard a car engine start.

"I see police car lights at Akiko's house. I'm coming to get you and we'll go there."

The phone disconnected and I held it out in front of me. The police went to Akiko's house — Akiko, my best friend growing up and friend to that day. I threw my phone in my bag and started running home until my mother's headlights approached me from around the bend.

———

"Akiko!" I jumped out of Mom's car and slammed the door behind me. "Are you in there?" I shouted, cupping my hands over my mouth.

The two police cars waited silently outside of her home, but the door stood open and the lights blazed inside. Soft cries leaked out towards Mom and me, and a chill ran up my back.

"Maybe we shouldn't interfere," Mom said, clutching at my arm. Hadn't she just picked me up from the road so that we could get there quicker? I thought we planned to interfere.

I ignored her. "Akiko!"

"Mei? Mei, is that you?" Akiko, her eyes red and face wet with tears, poked her head out of the house, and upon seeing me, sprinted in my direction. I opened my arms just in time for her to land in them. She sobbed against my shoulder, and my mom patted her back.

"What happened, dear? Is everything okay?" My mother asked, looking between the police cars and Akiko's front door. I couldn't imagine that anything was okay.

"Dad... Dad is dead. I came home from doing my rounds, and he was on the floor. I thought maybe he passed out somehow, but his skin was cold and he had no pulse. He probably died early in the day while I was gone."

Oh no. Akiko's dad was the only parent she had left, her mom having died ten years ago from a bad flu outbreak. I looked over her shoulder and saw her brother, Tama, watching us from the front porch. His face had changed a lot in the last couple of years, and the long days as a high school teacher had taken their toll, his sunken eyes red and his hair jutted out in a million different directions.

Akiko pulled away from my shoulder and sniffed. "I can't believe he's gone. He had been doing so well lately. He even met up with his friends more often, and his stomach aches had all but ceased."

Tama came forward and took his sister's shoulders in his hands. "There was only so much you could do. He was sick for a long time, and it was just his time to go."

Akiko shook her head. "I just don't believe it. He was fine when I saw him this morning."

My gut told me Akiko was right. She had been a nurse for a few years already and had always been good at divining sickness in her patients. When we were kids, she was always the kid who could correctly identify which ailment everyone had at school. I never understood this. I hated being sick, I hated being around sick people, and I hated blood most of all. But Akiko loved everything about the human body and how it worked. She flew through nursing school faster than anyone else her age. Now she worked for a visiting nurse service and attended to the elderly and sick around town, including her father. Well, including her late father.

"He said he was going to go out and visit friends. I wonder if he even made it out of the house."

Tama shook his head. "Every time I saw him recently, he was unwell, shaking and pale. You *wanted* him to get better. That's not the same as actually healing."

Three police officers exited Akiko's home, and one of them turned off the blinking lights in each car, plunging everyone into semi-darkness before the motion sensors outside of the porch clicked on. One policeman, a rounded, barrel-shaped and tall man, approached us, and it took me a full moment to recognize Goro, son of my mom's best friend, Chiyo.

"Akiko, Tama." He nodded to each of them before he caught sight of Mom and me. "Ah, Mei Yamagawa. It's been at least a year since I last saw you. How are you?"

I inclined forward in a slight bow. "I'm well. How's your mom and Kumi?" Kumi, Goro's wife, was a sweet, young woman a year younger than me. I had attended their wedding a few years ago.

"They're both well. I'm sure they'd love to see you. Mrs. Yamagawa," he said, inclining towards my mom, no doubt addressing her formally because his coworkers hovered nearby. He saw her enough to call her by her first name, Tsukiko.

Mom directed her eyes at the house, her hands worrying together. She was friends with Akiko's father and mother, though they had been a few years older than her. I remembered how upset and depressed she became after Akiko's mother died. They used to spend their days together when they weren't working the farm, and Akiko's mom had been an avid cook, like my mom.

Goro nodded at Mom and the two acknowledged each other enough to be considered polite. Everyone turned as an ambulance arrived, lights on but sirens muted. "Are you in town this weekend from Tokyo?"

"I... Yes." I coughed to cover up my lie.

Tama, Akiko's brother, glanced my way and a warmth flowed over me from head to toe. Tama was an old flame, and his smile still had a magic spell over me. It used to be that Tama and I would sneak out after dark and meet up in the grapes arbor to make out once our parents were asleep. We had dated during my high school years, but then he cheated on me, we attended different colleges, and we hadn't spoken since. Despite the bad breakup, it never stopped me from being attracted to him. Unfortunately.

This is not the time, Mei.

"We'll have to take your father in for a postmortem exam, Akiko," Goro said, as Akiko's head dropped and she began to cry again. I pulled her shoulder to me and squeezed. "But you'll need to stay here and answer questions for a little while. We just need to double-check everything. It's standard procedure. I'm sorry for the hassle." He bowed, polite and yet forceful but empathetic. Law enforcement was a good choice for Goro. He was always good at following the rules.

I squeezed Akiko's shoulders again and leaned into her ear. "I'll come by and check on you tomorrow morning. Get some rest tonight." Releasing her to her brother, I stepped back next to Mom and gave them room.

"This is no good," Mom whispered, as she took me by the elbow and directed me back to the car. "The whole town will be crawling through here the next few days. Akiko and Tama will get no peace."

I opened the door and sank into my seat, pinching the bridge of my nose, my headache resurfacing. "I'm sure it won't be that bad. I know they were popular and all, but he was an old man. It was expected."

Mom shook her head. "You don't know the half of it. Come. Let's have dinner, and tomorrow I'll fill you in on everything."

CHAPTER
THREE

The sound of pots clanging in the kitchen brought me up from a deep sleep, and I squinted my eyes against the bright morning sun streaming in through my childhood room's window. Rubbing at my eyes, I rolled over and disconnected my phone from the charger. It was 8:30, and my mom had already been up for hours. She took care of a dozen chores every day after waking at 5:00, and by the sound of it, she was in the midst of making morning breakfast.

I curled over on my side, putting my back to the bright morning window. My email inbox was empty, work having already cut off my incoming emails from clients. All I had now were personal emails to attend to. I turned off my phone, set it on the bed, and curled up into a smaller ball. I didn't tell Mom last night about getting fired or why I came to town. Mom only cared about feeding me and sending me to bed. Akiko's father's death had shocked us both.

My futon shifted and a soft head rubbed along my back, purring. Mimoji had come to see me. "Hey Kitty, come to wake me up?" My mom's orange cat purred as I rolled over. His yellow eyes gazed deep into mine before he head-butted me straight in the face. I laughed and swiped the fur from my mouth. "Okay, okay. I'll get up."

It had been a few months since I stayed at home for more than an afternoon. Sometimes I only had enough time to drop by for dinner. I hadn't spent the night in this room in at least a year, maybe two. When I got up from my spot in the bed, Mimoji burrowed into the warm blankets I left behind. Of course. It was the reason he got me up anyway.

My rolling bag, parked next to my old desk, contained all my traveling clothes, so I unzipped my bag and threw on a *yukata* before going to see Mom in the kitchen. I didn't know where my house slippers were, so barefoot would have to do. I nudged open my bedroom door and made my way down the long hall towards the kitchen. Sliding the soles of my feet over the warm, wood floors brought a comfort I hadn't felt in a long time.

This was our family house, the house my parents inherited from their parents who inherited it from theirs and so on. After my father had died, my mother had had the entire farmhouse updated. The rooms stayed warmer in the winter and cooler in the summer, and the kitchen and bathrooms were renovated. What used to be a creaky old Japanese farmhouse was now a modern homestead, even with Wi-Fi. Someday when my mother died, this house would go to my older brother, even though he had no use for it anymore. He did fine with his businesses in Osaka.

"Mei, I'm sorry. I didn't want to wake you." Mom stirred rice in the rice cooker, bowls of miso soup steaming next to it. On the stove grill top, fresh fish smoked away. A typical Japanese breakfast.

"Don't worry about it. I should've been up an hour ago anyway. I know you wanted help with the chores this weekend, and I slept through the morning work. Sorry." I yawned as I crossed the kitchen. "Do you want me to bring this to the dining room?"

"Yes, please." She pointed to the bowls of soup, so I loaded up a tray with the soup, rice, and chopsticks, and I carried everything into the dining room, a small room off the front of the house. The long table could seat at least a dozen people on their knees, but when it was just Mom and me, we sat at one end.

As I unloaded the tray onto the table, Mom entered with a heavy sigh, carrying the fish. "I picked a lot of potatoes this morning, and the second planting of greens need to be picked this afternoon. There's always too much work in the autumn!" She laughed as she sat down next to me. *"Itadakimasu!"* We chimed the usual before-meal prayer, and she clapped her hands once and bowed to the food on the table. I closed my eyes and followed suit.

We both started with the rice and miso soup, and Mom stayed quiet for some time. She looked between me, the food, and the window that pointed towards Akiko's house. "I wonder how Akiko is doing today. Do you think she got any sleep last night?"

"Probably not." Akiko had always been a little anxious growing up, and I doubted she could easily sleep after what happened.

"So, do you want to tell me why you're really here?"

I spluttered in my soup, trying not to choke on it. Great. What had I said to give myself away? She took one look at me and knew.

"I'm here to help out just like you asked me to."

She huffed. "I asked you to come in the spring too, but you only came for a few hours. It's not like you to stay for a whole weekend." She set down her chopsticks and narrowed her eyes at me. "You lost your job, didn't you?"

I only stared at her. I imagined laughing or smiling and waving my hand, telling her that she was crazy, of course I didn't lose my job. I was great at my job. But those thoughts were only dreams in my head.

I set down my chopsticks and dropped my head. "I was let go yesterday. I guess I'm just not good at selling things."

"Of course you're not good at sales. I could've told you that years ago." Mom laughed and I sulked. "You're too creative for a sales job. You received high marks in business school, but your passion is in creating, not selling."

Mom nodded at the end of the dining room and one of my original paintings on display, the local rice fields at daybreak. I did love that painting, and I had loved to paint, but who was going to pay me money to be an artist? No one.

"I can dream and paint until the cows come home, but earning a living doing either of those is not going to happen. I'm a good project manager, and I'll have to work hard at finding a project management job. No more settling for selling."

Silence fell on the room as we both sipped our soup and ate rice and fish. I may have been an artist at heart, but I was a modern woman. I loved my mobile phone, my computer, the city trains, the night time fun in Tokyo, and the convenience store food. Too bad all of those required money. I ran my fingers through my wavy hair, twisted it, and let go. Mom had never cared for the city.

"Well, you could stay here for a few days while you look for a new job..."

I tapped my nails on the table and avoided eye contact.

"What else is going on?"

"Well... You see... I can't afford another month's rent in the city. And if I come home now, my landlady is going to demand the back rent. Actually, she'll evict me, if she hasn't started the process already."

Mom sighed. "How much money do you need?"

"180,000 yen to cover rent and the bills I owe." Mom's face blanched. "But don't worry about it. I'll find the money some-where." I could sell a few things and offset at least half of what I owed, but this debt spelled the end of my life in the city.

"I've had just about enough of this. I will give you the money and help you find a job."

"Mom, there's no way you'll be able to help me find a new job in Tokyo. And even if you did, you'd have to help me find a new apartment as well because my landlady is sick of me always being late with the rent." I dropped my face into my hands and rubbed my eyes. "I'm not even sure what to do anymore."

It's not like I had any marketable skills other than general business and project managing. And I didn't want to do either of those for the rest of my life. If only I had figured out my life like Akiko had, I wouldn't have been in this mess. I glanced out the window towards her house and wondered how she was doing.

"Hear me out on something," Mom said, patting my shoulder. "I know how much you love the city, but maybe you need a break. Why don't you consider staying home for a year, saving up some money, and trying again when the timing is better?"

As much as I hated to admit it, her words were sensible. I had no savings, and I was up to my eyeballs in debt. And since I didn't know what to do with myself, I might as well stay home. I was such a failure. Even though it made me sick to my stomach, I nodded at Mom, and she nodded back. If I could come up with an alternate plan in the next two days, I would talk her out of this. It's not like I'd ever be happy living in Chikata anyway. I needed to return to the city. Needed to.

"Okay then. I'll drive you into Tokyo on Monday, we'll get your belongings from the apartment, and pay your landlady what you owe. Then you can come back here and help me with the harvest this fall. You can assist me while I teach classes during the winter and seed the fields in the spring. We'll see where we are once that's complete."

I wanted to die of embarrassment. A farm girl once more.

Time to change the subject.

"I'm worried about Akiko, so as soon as were done with breakfast, I'd like to get dressed and go over to her house."

"That's a good idea. She seemed very distressed last night. I'm sure she could use a strong shoulder to cry on. Everything is about to get very hectic for her."

"Why do you say that? I'm sure Tama will handle the funeral details." I picked at the fish in front of me with my chopsticks.

Mom stared at me for a long moment. "Has she not told you about the offer on her land?"

"No. What are you talking about?"

"Well... It's not really my place..."

"Mom," I said forcefully. "Don't hold back now. It's not like you ever keep any secrets."

She sighed again, her round face deflating in a frown. "Did you see all of the new businesses in town?"

"Yeah. I saw a Midori Sankaku is almost open and a popular restaurant that had a line out the door. What does that have to do with Akiko?"

Mom dabbed at her lips with a handkerchief. "About three years ago, the town council got a great idea for revitalizing the businesses here. We have all of this space, what with all of the abandoned farms, but we didn't know what to do with it. Mayor Tajima decided to ask a few economists what could be done, and they came up with this plan that has worked in other prefectures."

I nodded and remembered Shin Tajima, the mayor of Chikata, a perfectly capable and pleasant man who'd been running the city for some time. He'd always lamented that there was nothing he could do to make people stay in the countryside. The city had pulled them in with better jobs and a more modern life, and many of them abandoned farms they couldn't maintain.

"The neighbors that own abandoned farm land have been selling their land to the town council, and the council has been consolidating it and selling it to Midori Sankaku."

"Really? What would a grocery store want with land in

Chikata?" Midori Sankaku conducted the majority of their business in the cities, with smaller stores in suburbs.

Mom gathered up the empty bowls and placed them on the tray. "They're building something on the land — a few greenhouses and administration offices. Maybe a warehouse as well. I'm not entirely sure. I stopped going to the council meetings once I decided I wouldn't need to sell my land to them."

She rose from the table to bring the dishes to the kitchen, and I followed close behind with the leftover bowls.

"Which pieces of land are being sold off?"

Mom jerked her head in the direction of Akiko's house. "Everything on that side of the road but Akiko's family and the one next her, Senahara's land."

"Daichi Senahara is still alive?" I laughed. "I thought he would have drank himself to death by now."

Mom's lips twitched in a crooked smile. "He's pickled his insides. He could live forever at this point. A few weeks ago, I was coming back from the city, and I saw him pissing in his fields with a saké bottle in his hand. He didn't even have the decency to cover up his bare butt."

We both dry heaved dramatically. "Gross." I paused to clear my head of the awful image. "Huh. I had no idea anything was going on. Akiko and I talk every other week, but she was always so busy, either working or taking care of her father. She came into the city to see me two months ago, and we didn't talk about the town at all. We gossiped about the weird medical cases she sees in her patients and that guy she was dating for a while, and then she took the last train home."

"She's probably been keeping it from you. It's been a stressful time for her family. Her father didn't want to sell the land, and the regional manager of Midori Sankaku, Fujita Takahara, has been nagging at them for months."

I placed the bowls and plates in the dishwasher and turned the water at the kitchen faucet to hot. "Hmmm, I wonder what

Tama thinks of this." I grabbed the yellow sponge, rinsed it out, and wiped down the counters without even asking Mom. When we worked in the kitchen together, we were in sync. She cooked and I cleaned. I hated cooking, and I couldn't stand most of the traditional dishes she made. It looked like I'd have to sneak in food from the convenience store once I started getting some money of my own.

"I'm not sure. Tama works and travels, and that's about it. He only came to see his father once a week, if that."

That didn't surprise me. I could hear Akiko's voice, slurred with *shochu* during our last meet up, complaining about her brother and how he never helped out around the house. But he had been that way forever, so I never gave it more than a passing thought.

Mom grabbed her gardening apron from the hook by the door and placed her hat on her head. "So, if anything, I'm sure the nagging will continue now that Akiko's dad has passed away." She grabbed a pair of cutting shears from the cubby next to the door and slipped on her gardening shoes. "I'm going out to pick *mizuna*. When I come back, we'll bring food over to Akiko's house and make sure everything is okay. Then I have a cooking class to teach this afternoon. You should come!"

She slipped out the door and left me in the kitchen.

I took a deep breath as I tossed the sponge in to the sink. Live at home again? Was I crazy?

No, I'd have to return to the city again as soon as possible.

CHAPTER
FOUR

My mom spent so much time in the fields picking mizuna that she sent me over to Akiko's house with a gift and an apology. She had to get the greens to the local store before they went bad, and she promised to drop by Akiko's house later in the evening. I arrived on Akiko's doorstep with a bundle of *mochi* rice cakes wrapped in a purple and red *furoshiki* cloth.

The door opened, and I bowed to Tama, looking like death took him last night and spit him back out that morning. "I'm sorry to bother you, but I wanted to bring you these rice cakes my mother made. I hope you and Akiko are doing okay."

Tama reached out and took the rice cakes from my hands, but he didn't step aside to let me in. "I'm doing fine, but Akiko is very upset. I think she hoped our father would live till he was two hundred." He rubbed at the stubble growing on his cheeks, his eyes rheumy and red. "She just fell asleep for a nap. She was up all night crying after the police left."

"Don't bother her then," I said, waving my hands. "She should get some rest."

Tama lifted the package of rice cakes. "Thanks for this. Your mom is such a great cook. I'm honored that she would send these to us."

"Of course. You know she loves you both." I laughed and raised my eyebrows. "It's a good thing I didn't make them. Too bad that gene skipped me by a generation at least."

Tama smiled and nodded his head. "Remember when we were dating and you tried to make me dinner? I'm just glad we didn't have to call the fire department." He laughed as I rolled my eyes at him. That was awkward. I had wanted to impress him since everyone knew my mom held the title of "world-class cook." But instead, I almost burnt the whole house down. I should have stuck to paints and charcoals.

"Me too. I'm glad the house is still in one piece." I shuffled back-and-forth on my feet and avoided eye contact with him. I could never forget he had cheated on me and made me the laughing stock of the town. But I needed to put those things behind me so I could help Akiko.

"Anyway, I'll let Akiko know that you dropped by."

"Thanks. I'll give her a call later."

As I walked down the long driveway away from Akiko's house, my stomach began to rumble. Since Mom was busy and I couldn't cook, I decided to head into town to pick up something to eat. The early October sun hung just overhead, and it was a beautiful day to be out for a stroll. I missed this, working in the city. I'd only ever had the time to walk to and from work or walk on the weekends when I ran errands. Our farming neighborhood was only a kilometer from town, and I could make it there in about fifteen minutes.

With the shining and golden rice fields off to my right, I aimed towards town and hit the convenience store next to the gas station before the main strip. I grabbed a sandwich and a drink and paid for it with cash Mom had given me in the morning. True to form, I had no money of my own.

I found a bench in the park next to the town hall and sat

down to eat. Since it was the weekend, families lounged on the grass having picnics. Their kids laughed and played while the parents exchanged plastic containers of food and talked. I remembered growing up when this park didn't exist. The town council had built it when I was in high school. During the year, the park became a focal point for all of the local festivals, including my favorite fall festival that encompassed giant floats, a nighttime party with lit lanterns, and a trip to the Buddhist temple to the north of us.

My eyes settled on the kids playing with sticks near their parents. Someday, I wanted a family of my own too, and already this one dream remained unfulfilled. I thought it would be easier to meet someone in the city where I'd have more men to choose from, but it was even harder. Most of the guys I worked with were only interested in advancing at their job, staying late, and coming in early to get ahead. No one wanted to date, and after-work drinking parties were the extent of socialization.

For a long moment, I dreamed the kids in the park were my own. I held their hands and swung them around. I called them to the blanket to sit and eat, and I sang songs with them before they ran off to play some more. Concentrating as hard on the daydream as I could, Tama popped onto the blanket next to me, a smile on his face and laughter playing about his lips as our kids ran to him and screamed for Daddy.

"Daddy! Look!" One of the little boys across from me ran to his father with a big piece of bark in his hand.

Nope. These were not my kids. Just a dream. And Tama? Really? He was my *old* boyfriend, the one who had cheated on me, and I had vowed never to go down that road again. Still, I'd liked the way he smiled at me today, even though he looked awful.

I packaged up my garbage and walked to the center of town. The Midori Sankaku bustled with activity as people inside stocked the shelves and a large banner that read "Coming Soon!"

fluttered in the wind over the main door. The new restaurant, Sawayaka, had a small line out the front door and their specials blackboard on the sidewalk boasted of the homemade ramen soup with pork and local fresh greens. My mouth watered as the door opened, and the scents hit me dead in the face. I should've saved my money and came here for lunch. I promised to remember to ask my mom about the place. She must know the owner since she was the reigning queen of cooking in this town.

Wandering the main street, I was pleasantly surprised by all I saw around me. A year ago, Chikata had been failing with more businesses boarded up than ever before. Now, a new life had been injected into it. Was this because of the Midori Sankaku and their plans for a greenhouse that Mom told me about? With a new big business in town, more people would come to this area to shop or to work. The town council and mayor had gone well above and beyond duty in trying to revitalize the town. Could I open a business here? Plenty of abandoned buildings remained empty and unused. But what kind of business would work well for me? What would I even sell? I had no idea.

"Mei?"

The voice that came from my right jolted me out of my thoughts.

"Mei, it *is* you. Wow. I haven't seen you in years. How are you?"

I froze as I tried to say something appropriate. My old high school rival, Haruka Shinaya, came out of the doorway of an elegantly designed hair salon and bowed to me. Right. This was her family's salon, both her mother and father worked here as a hair dresser and barber, and now it looked like it belonged to her. Her family had been in Chikata for over a hundred years, and I'd always wondered if Haruka would take over this business some-day. She never struck me as the type to stay in our town and cut hair for a living. She'd been the head of our class, beating me out by half a percentage, and naturally gorgeous with her long straight hair and glowing skin. She was the most ambitious person I knew, and I hated her to my core, mainly because I was jealous. Who wouldn't be? She got to hang out at the hair salon all day while I had worked in the fields before and after school. I had figured she went on after college to become a high-ranking executive in some Tokyo or overseas business, and I'd never see her again. No such luck.

"I'm... good. In town for the weekend." I swallowed the lie. I would be here forever by the looks of it. "How are you? Looks like the salon is doing well." I gestured at the window and the chairs occupied, hardwood floors gleaming and brand-new rice paper lanterns lit up along the aisle between stations.

"It is. We remodeled last year, and since we're close to the station, we get a lot of business." She smiled at me warmly, and I tried not to shrink away. She hated me in high school. Why was she even talking to me?

"That's great. I'm sure your family must be proud —" I stumbled over the last word as she lifted her left hand to sweep her bangs out of her face. "Wow. That's a beautiful ring. Are you married?"

Jealousy burned in my chest. Of course, she was married, probably to a super hot man who's rich and talented and...

"Engaged," she said, clearing her throat. I'm glad I hadn't gotten any further into my imagination. "We're engaged."

"Ah, well, congratulations." I bowed to her to cover up my dumbfounded reaction to something I should have seen ten thousand kilometers away. "That's excellent news. Who's the lucky guy?"

Please don't see how I'm faking this. I want to be a better person than this.

"Oh. You don't know."

All the blood drained from my face. How could I know?

"Tama and I are getting married next year."

My failure was complete. The only way to save myself now

was to get back to the city and into the good graces of my land-lady, pay my rent, and find a new job. I couldn't stay here now.

She wrung her hands together at the sight of my obvious discomfort, my face white and brow sweating. "We started dating earlier this year. It's really kind of funny how it happened..." She cleared her throat. "Anyway, I have to get back inside and rinse someone out. It was good seeing you." She bowed again, a slight twist of her lips enough to show me she was pleased with herself, and the place she put me in.

Always second best.

CHAPTER
FIVE

Mom held her cooking classes in a teaching kitchen at the community center on the far side of town, past the police and fire department. She'd been teaching there for nearly twenty years, as long as I can remember and almost as long as Dad had been gone. And though the building had been updated throughout the years, her class always remained the same.

I arrived as the ladies were peeling and chopping, Mom instructing them to cleave the vegetables thicker so they'd cook up evenly once battered and deep fried. Tempura was on the menu today.

Standing outside the door so no one could see me, I took a deep breath and tried to forget the last twenty minutes. I left Haruka's hair salon and wandered about town, wondering what the heck had happened to me the last five years. How did I get so lost when I had it all? I'd done well in high school, had a great college education, an apartment in Tokyo, and a job. Granted, the apartment was the size of a bento box and the job sucked, but I had them. They were mine. Not anymore.

"Mei!" Chiyo, the tiniest woman on the planet, walked to me, her arms wide and welcoming. I snapped back from my dingy box of a room in Tokyo to the small town I grew up in. "Look at how beautiful you are! Your cheeks are so rosy, and I love your outfit." Chiyo always had the ability to compliment me, even if I had been sick and unwashed for days. Even if I hadn't slept in weeks! She could look past the dirtiest, most unkempt person and find the beauty inside of them without so much as blinking. A true gift.

"Thank you," I replied, shying under her exclamations. Other women in the room glanced up from their chopping to smile or nod their head at me. Chiyo already knew how to cook everything so she just came here to keep Mom company.

Mom was raised in Chikata, and she and Chiyo had been good friends since childhood. Chiyo's husband, a man who sold all his land when he could no longer farm due to a bad back, passed away a few years ago from a heart attack, and Chiyo moved to a townhouse. My father had died when I was five, so Chiyo and Mom lived the bachelorette life together. They cooked, gossiped, visited the temple, and even shopped together in Tokyo. Inseparable.

"Looks like tempura is on the menu today?" I followed her into the kitchen and sat beside her at her station, waving to Mom at the front of the room. On the counter, Chiyo's knife laid next to a pile of sweet potatoes and lotus roots, and a bowl full of fresh greens, probably from Mom's garden, awaited dressing.

"Let me cook for you, Mei," she cooed as she turned on the gas burner to heat up a wok of oil. "Oh, and I have a little gift for you, too." She smiled, the wrinkles around her eyes compressing like a paper fan. From under the table, she pulled out a pink and orange furoshiki, a cloth-wrapped bundle, and handed it to me.

"You didn't have to get me anything."

Inside, a red envelope wrapped in fancy gold ribbon, a selection of homemade sweets which I'm sure she made yesterday they looked so fresh, and a collection of newspaper clippings were packed in tight. I pulled out the envelope and opened it, finding six, brand-new 10,000 yen notes. I quickly stuffed them back in and rewrapped the bundle.

"Chiyo," I admonished her, "I can't take your money!" I kept my voice low so no one around could hear me.

"Shhh, I'm not giving you money. I'm paying you."

"For what?"

"I bought your painting of Mount Fuji, the one that's been in the barn for the last six years." She nodded her head at me definitively, as the color drained from my face. "I'm paying good money for it. 50,000 yen." She clasped her hands over her chest. "Oh, I've always loved that painting, and your mom said that you just lost your job. I'm so sorry."

My mouth opened but nothing came out for a full ten seconds.

"You bought my painting? But why?" It was a piece of junk and I hated it. I had stuck it in the back of the barn so I wouldn't have to look at it again. But knowing Chiyo, she'd been sneaking in there to look at my paintings. I'd tried to hide them, but I'd obviously done a poor job of it.

Her face lit up, a smile so broad I couldn't help but smile back. "I bought the local sentō! It needs a picture of Mount Fuji, and I thought it was perfect."

"Wait, wait. You bought the sentō?" Chikata's sentō, a public bathhouse, had been run by the Murita family since the dawn of time, or close to that. "Chiyo, you're fifty-five years old. Why would you do a thing like that?"

Her eyes glazed over as she stared at the wok of oil. "I've always wanted to run a bathhouse... And Mr. Murita is moving to America to be with his sons. I signed the papers four weeks ago, and I'm going to run it with Kumi. We'll have a blast."

Lucky Kumi! I hoped to see her soon. We weren't close, but I liked her a lot, and I wanted to hear more about this.

I opened the envelope again and thumbed through the money. 60,000 yen.

"You gave me 60,000 yen, but you only paid 50,000 for the painting." I tried to pull out the extra 10,000 yen bill, but her eyes widened in panic.

"No! It's bad luck to give an odd number of bills. Take the extra 10,000. It will keep away the evil spirits."

A chuckle leaked out through my clenched lips. Chiyo, superstitious until her dying day.

"Well, now I can pay my last month's rent. Thank you. And thanks for the newspaper clippings and the sweets. You know I love to keep tabs on what everyone's doing around here." I winked at her because it was so far from the truth, it might as well be in space. I'd distanced myself from the town the last five years because I believed my life would be in Tokyo.

I tried to keep my depression away while looking through the clippings. Chiyo kept tabs on everything going on here in Chikata from the Midori Sankaku opening, to their buy-up of local land, to the merits of local elementary and high school scholars, and weddings and birth announcements. I'd have to look them over sometime soon.

Akiko's father's obituary would be in the paper before long. My face fell into a frown remembering Akiko's tears and the way she squeezed me last night. My heart broke for her.

While everyone was cooking and otherwise occupied, I dug into my purse to find my phone. Looked like I'd be able to pay off a few bills and keep my phone for the time being! Thanks, Chiyo! And thanks to Mount Fuji for being such an inspiring image, I suppose.

I texted to Akiko, *"I stopped by earlier to see how you're doing and Tama said you were asleep. I hope you're okay."* I left it at that, not pumping her for information about Tama and Haruka, and why no one felt the need to tell me about anything happening around here. I didn't know about Tama. I didn't know about Akiko's father's failing health. I didn't know about this whole grocery store business and the land being sold to them.

"The Midori Sankaku is opening on Friday. Are you going to the sales?" One woman in the row in front of us asked the woman next to her. I didn't recognize either of them. They were maybe ten years older than me.

"I got the flyer in the mail," the other woman responded, a smile on her face. "So many discounts. Of course I'm going."

"Me too. We should meet up and go together."

"I'm *not* going," an older woman in the next row chimed in. "I'm going to support the smaller farmers selling at the farm stands." She nodded her head and glared at the two women, beaming shame on them from a meter away.

"But Midori Sankaku supports local farmers. They have someone who's in charge of local goods." My mother stopped her demonstration and cocked her head at the woman who planned on boycotting. "They've come by my farm several times to see if I'm interested in selling with them."

"Will you be selling with them?" I asked, surprised again that this was the first time I was hearing of this.

Mom set down her cooking chopsticks. "I hadn't decided yet. I would have to increase production and hire more people. It's a big undertaking. I already sell most of my produce to the local grocer and to Yasahiro Suga at Sawayaka."

"Isn't that the new restaurant in town?"

"It is," a low male voice said from the doorway. All the heads in the room whipped around and zeroed in on the tall, lanky man. Hello. Who did we have here? He shrugged as he smoothed out his hair, brushing it forward on his head with the palm of his hand, and then pushing his wire-rimmed glasses up on his nose. My cheeks heated reflexively as he looked straight at me since I had spoken last. I was also the youngest person in the room, by a long shot, and he couldn't be more than a few years older than me.

"Yasahiro!" my mother cried, looking from me to him and back again.

Uh oh. I had seen this look before, the I'm-meddling-for-your-own-good look.

"I'm so glad you made it. You remember my students from last week, right? Class, please welcome Yasahiro Suga again." All the women smiled and nodded or bowed, the two younger women tittering behind their hands. I rolled my eyes at them. Ridiculous. He was just a guy!

I glanced at him again and what he was wearing: skinny jeans, a short-sleeve button-down shirt with a tiny print on it, and shined shoes that came to a sharp toe. Well, he did know how to dress, whoever he was.

"I got your mizuna today, Yamagawa-sensei, and I was thinking about how to use it." He came to the front of the class and plucked off a bit of the greens at Mom's station, bringing them to his nose and sniffing. I blinked my eyes, trying to focus. I got it, fresh food was in. It was hot. But why was this man asking my mom about mizuna greens? And why was he calling her "sensei," teacher?

"Ah, class, Mr. Suga has dropped by again to talk about our local delicacies. Last week we discussed lotus root and where it comes from locally. We stir fried it with sesame and green onions most of us already grow in our gardens, and this week we're deep frying them with sweet potatoes we also grow around here. But mizuna is coming in as well this time of year. It grows in both the spring and the fall and has a mustard bite to it."

My mouth puckered in response, and he laughed at me. "Not a fan of mizuna?"

I covered my mouth and lowered my eyes. Caught.

"Not really. It's kind of bitter. I'm not a fan of fresh greens in general, though."

"No salads for you? I thought all women loved salads." His

lips quirked in a half smile, and my heart rate zoomed to dizzying heights.

"What's that supposed to mean?"

He blanched at my vehemence, frowning, his shoulders dropping. "I'm sorry. It was a joke."

I folded my arms across my chest and shot a deathly stare at him. Hey, I spent years in Tokyo trying to prove that women could be just as productive and reliable as men, working hard at jobs I hated, staying out to drink with colleagues, and sacrificing vacation days to work in the office. Even these little stereotypes about women bugged the heck out of me.

Everyone in the room froze in silence, avoiding looking at either of us. Awkward.

Mom cleared her throat. "Mei enjoys mizuna in hot pots, though, so she's not a total loss."

"I do," I muttered, some of the other women nodding in agreement.

"Then I'll cook up a hot pot for tomorrow's lunch special." He smiled warmly at me, and I looked away. "You'll have to come by and check it out."

I thought about my meager stash of cash now, thanks to Chiyo, and there was no way I would blow it on fancy food from this guy.

I didn't respond. I knew better than to open my mouth right then.

Mom and Yasahiro proceeded to show how to use mizuna greens but my phone buzzed, mercifully saving me from making a further spectacle of myself.

"Can you come by tonight? I'm a little better and would love to see you," Akiko wrote. Oh good. I blew out a long breath, glad she was feeling better.

"I'll come by with food around 17:00. See you then!"

I turned off my phone and lifted my eyes to the front of the class. Yasahiro was busy with Mom making a salad. Despite how

I had acted, I watched him closely, the strong cut of his chin and keen eyes made my heart do a dance it hadn't done in a long time.

Don't even think about it, Mei. No attachments. You're going back to the city!

I made eye contact with him and his lips jerked in a meager smile. Something told me I ruined his plan for a salad recipe for the class.

I was such a jerk.

CHAPTER
SIX

I arrived at Akiko's home around 17:00, just like I promised. I was hopeless with money and terrible at sales, but I was always on time. Punctuality was one of my strongest traits (unless I hated my job and then it took everything in my power to show up on time). Mom had packed a basket of food, tempura from class, salad, hot rice straight out of the cooker, and bottles of water, and I hefted it into the crook of my arm as I crossed the road and approached her house on foot. A number of cars were parked in her driveway, making me wonder about the other visitors she had today.

My mind wandered as I walked up the driveway. I remembered us running and playing outside as kids, racing across the grass and into the fields. Six years older than us, Tama was never around until we were in our teens, always out with friends or avoiding home. We had started dating when he was commuting to college, and I was in my last year of high school. The heady lust of years gone by knocked me sideways for a moment and I paused to catch my breath. We had dated in secret for the longest time before telling anyone. The loft in the barn was our favorite make-out spot. I lost my virginity there to him, though I wished I hadn't.

I slowed down as I passed each vehicle in the driveway, a blue BMW and a black Toyota, both nondescript and clean with no bumper stickers. I had a thing for cars; I loved them. A new model would catch my eye on the street and my head would turn of its own will and follow it. I wondered if I'd ever be able to afford a car.

At the front door, I hesitated, listening to the voices inside. Several male voices filtered through the closed door, arguing with each other.

"But this makes no sense!" Akiko's voice rose above the others in the room.

I cleared my throat and knocked on the door. Everyone inside fell silent as someone approached the front door, their shadow eclipsing the glass in the top half.

"Mei, what are you doing here?" Tama asked, a frown on his face. He had definitely gotten some sleep since I saw him last, showered, and shaved, but that didn't erase the dark circles under his eyes or the weight loss he'd experienced, probably in the last few months.

"I promised Akiko I would stop by with food. I have enough for all three of us." I strained my ears, hoping to hear more voices from the other room.

His frown twisted, obviously not ready to let me inside the house.

"She's expecting me. We texted a few hours ago."

He sighed and stepped to the side, allowing me entrance. I glanced around as I slipped my shoes off in the *genkan*, the entrance hall where all the dirt of the outside was left before entering a home. The place seemed sad and dark. The blinds were pulled on the windows and the screen doors throughout the house were closed. Incense burned in the corner shrine Akiko's father used to pray at every day, the image of Buddha staring out at the entire room. In the past, Akiko's father and mother opened up the front of the house during the summer, all the way back to the kitchen and garden, to allow movement of air and keep the house cool. During the winter, they would get out the heavier doors and bring out the *kotatsu*, a heated floor table, and floor cushions.

Now the place felt deserted and vacant, even with people here in the room. On the right, at the Kano's usual low table, sat two men I didn't recognize sitting across from Akiko.

"Oh, excuse me. I'm sorry to interrupt." I bowed to them and Akiko rose from the table to come to me. I thought she'd been crying, but anger flushed her cheeks, her jaw set and her eyes clear.

"That's okay. I'm done talking to these people," she said, grabbing my elbow and pulling me to the kitchen. Her fingers dug into my skin, painful shocks reverberating up my triceps to my shoulder. I tried to twist away but she had me firmly in her grip.

"Akiko, be reasonable," Tama pleaded, and she stopped in her tracks, turning slowly to face him.

"Be reasonable? This house, *this property,* should belong to me. I've lived here *all my life.*" Her vehemence punctuated every word with a growl. "I took care of Dad every day while he was sick. I cooked and cleaned and worked hard to keep this place functioning. It belongs to me."

Tama shifted on his feet, while the men at the table dropped their gaze from Akiko.

"Can you believe this?" she asked, turning to me. "Dad said I would get the house and the land when he passed away, since Tama is getting married, has a job, and a house of his own on the other side of town. But no!" She threw up her hands. "I just found out earlier today Dad never changed his will, and now Tama gets *everything.*"

My temper, steadily rising throughout her missive, boiled over. "That's crazy! You deserve this house."

"I do," she said, pointing her finger at the men at the table. "You are not getting my land."

"Akiko..." Tama pleaded once more, but she stopped him with a deathly glare.

"Who are these guys?" I whispered to Akiko, but they overheard me, standing up to face us.

"Miss Yamagawa," the older, graying man said, addressing me, and I pulled back in surprise, "I know your mother. I'm Shin Tajima, the mayor, and this is Fujita Takahara, regional manager of Midori Sankaku."

I swallowed past the lump in my throat. These men, dressed sharp and ready for business, sat here in Akiko's home, on a Saturday evening. This couldn't be good.

"We came to offer our condolences and speak with Tama Kano about our offer to buy the land and sell it to Midori Sankaku. Her father hinted he might be amenable to our plan before he died."

Ah. Now everything came into sharp focus. Mom said most of the land on this side of the road was sold to Midori Sankaku to build their state-of-the-art greenhouse. They must have been eager to buy up the rest so they could get on with business as usual.

"Never. Going. To. Happen." Akiko punctuated each word with a stab of her finger. "I will fight for this in court if I have to."

Both men hardened, looking sideways between them, their shoulders sharp angles.

"Please think about our offer before you do anything else. It's just an offer, not a threat." Tajima stood from his spot and Takahara followed. "We'll give you some time to think about it and come back next week after the funeral."

Akiko glared at them as they slipped on their shoes and headed out the front door.

"You're acting crazy." Tama pushed past her, huffing, his face red and angry.

"I'm being crazy? You loved this house growing up. Just six months ago, you were talking about moving back here with Haruka once you had kids. And now you want to sell it to those people?"

"I did not love this house, and it's Haruka who would love to live here, not me. They're offering *a lot* of money. We would never make the same amount selling it to other farmers."

I stepped into the shadows to avoid getting in the middle of this sibling fight. I fought enough with my older brother to know that fists can fly when people are angry enough.

"But they'll bulldoze the house, the land." She swept her arm out to encompass the last of the family land. She still farmed part of the back acreage with help from my mom, but most of it belonged to the neighbor, who had probably already sold his portion to Midori Sankaku.

Akiko's hand covered her heart, and mine ached for her. This was all she had left.

But Tama didn't care.

"Look, if you're going to fight me in court, you know they'll side with me. I'm the older sibling *and* I'm male. Property rights have always fallen to male heirs in this country. We don't even let the empress rule without an emperor."

All the blood drained from my head, and I stopped myself from launching forward at Tama's throat. What a ridiculous load of crap! Akiko obviously felt the same way because her face brightened five more shades of red. Most of the women in our generation were tired of being pushed around and marginalized in Japan. I could imagine Akiko up and leaving the country over this.

"Tama," she said, lowering her voice, "think about our mother. She would be so disappointed if this were to happen."

He bristled, shaking his head. "Mom and Dad treated me like dirt, so if anyone has any say here it's me. I deserve it."

He whirled around and headed for the front door. Shame

poured over me for witnessing such a personal, family dispute. Their parents had been hard on Tama, but I never suspected he would hold a grudge big enough to kick Akiko to the curb.

Tama swung the front door open and police lights reflected into the room. Both Akiko and I leaned forward to look out the front door and found Goro exiting his squad car in the parking lot as Shin Tajima and Fujita Takahara drove away in the BMW.

Goro hiked his belt up and straightened his tie as his female partner came around to meet him. They both stared into the house at us and Tama frozen in the doorway. He didn't have the time to beat a hasty retreat from the argument.

My neck began to sweat, dread welling up in my belly as I studied Goro. His face was set in stone, his shoulders straight, and his gait confident and precise. His whole demeanor said, "On duty."

I set the basket of food on the kitchen island and followed Akiko out into the main room. Goro and Tama spoke in low tones and Tama invited him into the genkan. Japanese sensibilities being of the utmost priority, Goro didn't come in any farther or else he'd have to remove his shoes.

"Tama, Akiko," he said, nodding to both. "Mei, I hope you're well."

I nodded, unable to speak through the lump in my throat.

"Tama, we need to bring you and Akiko down to the station with us. We'd appreciate it if you got your shoes and coats on."

"What's the matter?" Akiko's voice was so soft, Goro had to lean forward and ask her to repeat it. She turned her pale and sweaty face to me, looking for reassurance.

"We'd like to discuss it down at the station."

"Are we under arrest?" Tama asked, his voice rising.

Goro cleared his throat. "Well, the autopsy came back on your father, and we have questions about his health and his last day here in the house." Goro glanced at his partner, obviously uncomfortable. I could imagine arresting friends you grew up with would be difficult for anyone.

His partner, having no such connection to any of us, had no problem conveying the information Goro held back.

"Your father was murdered. He didn't die of sickness. Someone suffocated him."

CHAPTER
SEVEN

I woke up the morning after Akiko and Tama's arrest hoping it was all a bad dream. I put myself back in the living room of their house and instead imagined the two siblings not fighting, all of us eating dinner together, and the evening ending peacefully. Mimoji popped onto my bed and head-butted me in the face again, reminding me I was home, in bed, and last night did, in fact, happen.

After Goro's partner dropped the news, Akiko and Tama left with Goro in the back of the police car, and I stood in their doorway and watched them go. The food I delivered to them would've gone bad so I brought it home and ate alone while watching NHK dramas in the living room.

What was going on with Akiko? Her father promised her the house and land, and when she heard the opposite from Tama, her temper skyrocketed. She'd always been so peaceful which was why we were inseparable as kids. I was the overly emotional one, and she was my down-to-earth, easy-going other half. Our moms used to say we were twins separated at birth. We even made it all the way to college without having one fallout, though she wasn't happy I dated Tama because those two never got along.

How could anyone think Akiko would kill her father? She loved him. She doted on him and he on her. When he was sick on and off these last two years, she waited on him religiously. Anything he wanted or needed, she got it for him. We would often speak on the phone in the late evenings, me in Tokyo and Akiko here in Chikata, because she had no time for socialization. Some days, she longed for a shoulder to cry on or someone to gossip with, and I was always on the other side of the phone. But the last six months, she had distanced herself from me, and I had heard from her less and less. I actually thought she had started dating someone. But I was wrong. Dead wrong.

And what about Tama? Would he kill his dad? I know they didn't get along, but Tama didn't strike me as the type to smother his own father. Even though he was a jerk to me, he had been a stand-up member of the community. He taught at my old high school, ran frequent fundraisers, and volunteered during his vacations. Chiyo, the town gossip if ever there was one, had told me about his good deeds every time she came to see me. Come to think of it, she did mention once or twice Tama was dating someone new, but I didn't want to hear about it so I never asked who. I should have asked. I would've been better prepared to deal with Haruka when I saw her.

"Mei! I'm making breakfast!" Mom called from the kitchen.

"Five minutes, please!" I called back, curling around the cat.

So, if Akiko's dad was murdered, then who did it? And why?

I closed my eyes and tried to imagine the scene of the crime. Akiko's father sat at his usual table, his health failing and wrapped in a blanket. His breakfast and a hot cup of tea steamed on the table, awaiting consumption. He flipped through the town newspaper while NHK news played on the TV across the room. What happened then? If there had been a struggle, the table would have been upturned, food would have been disrupted, tea would have stained the tatami mats, and the house would have been in disarray. I saw none of that yesterday. And if the police had seen that, they would've declared the house a crime scene. They'd thought Akiko's father died naturally, and so did everyone else. So it was safe to assume Akiko's father knew his murderer. They'd probably spent time together that day and he or she had killed him when he least expected it. Or maybe they fought briefly before he was killed. Who could say?

I'd watched enough crime dramas on TV to know that the next month would be hard for Akiko. She'd already lost her father, and now her brother wanted to take away her only home. In my heart, I knew she couldn't be a murderer. She would have gladly helped her father for years and never complained.

My phone, plugged in next to the bed, buzzed. I reached past the cat to pick it up. Ugh. My landlady's name displayed on the screen as an incoming call.

"Hello?" I cringed, hearing my tired voice.

"Hi Mei, I'm sorry to call you so early on a Sunday," she said, sighing, "but it's necessary to speak to you before the weekend is over."

My landlady, always so proper and respectful, made me feel like a complete loser when I conversed with her.

"Okay..."

"You're behind on the rent over two months, and it's already the fourth of October. I spoke with a lawyer and I'm afraid I have to evict you. I'm sorry to spring this on you so suddenly."

I held the phone away from my face and groaned, keeping my tears at bay. I knew this was going to happen.

"I understand." I rubbed my face with my right hand and sat up in bed. "I'm sorry I've been such a bad tenant. I enjoyed living there, but I understand. I have the money to cover the rent."

This was it. This was the end of my big city life. My apartment, my job, my few city friends, and my fast-paced, eat-on-the-run existence were dead.

"The eviction process is long, and I don't think it would be any good for your credit. I'd like to advertise the apartment and get someone in now. So I thought, if you wouldn't mind, if you came and vacated now, I'll give you a break on the last month's rent."

Considering she had a deposit, key money, and a cleaning fee from me, I didn't think I'd set her back a large chunk of change or anything. She'd just rather have someone in the building with a regular job and a consistent income. Since my mom was my guarantor, I didn't want to bring any hardship on her either. I'm glad my landlady was letting me off the hook so easily.

"That's really generous and nice of you considering how bad of a tenant I am. I'll be there tomorrow to get my things. My mom said she would drive me in to the city, and I can pay you in cash for what I owe you."

My landlady sighed on the other end of the phone. "That would be great. I appreciate it. Miss Yamagawa, I believe you're a good person and would be a great tenant if only you hadn't lost your job. If you ever need anything, you can always talk to me."

My eyes teared up. I didn't deserve her kindness.

"You've been sweet to me. Thank you, and I'm so sorry again."

We hung up the phone at the same time. She was always nice to me, and I felt bad for letting her down. It must've been hard for her to evict me.

It looked like my plan to return to the city had failed as well. I couldn't find a new apartment without a guarantor, and Mom wouldn't do that for me again. And none of the guarantor companies would help me without a job. I was out of luck, bone dry.

I swung my legs out of the bed and scooped up Mimoji into my arms. Glancing around my room, I tried to imagine where I would put all of my belongings.

In a day's time, I'd be living at home again.

CHAPTER
EIGHT

I surveyed the eighteen meter row of vines in front of me and stretched my shoulders before slipping in my earbuds and listening to some AKB48 — not my favorite, but high energy enough to keep me going for the next hour or two. Harvesting was my least hated job on the farm, so I wasn't going to complain. I would've rather hired someone else to help with planting vegetables than hired people to harvest them. Taking a pair of shears in my gloved hands and adjusting the wide brim hat on my head, I started to snip away at the sweet potato vines. Snip, toss, pull. Snip, toss, pull. A pile of vines ended up to the side of the row as I made my way along.

"You're gonna need a better pair of boots for doing this," Mom shouted at me over my music. I turned it down, and she followed behind me with a potato fork, a large pitchfork she used to loosen the ground and unearth the sweet potatoes.

"I have old boots back in my apartment. We'll get them tomorrow." I closed my eyes and blew out a long breath, quelling anger at myself for getting into this situation. Normally on a Sunday afternoon, I'd be having coffee at a local café, reading a book, or going to the movies. I never imagined

I'd be digging up sweet potatoes and living in my old childhood room.

Snip, toss, pull. I turned up my music and threw more vines to the side. I would have to return and cut some of the vines to keep in water over the winter and replant them in the spring. Most people just bought their sweet potato slips at the store, but Mom had cultivated this crop from some of her best harvests. We always replanted our same sweet potatoes, and the local stores sold out of them quickly.

Tomorrow, we'd come back, add compost to the row, and pack it down for the winter. It was a lot of work but worth it. One hill of sweet potatoes from one vine could produce a dozen or more potatoes.

I finished the row after ninety minutes and then backtracked to help Mom dig out the tubers.

"Mei," she shouted at me, indicating I should take out my earbuds. I pressed pause and popped them out. "I'm so happy you're home." She smiled at me, and my stomach twisted. I wished I could say the same. "It's nice working with someone I don't have to teach. Chiyo helps out, but the other people I hire need to be instructed to do everything."

I had done this every year for over fifteen years, between school, homework, and cram school, too. Nothing was more like second nature than farming, and I hated every minute of it.

Or I used to hate every minute of it.

"I don't know. I despised all this growing up." I kicked at the dirt and sent a baby sweet potato flying into the next row. Mom frowned at me. "It's so different from working in a store or an office."

Mom hid her face under the brim of her hat as she bent over to throw more sweet potatoes into the basket.

"I know it seems lowly or backwards to someone like you, but this is a good life."

I chastised myself for being a jerk again.

"I raised you to be an independent young woman. Your father would have wanted that, too. I wanted you to have the good life and the college education I never got." She groaned as she straightened up and back bended to stretch her spine and shoulders. "But this land is paid off. We only have to pay utilities and taxes, and I make more than enough teaching and farming to get whatever I want."

I let my arms fall to my sides as I watched her fill up the basket.

"Really, Mei. You don't need a whole lot to be happy."

I bent over and got back to forking up potatoes. "I don't know what happiness is like. I haven't been happy in years."

"We'll have to work on that then."

Mom nodded her head, definitively, and I knew the gesture so well, I feared what may come next. When Mom had her heart set on something, a goal, a project, or a plan, she finished it.

I could imagine her going to every resource she had, scouring every corner of the town, or calling in every favor she'd ever been owed just to find me the perfect job. In my head, I saw myself working at the new Midori Sankaku, washing dishes at the new restaurant run by the handsome chef, running the register at a gift store, or even scrubbing out the baths at Chiyo's new bathhouse. Could I be happy doing any of those jobs? I jerked to the present as a handful of dirt hit my jeans.

"Hey, stop daydreaming," Mom chided me, laughing. "I swear your entire teenage years were spent staring out the window at the sky. What do you even do in your own head that's that interesting?"

"Hmph. Just thinking." I backed up a meter and kept digging. "Actually, I was wondering what to think about Akiko's dad, since the police say he's been murdered."

Mom shook her head. She was so surprised when I told her the news this morning. "I can't imagine why anyone would want to kill him. He was sure to die anyway in the next few years, and it's not like Midori Sankaku need the land all that badly."

I stopped and leaned on the handle of the potato fork. "So, who do you think did it?"

Mom stuck her hands on her hips, her gardening apron getting dirtier by the minute. I should get an apron. "Seems to me there are a few people who would benefit from his death."

I doubled over laughing, my voice bouncing off the barn back to me. "I remember all those Agatha Christie books you read when I was a kid."

She smiled, her eyes crinkling at the corners. "Every night by the fire. The library got a good workout from me."

"I know!" I shot my finger into the air. "Let's solve the crime. You and me. We'd make an excellent team."

"Ha," she scoffed, bending over. "If so, partner, then you have a lot of catching up to do. You'll need to go to the town hall this week and learn more about the Midori Sankaku business. If there's anyone at fault for this mess, it has to be them."

"Yes, Captain." I came to a stiff salute and smiled.

"Get back to work, Lieutenant. I want to spend the evening watching the new drama on TV and drinking saké."

"I love your priorities, Mom."

———

MOM AND I CLEANED UP AFTER GARDENING ALL MORNING and headed into town for lunch. She rarely ate out at a restaurant, so I came along happily. If we had been at home, she'd have made me sweet potatoes for lunch. I would probably be eating them for dinner the next three nights in a row. Thankfully, sweet potatoes were my least hated vegetable.

"Where are we going for lunch?" My mouth watered at the thought of the Japanese curry place in town, a chain restaurant but one of the best around. I always went into a coma after eating their curry.

"Come," Mom said, hoisting her bag onto her shoulder and walking in front of me. Her short gait shuffled along, her kimono keeping her steps dainty. Growing up, I'd always loved when my mom wore kimono. She would save them for the weekend, just like now, and everyone would compliment her on her attire. I only wore kimono for special occasions. In high school, I had been into Japanese street fashion, jeans, skirts, and colorful clothing and didn't care about kimonos. After college, I morphed into a salary woman. I wore nothing but black skirts, button-down shirts, and black blazers. They filled my apartment's closet in the city. I would be so out of place here in Chikata. If only I had the money to buy a new wardrobe.

My stomach began to churn as we approached the corner, and I noticed the line of people at the new restaurant, Sawayaka. On the blackboard outside, a list of specials announced a seafood hot pot with fresh mizuna greens. I had totally forgotten about this.

"Mom," I pleaded, grabbing at her arm as she marched past the people waiting in line, "let's go somewhere else for lunch. This place is so busy."

"Nonsense, Mei. I have the chef's table here."

"You have what?"

I came to an abrupt halt as Mom reached the hostess and the two smiled and hugged each other. "Tsukiko! It's good to see you in here today. Yasahiro was just talking about your wonderful greens and sweet potatoes, and he was sure you'd stop by. Is this your daughter?"

When I thought my mom would start meddling in my life, arranging jobs for me, I had no idea she'd get to work so fast. It was literally two hours ago she vowed she'd help me out.

"Yes, this is Mei," Mom replied, gesturing to me. I bowed to the young woman, thankful I put on mascara and lip balm before we left the house. "She's moving back home for a while so I want her to get to know all the new faces in town. Mei, this is Ana."

Ana held out her hand to me, and I noticed the big diamond ring on her left ring finger. She must have been my age but already engaged or married and working here. I buried my jealousy deep in the soil of my gut. Maybe she was married to the chef?

"Nice to meet you," I said, bowing to her and shaking her hand. "Are you from around here?"

"I grew up in Saitama prefecture and went to college in the States. But now I live in Kawagoe with my husband. Thankfully, it's only a ten minute commute! Let's get the two of you seated."

Ana walked us to a two-top table next to the kitchen with a "Reserved" placard on it. She took the sign, seated us, and then returned with hot towels.

"Yasahiro will be happy to see you. I'll let him know you're here."

Once she left and I'd wiped down my hands with the hot towel, I leaned forward to whisper. "Mom, how come you never told me about this place?"

Mom smiled, sipping at the glass of water on the table. She wore one of her everyday kimonos and the color brightened her face and made her look five years younger. Not that she looked old to begin with. She could've easily passed for a forty year old on most days.

"Believe it or not, Sawayaka is one of my many investments around town."

"Investments?" I believed my brother would know this, but I did not. He got all the information, and I had to pry it from Mom months later.

"I've been investing in some local businesses since I've managed to save a lot of money over the years. I have a ten percent interest in this restaurant and another ten percent in Chiyo's new bathhouse. I've bought shares in Midori Sankaku and in the package delivery business that just opened a warehouse and distribution center a few kilometers from here."

I blinked my eyes and imagined my mom doing business in meetings or traveling to locations to inspect warehouses. Usually, I pictured her hunched over in the fields, storing vegetables in the barn, cooking and drying daikon radish for the winter, making pickles, or falling asleep at the kotatsu with Mimoji in her lap.

"Don't look at me like that," she said, laughing. "I know it's hard to believe, but I'm a business woman. I even hired an accountant and stopped using Hirata to manage everything. He was being such a pain about all the extra work I gave him." My brother, Hirata, was a complainer when it came to work. It amazed me he was married with kids since he'd always balked at having to take care of additional people.

"I just... I've been knocked over with one surprise after another this weekend. I'm shocked you never told me about any of this."

"Sweetheart..." She reached forward and patted my hand. "I could tell you were struggling at your jobs in the city. You tried so hard. I didn't want to tell you because I was afraid I made it all look too easy, you know? I've been blessed. Never once have I had to borrow money. Even in the years the crops weren't good, we were able to save and buckle down for the next year by dipping into our stores in the barn. I sold things, but I always stayed afloat."

I stared out into the restaurant full of people, sipping at iced tea or drinking beers, laughing over beautifully plated food or asking for the check. I imagined the chef I met yesterday cooking in the kitchen, happy at his job and pleased with the prosperity of his restaurant. Every single person in this room was, no doubt, successful or content. Everyone but me.

"It looks like it's a thriving business. Is it always this busy in here?"

Mom nodded and followed my gaze into the main area. "It is.

Yasahiro has done well for himself. He used to work in the city at a restaurant but wanted to move to the countryside and open a slow food restaurant of his own."

"Slow food. I've heard of this. All locally bought produce and meat, right?" I was not a foodie. As someone who ate almost exclusively fast food, slow food lived far outside of my realm of existence. But it was hot and trendy. All the celebrities swore by it. The movement was hard to miss.

"Yasahiro buys produce from the farms around town, mine included, and fish from a broker at Tsukiji. He has a farmer who raises and slaughters cows, pigs, and chickens, too. All local, all organic. That's why he does so well. This place was written up in The Japan Times and Tokyo Metro Magazine, and he has a Michelin star. Now, he often sells out of food, he's so busy."

"Are you talking about me, Tsukiko?"

We both jumped and laughed. Yasahiro stood at our table, in chef's whites, his hands clutching two plates of appetizers. We leaned back as he placed them on the table.

"I have some summer rolls for you today," he said, clasping his hands in front of him. I didn't know him at all, but he seemed nervous, the way his eyes darted between Mom and me. But Mom was one of his investors, and I had been abrasive to him yesterday, so I could imagine why he'd be apprehensive about approaching us. He probably expected me to be mean and bitchy.

I tilted my head and looked at the summer rolls. Finely chopped greens, carrots, cilantro, avocado, and radish were enclosed in a translucent rice wrapper with peanut dipping sauce on the side. I braced myself to hate it but still smile.

"And I'm sending out the hot pots soon. I hope you enjoy the mizuna greens, Mei. I, uh, feel bad about what happened yesterday."

"Don't mention it," I mumbled. "It's my fault. I should have known you were joking."

I picked up the summer roll, dipped it in the sauce, and took a bite. I expected it to be bland and awful, but everything crunched, bright and fresh, and the spicy sauce zipped across my tongue.

"Mmmm," I said, my voice rising. "It's pretty good."

Yasahiro laughed. "Don't act so surprised. Did you think I was trying to poison you?"

"No." I huffed, offended by his brusqueness. "I expect this organic food nonsense to be devoid of taste."

Mom kicked me under the table. "Ow," I hissed at her.

I had never fallen for the organic food hype, and it showed.

Yasahiro's face fell, his good cheer leeched out of him by my careless words. "If anything, all of this food is better tasting than anything you can get at a chain restaurant in the city." He pushed his glasses up his nose and glared down at me.

"Oh really? Do you think you could win me over with your slow food haute cuisine?"

"Mei..." If Mom could have, she'd have grabbed my ear and dragged me out of the restaurant right then. She'd probably had enough of my attitude over the years. If I felt threatened about anything, I needed proof that I was wrong and the other person was right. I had challenged hundreds of people over the years, lost many and won a few, but it never stopped me from challenging another person to prove their viewpoint to me. What could I say? I liked empirical evidence.

Yasahiro cocked his head to the side, tapped his finger against his lips, and narrowed his eyes at me for a moment. I got the distinct feeling I was being sized up. What did my opinion matter to this man? He didn't know me at all. But I glanced across to my mom and her face displayed the epitome of polite amusement verging on horror. This restaurant meant something to her. Yasahiro's opinion meant something to her, and I was acting like a rebellious teenager. Something about being home in Chikata made me revert to my bad habits. At twenty-six years old, I should've tempered myself.

"Forget it," I said, waving my hand in front of my face. "I don't want to embarrass Mom. I'm sure your food is very delicious. Just look at all the people here."

"No, no, no. I love a good challenge. Please, let me win you over with my 'slow food haute cuisine.'" He laughed at his own air quotes. "That's the first time anyone's ever called it that to my face. Give me a week to prepare, and then I want you to come here every day for lunch for a whole week. I'll save this table for you. After the week is up, you can tell me what you really think. I promise I won't hold it against you, whatever the outcome."

Mom cleared her throat politely.

"Or against you, Tsukiko. Ladies, enjoy your meal."

He backed away from the table, rubbing his hands together. I inserted a thought-bubble over his head that read, *"Muahahaha. She will be defeated by my awesome skills and delicious food. Just you wait. Just you wait..."*

Mom sighed as she picked up the summer roll and dipped it in the sauce. "You are going to be the death of me, I swear."

"What?" I asked, feigning ignorance.

"Eat your food," she responded. "And you're grounded."

CHAPTER
NINE

C hiyo's "new" bathhouse was actually the oldest bathhouse in Chikata. For the last fifty years, it had been run by the Murita family, a staple family in this small town. Otsuka Murita had even run for office a few times and served on the town council. He had worked hard and saved his money from the bathhouse to pay for college in the United States for his two sons. Funny how that one decision changed his life. The sons turned out to love America. They had both married American girls and decided to settle down outside of New York City, where they each had two kids. Murita's wife didn't want to miss out on her grandkids' lives so she persuaded Otsuka to sell the bathhouse and move to the U.S.

Chiyo was in the right place at the right time. She was shopping one day when she heard Otsuka's wife talking of their impending move to the States, and she offered to buy the bathhouse right away before anyone else could. She didn't need to see the place or even have it inspected before she bought it. As one of only a few bathhouses in town, we had been there hundreds of times for soaks in the baths and gossiping. It was a regular Saturday tradition when I was growing up.

Outside the door to the bathhouse, a sign that read "Opening Soon!" flapped in the breeze and a new name placard with the *kanji* for "Kutsuro Matsu" ("relaxing pine tree") hung next to it. Mom rang the bell and waited for someone to come and let us in.

"Tsukiko! Mei!" Kumi smiled and beckoned us inside. She was a year younger than me, and we were in the same school together growing up. I'd always liked her and was pleased when she married Goro. Their wedding was the talk of the town! They made an excellent pair, and my mom happily confirmed that for the last few years. "It's so good to see you both! Mei, you look gorgeous. I'm so glad you're here."

"Oh, stop. You look gorgeous yourself," I replied, and we both giggled at each other like kids and then laughed because we're adults.

Kumi slid the door shut behind us, locking it. "People keep trying to come in even though the sign says we're opening soon. It's like they don't believe it or something." She shook her head. "I know the bathhouse has been around for ages, but everyone here knows it's under new management. We open in two weeks. They can wait. Come in, come in! Take a look around!"

She wiped her paint-covered hands off on her jeans as Mom and I looked around at the place. Wow. They'd done a lot of work! They replaced the old cubbies with new wooden ones, lacquered a dark brown. LED lights shined bright in the front vestibule and the payment desk had been torn out and a new standing desk had been situated in its place.

"We just installed a new payment system," Kumi said, showing me the iPad register. "We also have our own loyalty card people can load up with money for a discount. It's really fun." She smiled tapping through the screens. In high school, she programmed apps for everyone's phones and even made a dating app once where you could date different members of a famous manga. She was the perfect person to have running a business. I could never do that kind of stuff. I loved my phone, but I had no idea how it worked.

"I just updated the website, and I'm getting ready to start up the social networks for this place." She rubbed her hands together, and Mom nodded at her. I could see why Mom invested in the bathhouse. With someone handling all of the business and bringing the place into the twenty-first century, it'd be even more successful than it used to be.

They didn't change the basic layout of the bathhouse. The men were to the right, and the women were to the left. To the rear of the front desk, a set of stairs led up to the observation loft. Up there, Chiyo would sit and watch both sides of the bathhouse, making sure both men and women behaved themselves. This was common, and I loved watching foreigners freak out that someone observed them while they got naked, washed, and sat in the baths. I'd only seen it a few times, though, because I only frequented sentōs where I knew the staff or they knew my family. I had to be careful because I had been kicked out of bathhouses before. I shrugged my shoulders to move my bra strap across my back and tried to push the memories from my head.

We ducked into the ladies' side of the bathhouse. Here, Chiyo directed two younger men, helping them install new mirrors at each of the bath stations. I was about to compliment her on the new decor when a reflection in the mirror caught my eye.

I turned and found my giant painting of Mount Fuji up on the opposite wall, over the baths. I suddenly began to sweat. I'd never displayed my work anywhere but home, and now, one of my paintings hung in a bathhouse with my name right next to it.

"See?" Chiyo said, coming up beside me. "I told you it's perfect for this space. Most bathhouses have Mount Fuji painted straight onto the wall. And remember there was that dreadful painting of the Tokyo skyline in here?"

I nodded my head, remembering it. I used to stare at the mural and wonder if the original painter had been on drugs. It was horrible.

"I had it painted over and your painting hung in its place. It's wonderful!" Chiyo threw her arms out at the painting and sighed. She'd always been this way, a bit starry-eyed and gushing over everything. "I was wondering if I could commission a new painting from you."

I began to sweat buckets, and I pumped my shirt a few times to get cool air to my body. "Chiyo, you're so kind, but I haven't painted anything in five or six years. I don't even think I could paint anything if I wanted to. All of my supplies are so old —"

"Nonsense," she exclaimed, interrupting me. "I'll pay you up front so you can buy the supplies. The bathhouse's new name is 'relaxing pines' so I'd love a pine forest for the men's side."

"What was on the wall there before?"

She frowned. "A painting of Tokyo Harbor." She sighed, shaking her head. "I don't know what they were thinking when they decided on that."

"I'm sure it was as bad as this side."

I took a deep breath and studied my original painting. One of my more inferior works, it was messy and discordant. At the time, I had been studying color theory and blending, and many parts of the landscape and mountainside were downright sloppy. I wanted to take it down and throw it away. I imagined sneaking in in the middle of the night, taking it off the wall, and leaving a pile of money in its place. But it was huge, just over a meter wide. I could never carry it. The materials for it alone set me way back. I spent New Year's money on the canvas and paints for it, but once I completed it, I never framed it. I just left the painting in the loft in the barn. It was probably pretty dirty and worn when Chiyo rescued it. But she'd already shown the canvas and framing some love by cleaning it up.

Guilt blanketed me from head to toe. I couldn't believe this awful painting hung here in Chiyo's new bathhouse.

"What's the matter?" Chiyo asked, glancing between me and Mom behind me.

"You should take it down." I shook my head and backed away from it. "It's just so... amateurish and embarrassing."

"It is not," she said, stomping her foot. "It's lovely. *I love it.* And it's mine now. I will not take it down."

"At least take down my name? Please?" My voice cracked, my whole being overwhelmed with how much I hated it. My breathing came in short bursts, and I felt like I was drowning.

"I'll do no such thing. This is something you should be proud of, Mei. Stop being so hard on yourself."

I turned my back to it and exited out of the bathing area to the front desk. Kumi followed me out and touched my shoulder.

"Hey, it's okay. It's never easy looking at your own work like that."

I folded my arms across my chest and paced around the waiting area.

"Oh yeah? What makes you an authority on this?" I stopped and closed my eyes against my loose tongue. "Sorry. That was mean."

She laughed. "Well, I do graphic design on the side to make extra money, and you wouldn't believe how many times I've drawn or colored something only to hate it the moment it went online. People would comment and say it's brilliant or whatever, and I'd immediately delete it. Then I'd put it back a day later." She waved her hand in the air. "Repeat as necessary. I do it all the time. It's like a sickness. But all creative people are like that. Very few actually like what they produce. Most of them hate it."

Huh. I hadn't known this about Kumi. Sure, she was the girl with pink hair and doodles all over her notebooks, but I didn't think her artistic talent went anywhere after that. How she managed to marry a cop was beyond me.

"Next time you come, you should just go in there and stare at it for a while. Get used to it. Mom loves it. It's not going anywhere."

The front door bell rang and Kumi went to unlock it. Goro entered, his police uniform absent, wearing jeans and an old rock concert t-shirt. The two of them kissed and embraced, and I turned my head to give them space.

"Mei, it's good to see you again." Goro said his usual greeting. "Are you here to see your painting up in the washing area?"

Kumi patted him on the chest. "Don't stir up bad conversation. Mei isn't used to seeing her work on the wall. She would probably burn it if she could."

"Indeed," I said, and Goro eyed me suspiciously. "Honestly, though, I would never commit arson on this place. You know how I feel about fire." Visions of me standing outside and chopping it into a pile of wood danced through my head. That would've been acceptable.

"Good," he said, nodding in my direction, and I pictured him again, the last time I saw him, taking Akiko in for questioning.

"Hey, I hope this isn't out of line, but I was wondering what's going on with Akiko?"

Kumi grabbed her phone from the front desk. "I'm going to get coffee. Anyone want some?"

We both shook our heads and she left Goro and me alone.

"Akiko will be fine. We were just checking on her alibi and whereabouts. The usual stuff. What do you think happened?" I loved this about Japanese police. They were helpful and fine with the community policing itself, nothing like cops in American dramas I watched online. Goro's inquiry was typical. The police were the protectors and arbiters of our world, not our antagonists.

I bit my lip and shrugged my shoulders. "She's my best friend. I can't believe she would kill her father."

Goro stared at me without saying anything.

"Look, I'd like to help out."

"You? Help out? You think you can do better than us?" Goro cracked a half-smile and folded his arms across his chest. He was goading me, and I laughed.

"You know it's our duty to help out, right? At least, that's what *I* was taught growing up." Chikata was small potatoes. They didn't have a huge police force with detectives and forensics experts, so they relied on the community to gather evidence.

"You're not insulting my wonderful mother, are you?"

"Absolutely not." I cracked a smile.

"Do you know the last time we had a genuine crime here?"

"No clue."

"Way before my time." He released his arms and shrugged his shoulders.

"It's an easy guess it has to do with all the new improvements in town," I said, sitting on a bench near the cubbies. "The grocery store? The Midori Sankaku greenhouse? The new restaurants and stores? Suddenly this town is getting a ton of attention."

He leaned against the wall. "We're just talking, right?" Meaning: *"You're not going to go around telling people I'm talking about this, are you?"*

I opened my arms and swept them in front of me. "Just chatting. We're old friends who are concerned about Akiko."

"And Tama. Don't forget he's being questioned, too."

"This is insane. There's no way either of them would kill their own father."

Tama's words as he yelled at Akiko rang through my head. *"Mom and Dad treated me like dirt..."* Which I couldn't believe. Both Akiko and Tama were fawned over as kids. But Tama did have a huge chip on his shoulder. Always had.

Goro shrugged his shoulders. "They're both back home now, so I don't think they're in trouble."

"Really?" I pulled my phone from my purse and checked my messages. Nothing. Hmmm. Maybe she didn't want to talk after what happened.

"Akiko's story checks out. She was attending to patients all day long. Tama was at school teaching."

Goro glanced over his shoulder and then at the entrance to the women's bathing side. My mom stood in the doorway.

"Good afternoon, Tsukiko."

"Are you talking about Akiko and Tama?" she asked, coming forward.

"Mom and I said we were going to solve this crime in our spare time," I boasted, sure that we'd figure it out before anyone else.

Goro laughed, a deep belly laugh that doubled him over. "Are you serious?" he asked, wiping a tear from his eyes. "You both think you'll solve a *murder*?"

"Don't get smart with me, Goro," Mom admonished him, and he had the good sense to stop laughing and straighten up. "We know this town as well as you do, and Mei and I are smart and resourceful. We can do the job as well as any of you."

"Sure." He bit off the one syllable to a clip. "But both of you should watch yourselves, so you don't get hurt."

I waved him off. Whatever. How much more could I be hurt? I couldn't be fired from my job or have my savings plundered. I had neither.

"Who do you believe will solve this case first? You, or Mei and I?"

"Me, of course. You want to put a wager on it?"

I rubbed my hands together and smiled. I loved betting, I loved challenging, and I loved to win. "Yes, let's make a wager on it. You versus me. Winner gets all the credit. Loser has to raise 50,000 yen for charity by running the town's 3k race in November in their underwear."

Goro paled and gulped. The 3k race in November was a huge local hit because it was also a part of a marathon. Everyone attended. There would be no hiding from the prying eyes and phone cameras. And though I wasn't in the best shape, I could definitely start running again. I had been on the track team in high school.

Goro thought on it for a moment, his mouth twisting to the side.

"Deal."

CHAPTER
TEN

Akiko's father was finally released to her on Tuesday morning and she was ready with a wake and funeral prepared. After the autopsy, they kept his body on dry ice and stuffed his orifices with cotton as was the usual custom. Chiyo and I arranged small gifts of sweets for everyone we thought would attend the wake and arrived at the funeral hall dressed in black. Mom offered to man the front table for the day, greeting guests and collecting the *kodan*, condolence money, which Akiko would use to pay for the funeral.

I smiled solemnly to Tama, standing next to his father's casket, and he nodded back to me. Glancing around the room, I counted only five people, people I recognized from around town but didn't know by name. My face slipped into a frown. This was the loneliness of old life. Kano's wife had gone and many of his friends were dead too. In those last few years, Akiko said his health was failing and he had stopped visiting his favorite spots in town. I wished there were more activities for the elderly to do to keep them busy and happy in their final years. Imagining the lonely days for them saddened me.

Akiko emerged from the room next door, a place to go for

food and drinks after guests paid their respects. Her pale and sallow face did not look much better than her father right now, and her crisply pressed black suit did nothing to help her complexion.

I wrapped my arms around her and squeezed, tried to squeeze life and love back into her. She deserved so much more than the treatment she'd received so far.

"Hey, how are you doing?" I hadn't wanted to bug her too much, especially after the police hauled her off on Saturday.

She pulled away and straightened her suit jacket. "Can you believe I had to go out and buy this thing?" She frowned down at her outfit. "I want to burn it after today."

I nodded, feeling the same way about several outfits of mine that I wore to sad events. The outfit I had worn to my grandmother's funeral sat in the back of my closet for years until I sold it at the age of fifteen to a consignment store.

She took a deep breath and let it all out in a huff. "I'm okay. Well, I've been better. The food and drinks were mostly donated and the priest will be here at 11:00 to say the sutra. He's going to the crematorium tonight, funeral tomorrow morning."

She rubbed her eyes and yawned, and I peeked over her shoulder at Tama who greeted a few people and nodded at their condolences.

"Did Tama help you at all?" I kept my voice low.

"Him? No," she grunted. "His job was to show up and be the first-born male. Just like it's his job to take the money and run."

"Shhhh," I quieted her and glanced around. "Don't let anyone hear you."

"What?" A bitter note in her voice took me by surprise. "He always gets what he wants. Always."

Movement at the door caught my eye. Haruka, dressed in a knee-length black wrap dress, walked across the room, her bouncy hair flowing behind her. Tama's face lit up when she smiled at him, and I may have been imagining it, but I could've sworn Tama threw a glance at me over her head.

What was he trying to do? Impress me? I really didn't care. Tama was way in my past, and I had no interest in him, even if his attention brought about a warmth in my body I hadn't felt in years. Still, that warmth was lukewarm, at best.

Akiko looked between me and Tama with Haruka. "Are you interested in my brother again?"

"What? Me? No. Not even close."

"He's been talking about you a lot the last few days. Wondering what you've been doing the last five years, how long you'll be home, if you're returning to Tokyo..."

"Tell him to mind his own business," I said, squeezing her arm. "I'm too good for him." I winked at her, and she smiled weakly, but it was something.

"I have to go. I don't expect a lot of people, but I'm sure most of them will be here this morning."

She walked off, giving me a good view of Tama and Haruka, holding hands side by side, and speaking to people quietly. Why in the world would Tama be interested in me anyway when he had her?

Wanting to leave the wake as soon as possible, I hustled across the floor to the separate room where tables covered with flowers, trays of vegetable sushi, small sandwiches, and salads awaited hungry mourners. At the center of each round table, bottles of saké practically called my name. It may have only been 10:00, but I was ready to sit, eat, and drink the entire day away. Between losing my job and becoming a farmer's daughter again, and my best friend's father dying, I couldn't think of a better reason to get drunk.

I chose a spot in the corner, set my purse on the table, poured myself a cup of saké, and got going.

This idea that Tama may be interested in me again bugged me. I'll admit that I still thought he was handsome, and with a successful job, he was quite the catch. But I wasn't one of those girls who got burned and forgot about it. I dropped Tama like a hot coal from the stove when I heard he cheated on me and I never looked back. If he didn't want me then, why would he want me now? Besides, I found Haruka disgusting and him doubly so for being with her. We were so over.

I sipped on the saké, knowing that if I pounded it, I would regret it in about two hours. For a solid thirty minutes, I sat alone in the party room, waiting for someone to join me until Chiyo, Goro, and Kumi arrived. We waved and smiled to each other, and they took a moment to gather some food before coming to sit with me.

"Your mother says she'll be in around lunchtime and then they'll be done for the day. The priest will be here soon to say the sutra, but that should only take fifteen minutes or so."

I drank more saké as the three of them discussed bathhouse plans. That must've been nice, to have a clear-cut job and business plan into the future. I stared into the clear liquid of my drink and tried to imagine my new life on the farm, one filled with hard-working days earning good money, and nights spent out with friends, going to art galleries or eating at fancy restaurants. Instead, I saw me at my mom's age, a crazy cat lady, worn and brittle from the sun and working outdoors, no family, and no life outside of what I had at home. My mom had had it better than me. She actually met a man she loved and had children with him. I doubted I'd have the same kind of luck.

I looked up at the door in time for Shin Tajima, the mayor of Chikata, to walk in. I felt the urge to jump to my feet, like one does when your boss walks in the room or someone much farther up the chain of command. Chiyo, Goro, and Kumi just nodded and greeted him like they would any other person, so I did the same.

"Do you guys know Mr. Tajima?" I whispered. He had

pulled his phone out and was listening to it while picking up sushi rolls and depositing them on a plate.

"Of course," Chiyo whispered back. "Most people in town know him."

"Don't you think it's weird he's here? Last I saw him, he was in Akiko's house, and she was yelling at him that she wasn't going to sell her land to him."

"Hmmm," Goro said, rubbing at his chin and training his eyes on Tajima, oblivious to us, though we were the only people in the room. He sat down at a table on the other side of the room, scrolling through something on his phone.

"Hey," I whispered at Goro, swatting my hand in his direction. "No free tips. It's me against you, remember? And I want to see you run in your underwear."

He huffed a laugh. "Fat chance but fine. Have you looked at Fujita Takahara?"

"He was also at Akiko's the other night. I didn't like him. He seemed... too slick. A little too polished to be a regional manager of a grocery store."

"Yes, that's right." Goro snapped his fingers. "They were both leaving in a BMW when we arrived. I thought I saw them but they were driving too fast. Well, we've been looking into him. I can't say what I've found yet, but we *are* looking."

"Hmmm." I leaned back into my chair and sipped more saké. "I'll keep that in mind."

Goro jerked his head towards the door as Fujita Takahara entered. He avoided the table of food and sat next to Tajima. They tilted their heads close to each other and whispered, but I couldn't hear anything.

Would the murderer show up to the funeral of the man he killed?

Maybe he would to throw anyone off the scent.

My body began to warm as the saké flowed through me. I pressed my cold hands against my cheeks and tried to calm the alcohol flush response, the one thing that totally gave me away when I drank. I was a stone-hard kind of drunk. I didn't get mushy, lovie, or sloppy. I merely became a rock — silent and immobile. Unless I was alone with someone I liked and then the truth poured out of my mouth like a waterfall in the spring after the snow had melted. I was safe at a funeral, though.

I rose from the table to slowly walk past Tajima and Takahara, hopeful I could overhear what they were saying.

"... But the fourth hole is tricky because of that sand trap just around the corner..."

Damn. They were talking about golf? What could be more boring than that?

Disappointed, I stood at the food table and piled a plate with vegetable sushi.

"Better save some for the other guests," a voice at my shoulder said, scaring me and sending my plate jolting forward. His hand snapped out and caught it before the food tumbled off. Yasahiro, the chef I challenged, smiled at me. Oh no. I wasn't prepared to deal with him again until lunch next week.

"I... I get hungry when I drink." This was true too. Alcohol meant a whole lot of truth and food. Both of which could leave me either someone's best friend or someone's greatest enemy by the time I was done.

He laughed, grabbing his own plate and adding a few sandwiches. "Me too. I'm, uh, glad I bumped into you again, though I suppose I should have known I'd see you here today —"

"Did you know Mr. Kano?" I asked, my voice ten times louder than it should be. I closed my eyes and cursed silently at myself. "Sorry. Sorry. I didn't mean to interrupt you."

"That's okay. Yeah, I did know him. He liked to go to Izakaya Jūshi in the evenings, and that's one of my favorite hangouts. We used to drink together before he got sick."

"Ah. I see. He did love that *izakaya*." I set my plate down and tried not to waver as I crossed my arms. "How long ago, would you say it was, when he got sick?"

Did it sound like I was pumping him for information? I couldn't tell.

He popped a sushi roll in his mouth and thought, his eyes turned to the ceiling. I followed them upwards and marveled at his hair, so stylishly messy, but not immature. I hated all those trendy, moppy boyish cuts. He seemed much more polished.

"About three months ago. Maybe the beginning of summer. I haven't seen him there since."

I thought back to my conversations with Akiko. He had been sick a lot this past year, but Akiko swore he had recovered.

"So," Yasahiro said, clearing his throat. I snapped my attention to him. "I was wondering if there are any foods that you absolutely hate."

"What?" That was such a strange question, especially since we were just talking about Akiko's dad.

"For next week. The challenge." He pushed up his sleeves on his sweater over a button-down shirt. My gaze settled on the ripples of muscle in his forearms.

"Do you get that from working pans in the kitchen?" I asked, pointing to his arms.

Oh my god, did I ask that out loud? I glanced around to make sure no one else heard me. I thought I'd be safe here with so many people in the room, but my mouth had switched to TRUTH ONLY and now my face bursted into flames.

Yasahiro smiled as he coughed and cleared his throat. "Yeah. I suppose I do."

God, kill me now.

"Eggplant. I don't know why but I can't stand eggplant." I could handle this truth, and it spurted from my mouth like water from a fire hose. "Hopefully that's not like your signature dish or anything."

"Nope. That should be fine."

I blew out a relieved breath as I stepped back. Saved that one!

Akiko appeared at the door, mercifully stopping me from embarrassing myself further.

"The priest is here to perform the sutra. If you could step into the main room now..." She gestured to her side and everyone stood up from their tables.

I ducked my head away from Yasahiro and ran to Chiyo's side.

She giggled in my ear. Great. She caught me being awkward with Yasahiro. I would never live that down.

"Not a word from you," I hissed back as we joined everyone for prayers and incense.

CHAPTER
ELEVEN

"I can't find a shirt to wear to this thing!" I tossed one piece of clothing after another out of my suitcase and across the room. The place had been a mess since Mom and I brought home everything from my apartment on Monday. Now, extra furniture, suitcases, and boxes filled with my entire wardrobe lined both open walls of my room.

"Maybe if you took some time to put things away, you'd be able to find what you want." Akiko rested on my bed, plucking at her pants and stretching her legs out in front of her. She was on leave from her job for the next week until she heard more from the police, but she wasn't allowed to go anywhere or do anything. A cop sat in a car in our driveway, waiting for her, no doubt getting caught up on paperwork or playing on his phone because watching Akiko must have been the most boring job in the world. She was *not* a murderer, and she was definitely not going to skip town.

"Here!" I yanked a light sweater from the pile and pulled it over my t-shirt. "Good enough."

Turning around, I faced the destruction of my room. Clothes

laid everywhere, boxes overflowing, and I couldn't see one open spot of floor space.

"Ugh, I'm going to have to clean this up before Mom sees it. Anyway, yes, I'll have to officially move in before the end of the week or I'll go crazy. In the meantime, I've got to head into town and go to this informational meeting on Midori Sankaku. I need to vet all of my potential suspects."

Akiko rolled her eyes at me. "What makes you so sure I didn't kill my own father?" She looked up at me and blinked her innocent and wide eyes.

"You? Remember that time you couldn't kill the giant spider in your bed and your dad had to come and get it for you?"

"That was a spider."

"And this was a human being," I reasoned with her. "One deserves to die. The other does not."

She smiled. "True, but I'm glad you have faith in me. Someone should."

If I'd had time, I'd have given her a big hug, but I pulled my hair back in a ponytail and slapped on some lip balm instead.

"Besides, there's a price to pay if I don't find the killer," I said, winking at her.

"You don't have to do this, this bet with Goro. What if things get out of hand?"

I shrugged my shoulders. "Out of hand how?"

"What if it takes up all your time?" Akiko rose from the bed and slipped her socked feet into a space between my clothes.

"Just kick them to the side so you can get through. What time do I have to worry about? Right now, I'm just helping Mom around the farm. I have no job, no boyfriend, and no money."

Akiko smirked. "You and me both."

"That's not true. I bet you have money saved, and you'll be back to work in a week."

"Okay then, at least we both don't have boyfriends."

I laughed as I followed her out to the main house. "I don't think that's something to be proud of."

We gathered our coats and shoes at the door and stepped outside into the dwindling evening light. Akiko had come over for dinner (Mom made sweet potatoes, of course), and now the sun was almost set, leaving the whole countryside in a cast of gray and dark blue shadows. We walked past the police car and the cop inside rolled down his window.

"Going home?" he asked, sipping at a hot cup of coffee, a thermos on the seat next to him.

"She's going home, and I'm walking into town for the meeting at 20:00."

He nodded his head, not offering anything more in the way of conversation, so we headed to the end of the driveway.

Akiko sighed as she laid her head on my shoulder, her arm wrapped around mine. "Why do I feel like this ordeal is never going to end? I'll be the town pariah forever and no one will ever want to talk to me again."

"Nonsense," I said, grabbing her shoulders and looking her in the eyes. Her flat long hair looked like it hadn't been brushed in days, and her face gleamed with a waxy sheen. If she hadn't been walking and talking, I would've suspected she was already dead. "Everything will be fine! Go get some rest. Take a hot bath and relax. Tama's at his place, right?" She nodded in response. "Then you have the house to yourself. Enjoy it."

"Not exactly to myself," she whispered, as the police car slowly turned around in my driveway and followed us. "And it won't be my place for long. Tama's right. There's no way I'll be able to win against him in court."

"Shhh. Don't say those things." I left her at the end of her driveway. "I'll go speak with him later this week and see what I can do. Until then, we'll all sleep better if we can figure out who murdered your dad. *That's* the most important thing."

I speedwalked to the town, only glancing back once to see

Akiko heading into her house and the police car firmly outside. Didn't they think that was a waste of resources? I was sure that cop would rather have been doing something useful instead of babysitting a bookworm, homebody, and manga geek like Akiko.

I stayed far enough off the road, walking in the gravel, but not one car passed me on the way into town proper. I would miss living in the city. I loved the energy, the buzz, and the constant movement of the people, cars, and trains. Out here in Saitama prefecture, everything felt slower, sleepier. I had had to start running a fan all night long while I slept because the house was too quiet. How could anyone sleep when it was that quiet? I had no idea. I couldn't hack it more than one night.

The lights blazed brightly at the community center when I arrived. Mom's usual cooking class room remained dark and empty, though. She was one of two people in town that taught there, and she was at home making pickles tonight. The other woman who taught here instructed people on how to make baked goods. I'd heard her classes were informative and you got to eat everything. Mmmm, I'd love some warm bread.

My stomach grumbled imagining a thick slice of bread, spread with butter and preserves, and an older woman walking next to me laughed. I shrugged my shoulders at her and smiled. What could I say? My brain would daydream about anything.

In the main meeting room, a panel of people sat and waited for others to come and join the crowd. I use the term "crowd" loosely. It was just me and five other people. But I sat down, shrugged off my coat, and grabbed my pen and paper from my bag.

Right away, I recognized Fujita Takahara and Shin Tajima. Another woman sat with them, but she held a pen and paper, so I guessed she must be the meeting's secretary. Opposite them, another man ran a computer and projector.

"Thank you for coming. This is one of the last information meetings we're holding for town residents before the winter sets in, so it's good you made it," Tajima said, smiling out at everyone from a spot at the podium. "Tonight, we're going to go over the numbers for those of you considering selling your land to the town. Please look to your right and take a packet of information from the chair on the aisle. This contains all the statistics and details you may want to know about land uses, profits to the town, and Midori Sankaku's long history as a prosperous business in Japan."

I slid to the right and grabbed a packet but left it closed on my lap. In my notebook, I started a new page entitled, "Suspects." Down the length of the page, I wrote out my considerations and what I knew about them.

First, *"Tama Kano: Son of the deceased. Was bitter and angry last time I saw him. Wants to sell land to Midori Sankaku."*

That covered motive but not opportunity.

"Was at school all day when father was killed."

I thought for a moment and put my pen to paper, but stopped. Who else could have committed the murder? My own mom? She was right across the road all day and had the opportunity. My scalp prickled and I glanced around, as if everyone could peer into my brain and see my traitorous thoughts. *Calm down, Mei.* But she had no real motive the more I thought about it. Nothing that Kano had done would have any affect on her and the family home. She would be upset to see him go, but she had said good-bye to many friends throughout the years. I racked my brain and couldn't come up with anything. If Mom had been too involved in their lives, Akiko would have said something.

I chewed on the top of my pen while I turned my attention to the front of the room. The lights dimmed, and Tajima began his PowerPoint presentation while Takahara sat next to him and stared up at the screen. "It's important both for the health of the town and for the surrounding areas that we continue to work towards a boost in economic resurgence. With the help of Midori Sankaku, we've seen new investment in local businesses, with several new restaurants and service oriented shops opening in the last few months. We have a brand new grocery store opening, which provides more jobs to the local residents and keeps people purchasing groceries locally instead of driving out of the prefecture to shop at big box stores. And now land that has sat vacant or unattended will be put to good use."

I leaned forward and placed my elbows on my knees, absorbing all of this new information. Tajima was right; this greenhouse and new grocery store would be good for Chikata and the surrounding towns. The greenhouse would provide more vegetables that couldn't be grown during the winter months, but it would bring jobs as well. A lot of out-of-work farmers could run or harvest a greenhouse. Not only that but the new grocery store would bring people from other towns *to* the area, and that would be great for other businesses around here.

Tajima pointed to a line graph on the screen that climbed steadily over the course of the last few years and into the future. I couldn't help but agree with him. Yes, this sounded like a great idea. And if I were Tajima, I'd be doing everything in my power to win over the residents that didn't want to sell their land. Midori Sankaku could have taken their business elsewhere, and still could. Though the grocery store was built and ready to open, they hadn't yet broken ground on the greenhouse, and that was what the town stood to gain the most from.

"When you sell us your land at anywhere from 80,000 yen to 120,000 yen per square meter, which is a very fair price for land that's been abandoned, we turn around and sell it directly to Midori Sankaku at a ten percent markup."

"Why wouldn't I just sell directly to Midori Sankaku and get more money?" asked the old lady who entered the room at the same time as me. Good question.

"We have a contract with Midori Sankaku that will allow you to sell the land to the town and avoid any legal costs because they will cover those costs for you. You can even choose your own lawyer, and they will take care of it. All of that information is on page twenty-two of the handout. We want the process to go smoothly for everyone."

I shuffled to page twenty-two of the handout and found information on tax breaks, legal cost negotiations, and timelines for selling and vacating the land. The other thirty or forty pages of information covered everything I could think of to ask: how this worked in other parts of the country, statistics on jobs and displacement of individuals during construction, how long construction would take, who would be in charge, new roads that would be built... I flipped aimlessly through the information and set it on the chair next to me.

After another fifteen minutes of slides, Tajima opened the floor for questions. I sat back and let other people go first since I was attending to feel out both Tajima and Takahara for their personalities, not what they wanted out of the land grab scheme.

On my Suspects page, I wrote: *"Shin Tajima: Mayor. Wants what's best for Chikata. Will be voted out if he doesn't get the job done. Possible kick-backs from Midori Sankaku?"*

That was a thought. Maybe he stood to get more out of the deal than what floated on the surface. Was it something he'd kill for?

I raised my hand and waited to be called on.

"Miss Yamagawa," Tajima said, nodding to me. It took me a full second to realize he was not addressing my mother. Even at work, people had called me by my first name. "It's good to see you here, but I didn't think your mother was interested in selling her land."

"She's not. Sorry. I'm going to be living in town for a while, so I thought I'd come and learn what this business was all about."

Tajima smiled. "That's good to hear! I like to see our citizens concerned with the welfare of the town."

I swallowed down a confession. I *should* have been

concerned with the welfare of the town, but I was more concerned with my best friend not going to jail.

"I was wondering where the money goes that the town makes in this exchange? Does it pay for... infrastructure, or does it pay for salaries, or...?" I let the question trail off.

"That information is on page thirty-five. You'll see how we've designated the money we'll earn from these deals. Most goes to pay for city infrastructure updates and education."

I returned to the handout and flipped to page thirty-five. Everything seemed above board, but how could I know if they were being honest or not?

I tried to imagine Shin Tajima funneling money to pay for hookers and drugs, to pay off gangsters, or a blood debt of some kind, and it just didn't stick. His family had lived here for generations, his kids successful, and his social credit strong. I'd look into it, but I couldn't see him smothering Akiko's dad in the middle of the day.

Fujita Takahara on the other hand — I didn't know him at all.

"Is that it, Miss Yamagawa?" Tajima's question crashed into my daydream of Takahara wearing his expensive suit, his high-end watch, driving his BMW, and paying off yakuza for protection. That I could believe.

"What happens to the people who don't want to sell?"

"I don't understand your question," Tajima replied, seeming to be genuinely perplexed. I glanced at Takahara and a small smile crossed his face before he leaned back in his chair.

"Will those who don't sell be forced from their land by legal matters?"

Both men squirmed in their seats and eyed each other.

"Absolutely not. Midori Sankaku has plenty of land to get started on their projects, and the offer will remain open for as long as necessary." Tajima wiped his hand across his forehead and cleared his throat. "Anything else?"

"That's it. Thank you." I didn't know how to ask any more

questions without sounding impolite, and Tajima's facial expressions showed his unhappiness. I couldn't push any further.

Takahara, sitting at the table, stared me down as I locked eyes with him. His cool and aloof demeanor echoed off of him as he smoothed his hair and raised an eyebrow. Now, he knew who I was, that my mother was not selling him our land, and that I was nosey.

Good job, Mei. I had just put myself into harm's way.

CHAPTER
TWELVE

I left the meeting feeling unsettled. It wasn't every day I came head-to-head with powerful people. Back in Tokyo, at my job — well, my old job — I had never even met my boss's boss. I worked on a team of peers and was rarely ever called into my supervisor's office, so I had no experience dealing with people in positions of power. Speaking to the mayor and this high-up guy at Midori Sankaku made me uneasy. I hoped Mom didn't get into trouble for what I did. I'd hate to ruin her reputation around town.

The pitch black sky hovered over me, and with the lights of Tokyo far away, millions of stars floated above. I stopped just outside of the main strip, pulled my sweater around me tight, and stared up at the heavens. I'd always wanted to paint the night sky or nighttime scenery. I used to concentrate on landscapes and objects, still life, but always well-lit and during the daytime. Shadows of objects in the night radiated a beauty I loved and craved. I had been dreaming a lot about painting lately, what with Chiyo buying my painting of Mount Fuji, and it was time I went into the barn and found my supplies. It looked like I'd have some spare hours on my hands now that I was home for good. Forcing myself to do it would be best.

As I walked home, I texted Mom to update her on my night. I didn't want her to worry about me, so I kept the communications' lines open at all times. I had a good thing going with her, and I didn't want to wreck it by being rude. She was my lifeline now, and I wanted to show her I appreciated it.

As I slipped my phone into my purse, I noticed lights approaching me from behind. I stepped off the road more into the gravel and waited for the car to pass me.

"Miss Yamagawa, can I speak with you for a moment?"

I shivered in the cool night as I saw who drove the car, Fujita Takahara. He'd pulled up next to me, his window down, and mirror light on so I could see his face.

I glanced left and right on the road, keenly aware I was alone. My heart rate picked up pace, panic seizing my brain and squeezing it tight. I'd always believed my hometown was safe. No one had ever reported break-ins or muggings. Now, with strangers around, I didn't know who to trust.

Takahara pulled his car to the side of the road, stopped, and stepped out. I turned towards home and kept walking, ignoring him as best I could. I wasn't going to stand there and let him do something to me.

"Miss Yamagawa! Please wait."

I couldn't ignore him with his car only a few meters away. He would just drive after me if I kept going, so I halted in his head-lights, staying in the light so I could see him. He approached me slowly, a small smile upon his face. He looked younger than he did in the community center under the fluorescent light. Maybe mid-thirties? His smile, genuine or not, unnerved me. The fact that he was approaching me here and not at the community center gave me pause. I wished I knew self-defense.

"What do you want?" I folded my arms over my chest and waited, hoping I looked strong and intimidating.

He chuckled, running his hand through his hair, perhaps a nervous tick because he did the same thing when I asked questions of Tajima.

"Sorry. I know this is creepy, stopping you on a deserted road —"

"Yeah, it's creepy!" I widened my eyes and stepped away from him while he laughed again. "What do you want?"

"I'm heading back to Tokyo and then to Singapore for a few days so I thought I'd try to catch you before this went on too long."

I tensed my muscles, ready to bolt.

"Midori Sankaku has no desire to force people from their land. You see, I also grew up in a small town like this, but my hometown is even worse off than this place. They don't even have a town council who is willing to do all of this work to revitalize the region." He sighed, and my muscles relaxed. "What you have here is an amazing opportunity. We're committed to growing the town and the region, and we're committed to bringing the freshest possible produce to the local community."

I gazed off into the land that I knew had already been sold to Midori Sankaku. I remembered when farms used to produce wheat in those fields, but they'd been abandoned before I was even out of high school.

"If people want to sell us their land, we want to buy it. But if they aim to stay and farm it themselves, then that's the best possible option. Honestly."

I narrowed my eyes at him. "I'm not sure I believe you."

He sighed, his shoulders dipping. "I didn't expect you to. I want you to know that my door is always open. You can come by and ask me anything, or..." He reached into his pocket and produced a business card that he presented to me with both hands. I bowed and took it with both hands. "You can call me and speak with me. If you don't want to talk with me, you can speak with my administrative assistant instead. She's very knowledgeable about the whole business. For the time being, I have an office on the second floor of the community center. The address is on the card."

He backed away from me and bowed. I examined his business card again as he got in his car, pulled away from me, and headed back to town.

I'd love to believe him, that their business had no ill intentions, but I knew how this worked in Japan. No one here liked to give up family land. It had belonged to our forefathers and the spirits of gods we'd loved for generations. We'd rather stay than go, but sometimes circumstances were unavoidable. It had always bothered me that so many people abandoned their land in our town, but with families to feed, it was the last possible option they were willing to take.

Still, when land needed to be acquired for use, the government didn't just take it, like they did in other countries. They'd tried that in the past and it led to riots. Instead, they would send in a team of people to butter up all the residents and sweet talk them until they were ready to sell. They wore those people down slowly, like water polishing a rock in a stream. Sometimes it would take a decade or more, but they wouldn't give up until everyone had sold their land. How long had Midori Sankaku been working on Chikata? I flicked the business card in my fingers, concentrating on Takahara's diminishing taillights. Probably two years now?

I couldn't be sure if it was a good or bad thing they chose Chikata.

Pulling my feet from where they grew roots on the road, I turned and walked home. I had more digging to do.

CHAPTER
THIRTEEN

I filled Akiko in on everything that happened the next evening while sitting at her kotatsu, drinking *shochu*, and eating a pizza I picked up before coming over. Pizza was a big deal for us. Only one place in town made it, and they were always swamped when I went there.

"You're not being harassed by the guys out in the patrol car, are you?" I filled up our cups with shochu and fruit juice. It was the only way I liked to drink shochu, a hard liquor similar to vodka I only liked in mixed drinks. I should've just bought *chuhai* (pre-mixed shochu and a juice) but this was more cost effective, and I was all about being cost effective.

"Those guys?" She waved her hand and scoffed, twirling her long hair over her shoulder and fluffing her bangs. "Please. I've known them half my life. I would invite them in for dinner like I do most nights, but I thought we'd gossip. I'm sure they'll be in to use the bathroom."

I sighed, relieved. "That's good. I've been worried."

"Mei, you've been living in the city too long. This is Chikata, remember? I see the same people practically every day, especially when I work in town. I walk into pharmacies and I'm greeted by name. I stop into the koban and check on the men and women working there, ask about their families and bring them gifts at the holidays. This is my life."

I imagined Akiko picking up prescriptions for her patients, smiling and laughing, cracking jokes with the police officers in the local police boxes. Her face fell into a frown.

"Well, it was my life. I hope it is again someday soon."

I covered her hand with mine. "We're going to figure out who did this so you can get back to normalcy."

Her eyes drifted over the area between the kotatsu and the TV, past the space heater blowing warm air on us from the corner. "He died right here, you know?" A wave of chills covered me from head to toe. I wished I could turn up the heater on the kotatsu. "He was laying here on the floor when I came home. Nothing weird or out of place. It took me a full minute to realize something had happened to him."

The hair on my head stood up, creeped out by being in the same spot Akiko's dad was in when he died.

"Did you burn incense?" I asked, sneaking a glance at the surrounding area and hoping his spirit was not floating over the table.

"Absolutely I did," she said, pulling back in shock. "I said prayers for three days straight, burnt incense, and brought his favorite pair of chopsticks to the funeral to be burned with him. I hope his spirit is resting in peace." She looked up at the ceiling and mouthed another prayer. "I'll have to go to the temple again soon."

"Good idea." I grabbed each of us another piece of pizza and took a bite. "Anyway, I'm glad you're doing okay, considering."

"I'm tired of being in the house, but I'll stay as long as I need to. Goro says they're checking evidence and following leads, and that the car outside is more for my safety than anything. They don't want the murderer coming back and killing me too." Her eyes sparkled with tears.

"Hey, hey. Don't worry about it. You'll be fine." I patted her back and rubbed her shoulder. Poor thing! I wanted to hug her and bring her home with me so she could feel safe and secure, like when we were kids. "We'll all be fine. Let's talk about something else."

"Okay." She sniffed up and dabbed at her eyes with a handkerchief. "Can you believe Haruka is dating my brother?" She stuck her tongue out. "I never liked her."

"Me neither. And they're not just dating, they're engaged. Do you know when the wedding will be?"

She sipped on her drink. "I'm not sure. They haven't set a date yet. Maybe next summer?"

"So, they got engaged recently?" I asked, trying not to pry too much.

"Earlier this year, in February, I think. I was going to say something but..." She stopped and looked at me, my mouth full of pizza.

"What?"

"Well, you know. You two dated, so I didn't know if there would be hard feelings."

I waved my hand and refilled our glasses. "That was ages ago. Ages. Have I even mentioned him in the last five years?"

"No."

"Exactly. I've dated three other guys since Tama. He's history."

"You're right. I should've known better."

Time to change the subject. "Tell me more about Takahara and Midori Sankaku."

Akiko quickly checked her phone as it buzzed at her. "So much email. Anyway, I'm sure your mom knows more than I do. They're opening that big store, which I can't wait to shop at, and then there'll be a huge greenhouse behind here next year sometime." She waved to the fields behind her house. "They plowed down the houses on both lots earlier this summer. It's been weird watching the land change over time." She ate more pizza, picking at the cheese. "And of course, they'd love to buy our land too, but I want to live here forever if I can. Besides, I can't stand Taka-hara. He hits on anything with a pulse."

"Really?" So my instincts about him were true. He seemed overly eager to get me on his side, and the way he followed me home gave me nightmares. I woke up in a cold sweat that night.

"He's already dated most of the eligible, hot women in town. He won't touch the ugly ones," she said, snickering. Then she threw her hair over her shoulder. "He even tried to ask me out on a date. Can you believe it? I refused him. I'm no fool. Supposedly, he's quite a player. If you Google him, you'll see."

I made a mental note to gather more evidence on him. He sounded intriguing yet revolting.

"Anyway, despite being hounded about selling my land, I'm excited about all the changes in town. So many stores had gone out of business or left. Lots of people abandoned their property and moved to Tokyo, too. Now, things are beginning to change. I think we got lucky because of our access to the highway and we have our own train station."

"I'm certainly curious about the new things in town. Maybe I could get a job somewhere local."

Akiko slid her eyes to the side at me. "Maybe you could work at Sawayaka?" She produced a small, sly smile.

I laughed, hard, my stomach cramping and the guffaws lessening into giggles. "Have you ever seen me work at a restaurant? I'd be a disaster. I couldn't work in a kitchen because I'd burn the place down."

I shivered when I thought about fire. I had the scars on my back to prove I should never be around things that flame.

"Yes, you're a horrible cook. I was thinking more of a hostess job."

"They have a hostess. I'm sure I'm over-qualified anyway."

Akiko paused, pursing her lips and looking to the ceiling. "You could help out with sales?"

My brain overloaded with irritation. I loved Akiko, but I hated her meddling. "What's up with all these suggestions for me and Sawayaka?" I tried to laugh it off, though I wanted to kick her under the table.

She laughed. "Well, with you challenging Yasahiro Suga, I was sure you liked him."

I grumbled, "Like him? I don't even know him. And he thinks that women only eat salads."

"I doubt that. He was just joking. He has a Western sense of humor. You should be fine with that, what with all the American TV you watch."

I did watch a lot of American TV, and Akiko was familiar with my love of *Friends, How I Met Your Mother,* and *The Big Bang Theory.* Their sense of humor had rubbed off on me the last few years. But I didn't expect Japanese people to have that sense of humor. When they said something like that, I expected them to act like a jerk, not be joking.

"You think he was joking around?"

"I do. I've met him a few times. He's a nice guy. Not my type but kind. Generous." Her phone buzzed again and she glanced at the screen. "He was dating someone kinda famous, though I don't know anything about it."

"Whatever," I said, brushing off the conversation. "I'm sure he has a girlfriend. He's too handsome and successful not to be single."

Akiko laughed at me, as a blush bloomed on my face. Had I really said that out loud? Damn alcohol. "Sure, Mei. You're probably right. He's super hot. I'm sure he's already snapped up some celebrity in Tokyo." Her phone lit up again and she sighed. "My patients miss me. Hey, it's almost 20:00 and Fuji TV has a new drama I wanted to check out. Want to?"

She wiggled the TV remote at me, so I smiled and nodded. I loved to see her happy.

"Sure. If I fall asleep at the kotatsu, wait till the last possible moment to wake me up." I sat back with my drink, relaxed and at ease. I could get used to this.

"You got it," she said, turning on the TV.

CHAPTER
FOURTEEN

The rest of my week encompassed all the little things in my new life. I worked the fields in the morning with Mom, trimming plants, pulling up weeds, harvesting turnips, daikon, carrots, and parsnips. My hands ached from the pulling, twisting, and digging, and my back suffered from the carrying. Baskets full of root vegetables sat in the barn for a day or two until they were picked up for delivery to the local stores. We kept as many vegetables in the ground as possible until the first light frost because they'd keep better through the winter. Mom had been saving newspapers for the past month so we could wrap up root vegetables after the season ended and store them in the barn.

Had I been doing any detective work? Not really. I spent some time with Akiko every day under the watchful eye of the cop outside of her house, and I listened to everything she had to say about Tama, her father, and her patients, but usually she just cried, and I held her hand or tucked her into bed before I slipped out the door and got back to work. I had a feeling I was going to lose my bet with Goro. I filled out my list of suspects and did some digging on each one via Google, but I didn't get far because

I had no real idea what I was doing. I had better start training for that run and get used to the idea everyone would see me in my underwear come November.

Every time I went into the barn during harvesting, I avoided the loft, but at the end of the week, I was finally ready to climb up there and inspect the remains of my past. The stairs creaked as I ascended into the dusty space above the tractor we used in the spring. On the right, under the window, sat the old couch I used to sit on and read, the spot where Tama and I slept together for the first and many times after. A plastic tarp covered it, and I could imagine the upholstery underneath was pristine. Mom was pretty thorough about taking care of this place. My old canvasses, some half drawn on or painted, others blank, leaned against the adjacent wall, next to my easel and tackle boxes of paints. On the left, Mom's fire-proof file cabinets sat against the wall, carrying her precious documents and other things she needed to run the farm.

The Mount Fuji painting used to take up the space to the rear of my canvasses, but the wide wall stood empty, begging to be filled. I grabbed the top tackle box and popped it open. Tubes of acrylic paint lined the top tray, like I'd left them in there yesterday. Several were unopened and moved when I squeezed them, but a few had seized up. Wow. I was lucky! I'd heard acrylic paint could last ten years or more, especially if they were kept in the fridge, but the temperature fluctuated up here and I expected worse.

I flipped through the few canvasses left and placed one on the easel. I had scratched a few hasty pencil sketches onto it, but nothing seemed familiar. Hmmm. I turned the canvas around 180 degrees and there! Yes. I had planned to paint a lake with a *torii* gate and a mountain in the background. I never understood this about myself. I loved modern life. I loved my phone, my computer, and the city. Yet, when it came to painting, I only ever wanted to capture the world in its splendor, natural and real. I didn't paint people. I didn't paint animals. I hadn't tried abstract or modern, though I loved to look at both. I was attracted the most to natural landscapes.

I was a host of perplexing contradictions.

"Mei?" Mom called.

"In the loft!"

The stairs squeaked as she climbed up.

"Wow. I haven't seen you up here in ages." Mom joined me at the canvas and wrapped her arm around my waist. "What was this going to be?" She turned her head to the side. "A lake?"

"Yeah," I said, sweeping my hand up. "Mountain and torii gate, too."

"Ah, yes. I see it. How are your paints?"

"Good." I set aside my first tackle box and looked in the second one. "Most are okay. I'll have to make a list of what I need. And I want to go back to oils for Chiyo's painting, so I'll have to reinvest in at least the basics."

"And new paint brushes and canvases, too. I've put money on your dresser in your room. We'll see if you can find it." She winked at me. My room was still a mess.

"Thanks, Mom." Normally I wouldn't have taken money from her, but I knew I'd earned a week's worth of wages already, so I wouldn't try to give it back to her like I used to.

"You should take my car into the city tomorrow. The canvas to make Chiyo's painting will be too big to bring on the train."

"Sekaidō and Yuzawaya are both open tomorrow, but I planned to stay home and help out around here."

Mom smacked me on the shoulder. "We don't work on the weekend unless we have to. This is the farm life. We make our own hours." She smiled as I looked at her in wonder. Make my own hours? For the last four years, I'd lived by office hours plus nights out drinking with coworkers. Before that, it was school, school, and more school. Never a moment to myself. This was a whole different life.

"Any chance you can pick up some things for us in the city while you're there?"

I broke into a laugh. "Like what?"

"Saké, of course! And shochu. We need to stock up."

My mom, the lush.

"Of course."

Mom glanced around the space, shuffling back and forth on her feet. "I'm not sure if you'll survive a winter in here, Mei. The barn gets so cold, and we only have the old electrical outlet downstairs."

"Can I bring up the gas space heater?" We had a few in the house for the dreadfully cold winter days.

"Sure. Just be careful. Only run it when you're in here." Mom turned to descend the stairs but halted. "Are you excited about your week of lunches at Sawayaka?" She tried to ask this innocently but excitement edged into her voice. "I heard Yasahiro is pulling out all the stops to prove to you his food is the best there is."

"Mom," I whispered, waving at her and trying to get her to stop nagging me. "I'm sure it's no big deal. He probably already hates me for challenging him. So many men can't stand that."

"Please. He's a chef. Being challenged is his life. He loves it or else he never would have done it."

Really? I'd figured he'd be angry, fitting in the challenge amongst his other work. Especially during lunch hour, which must be busy for him.

"How do you know him? I mean, how did you come to even invest in his business?"

Mom shook her head side to side. "It's funny the way it happened. I was looking at the same building to buy it when it was up for sale —"

"What were you going to use it for?"

She waved her hand around. "I wasn't sure. It was just a dream of mine to have my own storefront to sell my own produce and pickles and snack food..." Her eyes glazed over, perhaps imagining her own business where she would've served customers all day. Though this sounded a lot like torture to me, I bet Mom would've loved it.

"Anyway, when I heard a young chef, trained in France but interested in slow food traditional Japanese cuisine wanted the space for a restaurant, I immediately withdrew my bid on the building and asked to meet him. He started coming to my cooking classes about a year ago, and I gave him a lot of my recipes I've had for the last forty years. I know you hate to cook, and I didn't want those recipes to be forgotten."

Since I was eight years old, I didn't hate to cook, I was *afraid* to cook, afraid to use the stove. I had a healthy fear of fire, and I'd set things aflame in the kitchen a few too many times for my taste. I stuck to the microwave, rice cooker, or boiling water.

"Yasahiro trained in France?" I asked and regretted it as Mom smiled, her eyes gleaming with a devilish tint.

"Paris. He lived there for four years and learned from some of the best chefs in the business. I was pleased to hear he wanted to stay in Japan and cook here. He did well at his last restaurant too, but he wanted a place of his own. His parents are from Chichibu." Chichibu was only an hour and a half away by car, so he hadn't settled too far from home.

All of the times I'd daydreamed about Yasahiro being a chef these past few days, I never pictured him in Paris. Several people said he trained in France, but my brain didn't go there. I stared out the loft window and imagined him sauntering through the streets of Paris, wrapped in a big scarf, carrying a bag of fresh produce, cheese, and a baguette, living in a tiny, chic apartment, drinking wine with friends and eating amazing food.

"Mei —" Mom snapped her fingers in front of my face and laughed. "Oh, I've seen that look before."

"Mom. Stop it." I ushered her to the stairs. "I was just wondering what he's going to feed me." I followed her down, both of our steps making the stairs creak and bounce. Despite knowing how well designed the barn was, I wondered if the loft would come crashing down one day.

"He'll try to win you over with the basics first. And I must say, he's quite good at all the traditional dishes. You won't be disappointed."

She conveniently forgot how I detested traditional food. Would I be able to fake my reactions to Yasahiro's cooking? If I was honest, I might offend him, and I didn't want to make an enemy of him, especially since Mom liked him. I had gotten myself into a stupidly, sticky situation.

"We'll see, Mom. We'll see."

CHAPTER
FIFTEEN

On Monday, Sawayaka bustled with happy customers at the tail-end of lunch time, and I walked in ready to be wowed. I originally figured I would give him a hard time on purpose, but after hearing his history from Mom, I decided to be lenient and arrive on a positive note. I'd had a light breakfast and went for my first run in over a year, so I was starving and prepared to eat just about anything Yasahiro put in front of me. Ana, at the hostess station, squealed when I approached her.

"I'm so delighted to see you again, Mei." She bowed to me and I bowed back, a little self-conscious with all the people turning to eye me. "I can't wait to hear what you think of Yasahiro's cooking. He's been developing menus and testing out dishes on us all week long." She closed her eyes and hummed. "It was delicious. I wish you could challenge him every week."

Yikes. I'd had no idea he would take the challenge so seriously. I tucked my hair behind my ears and straightened out my shirt, nervous butterflies — no, nervous small birds — taking flight in my stomach and threatening to fly me straight to the bathroom. Whenever I got nervous, I wanted to puke. It wasn't pretty.

"Well, I hope I didn't cause him too much trouble!" I faked a smile and bowed again, hoping to calm the birds. "I've been looking forward to today since I was here last."

Ana crooked her finger in my direction. "Follow me."

We wove through the tables, most occupied, and she sat me next to the kitchen, plucking the "RESERVED" sign off the table and slipping it into the pocket of her apron. "I'll let Yasahiro know you're here. Enjoy the meal. Stop by on your way out and let me know what you think. I'm dying to hear all the details."

She winked at me as I sat, and I suddenly felt self-conscious about everything. How was my hair? Was it behaving? It was a little humid out this morning and my hair had this wavy kink to it that fluffed out in weather like this. I straightened my button-down shirt, annoyed that my whole wardrobe was meant for working in an office and not for a farmer's daughter out for lunch at a high-end restaurant. At least my flats were in good shape. I had a thing for shoes. It was quite possible that if I did not have a "thing" for shoes, I may have had an apartment in Tokyo still, but let's not dwell on that.

I had no one to talk to, so I took my phone out of my purse and checked for text messages. Akiko wrote, *I'm jealous of your lunch plans. Please take photos and send them to me. House arrest is no fun.*

I frowned down at the screen. Why was she still being watched? She had attended to patients the entire day her father died. She wanted to go back to her job, but the police needed to leave her alone for that to happen. Were they watching Tama as diligently as they were watching her? He had as much motive as she did, though I didn't believe either of them would kill their father. Tama had a job, his own place, and a fiancée. Akiko was doing well as a nurse and had had a roof over her head as long as her father was alive. It made no sense that either of them would commit the crime.

It must've been someone on the outside, and currently, my

only picks were Tajima and Takahara. Both didn't strike me as killers. I glanced around the busy restaurant, and an image of Yasahiro wielding a knife popped into my head. Maybe he was the killer? Oh no. What if I'm having lunch with a murderer?

Think, Mei! Motive and opportunity. What reason would Yasahiro have to kill Kano? And would he have the opportunity? If I suspected him at all, I'd have to find out if he ever took time off work, though he seemed like a workaholic. No one with a Michelin star works part time. He was àt the funeral and said he only knew Kano from late night drinks. I'd have to look into it.

So far, my detective life proved to be a complete failure. Why was I not surprised? I'd been plagued with bad luck my entire life, and I didn't see it stopping anytime soon.

"I haven't even served lunch to you yet and you're already frowning?" Yasahiro stood over the table, a plate in each hand, and a smile on his face.

He's kidding, Mei. Kidding. Remember? Akiko said he had a sense of humor, unlike most people around here.

I returned his smile and took a deep breath through my nose, smelling something of toasted sesame. "I'm definitely not frowning over food," I replied, careful to make eye contact. "Is this lunch?" I sat up to see the plates, but he glided them down to the table.

Yasahiro cleared his throat and raised his chin. "To start, we have a fresh green beans and lotus root salad. Crisp and tangy with toasted sesame seeds, rice vinegar, and ginger." He pointed to the plate in front of me, greens and thin slices of lotus root arranged in a neat pile. "And these are my pork and scallion dumplings with Sriracha, ginger, and lemongrass dipping sauce." Four plump dumplings sat on the other plate, and my mouth began to water.

"I hope you enjoy them," he said, bowing and turning to go.

"Wait." I snapped my hand out and grabbed the white fabric of his chef's coat. "Won't you be having lunch with me?"

I glanced around at the restaurant, crawling with people. Oh no. I'd honestly believed we'd have lunch together. He'd tell me about the food and his work and...

I blushed. Hard. I thought this was a date, didn't I? Deep down, way down in the cellar of my brain, I'd daydreamed a date out of this. I was so stupid.

This was the lunch rush hour, and he only did this because I challenged him.

Snap out of it!

"I mean..." I stammered, and letting go of his chef's coat, he smoothed out the wrinkles with his hand. "I know you can't have lunch with me. It's too busy in here. I just thought you might want to, um, explain a little more about the food?"

If only my lie sounded a little more confident.

A small smile grew across his lips, and my entire being died of embarrassment. "I'm sorry. I do have a lot of work to do, including your main course."

"Oh yes, of course. I completely understand. I'm looking forward to eating everything you bring out today. I'm sure I'll be won over by Wednesday, and we'll declare you the winner of this silly challenge."

Because I was not coming here and eating alone while everyone around me ate together. I was willing to do that once in a while, with a book, but not every day. I'd rather I ate at home with Mom.

"No, no, no. I said I was going to feed you lunch for a whole week, and you can't capitulate right away. You said this food would be bland, and I'm going to prove it's not."

I nodded slowly, resigned. What had I gotten myself into? I'd challenged a chef with a prestigious resume, a student of my mother's, and the town's newest darling. I should never have opened my mouth. I was close to making a complete fool of myself, and I regretted it to my bones.

Yasahiro paused for a moment as I took a sip of water.

"But, if you'd like to come and eat lunch a little later tomorrow, maybe after 14:00, I could eat with you. Lunch usually slows down by 13:30 and then we close the kitchen from 14:00 to 16:30 to prepare for dinner."

"I don't want to bother you any more than I already have —"

"It's not a bother," he interrupted, and this time, he stammered and seemed eager to keep me there. Hmmm. Interesting. The daydream of Yasahiro wandering the streets of Paris popped into my head again, and I stopped to add more details to it: the tiny scar through his right eyebrow, the shape of his ears, his white teeth (he must go to a private dentist). The daydream shifted and I imagined him at the dentist's office, in the chair. No! Back to Paris. Yes, that was better.

"Mei?" he asked, breaking into my daydream. "Is that okay? A later lunch? I wouldn't want you to be hungry all morning."

"No, that's fine." I cleared my thoughts and returned to the restaurant. "Sure. I'll come tomorrow at 14:00, and I'll be sure to eat a big breakfast."

He smiled and left, heading into the kitchen.

I took out my phone again and snapped a few photos of the meal, posting them to Instagram where I had exactly twenty followers, all of whom were old college friends or coworkers I actually got along with. I tagged the food photos with the appropriate hashtags and included the location. Free advertising for Sawayaka! Then I sent them to Akiko, hoping to brighten her day a bit.

Before I could put my phone away, the screen blinked with a new message. *"Hi! It's Kumi. Mom gave me your number. I was wondering if you could come by after your lunch at Sawayaka today?"*

"Sure." I texted back. *"How did you know I was at Sawayaka?"*

"The whole town knows you're there for lunch." She included a sticker of a fat, grey cat eating ramen.

"Omg, really?"

I glanced around the restaurant, and yeah, dozens of people were eyeing me and nodding in my direction. Damned small towns.

"I'm being watched." I sent a sticker of a panda bear with large eyes.

"Even if the food is horrible, pretend it's amazing. Our entire town is following your every move. Before Sawayaka, we'd never had a restaurant with a Michelin star. Save face!"

I laughed at my phone. *"I'll be there when I'm done."*

I set my phone down and picked up a green bean with my chopsticks, popping it in my mouth.

Mmmm, still crisp and sweet, like it was plucked from the vine only hours ago, and the ginger and sesame oil lingered on my tongue, balanced and perfect for each other.

I didn't have to pretend because this was delicious. I dug in and continually glanced towards the kitchen door wondering what to expect for my main course. I couldn't wait.

CHAPTER
SIXTEEN

"What did you eat for lunch?" Kumi pounced on me as I walked in the sentō. "We've been dying to know."

"We?" I asked, setting my purse on the newly painted front desk and taking in the changes that had been made in the last week. The space was coming together now.

"Me and about twenty of my friends. Twenty of my single friends who are all jealous of you right now."

Shame poured over me as I imagined the single women in town being edged out by my non-competition. "It wasn't a date. I swear." It would have been a date if he had sat with me. Tomorrow, maybe things would be different. Or they might be as pitiful as they were today. One could never tell.

"Sure, it wasn't." She winked at me. "Now, tell me about the lunch."

I retrieved my phone from my purse, showed her the appetizers, and the spectacular Thai curry he made me for lunch. Paired with the sesame oil and ginger appetizers, the combination melted me into a happy puddle.

"Ohhh," she breathed out. "I haven't had that there. I didn't know he cooked Thai food." She licked her lips. "Was it fusion?"

I paused for a moment, remembering the flavors from lunch, the heat on my tongue and down my throat. "It was mostly Thai with all local vegetables and shrimp. It was delicious. I hadn't had Thai food in a long time."

Kumi's eyes glazed over, a far off dreamy haze softening them. "I've heard he can make just about anything — French, Thai, Ethiopian, Mexican. But for some reason he's here to learn and recreate traditional Japanese dishes."

I replayed my meal in my head. The menu consisted mainly of Thai with a smattering of Japanese foods, but it was also his "slow food," all local and fresh. Why didn't he feed me traditional dishes if he specialized in them?

"Huh," I said out loud, belatedly realizing I didn't say anything else aloud. Kumi narrowed her eyes at me. "Anyway, here's some photos I took." I swiped through the ones I had on my phone and she sighed.

"That looks lovely. Are you on Instagram? You really should be if you're not."

"Of course I am." I gave her my username and we followed each other. She squealed when she started swiping through my photos, and I looked through hers. Kumi, obviously a prolific photographer, uploaded at least a photo a day. Her photos included those from around town or in Tokyo, self-portraits or Goro and their house, food, photos of her sketches and designs, and the bathhouse as well. I had no idea she was such a fun-loving girl. Goro was her complete opposite. He'd always struck me as by-the-book, never wavering from rules and regulations. Basically, a model police man. He was made for the job.

"So, I was hoping you'd come by today because —" She sighed. "— I'm dying to know how your bet with my husband is coming along."

I backed away from her. "If you think you're going to trip me up so that Goro will win —"

"No!" She jumped forward at me and broke into laughter. "No, the opposite." She rubbed her hands together, glee coating her face like a thick gloss of honey. "I want to see him run that race in his underwear. It would make my year."

"Really? But..."

"But what?" She laughed. "You don't think husbands and wives have their own bets? Because, yes, yes we do. I've been trying to get him to run a race for the last two years. He runs twice a week but refuses to commit to a race because he says he doesn't have time, which is crazy. I think he just doesn't want to lose or be seen as a loser. He has no idea you can run for the fun of it."

"Well..." I deflated and sat on the bench near the door. "I'm not sure you're going to get your wish. I thought I'd be a fantastic detective since I have the time to investigate, and I have the connections, but I'm not getting anywhere at all."

"What have you done so far?" She sat next to me and turned so her leg was tucked up on the bench between us.

"I went to the town meeting on the land buy-up and Midori Sankaku. The information they gave out is pretty thorough, and I got the feeling they will wait, years if they have to, to get the other land they can't buy right now."

Kumi nodded her head. "I've heard this as well."

"So I figured Mr. Tajima would be a suspect, but he was very sincere, and I just couldn't imagine him killing Mr. Kano to get his land."

"No. It's not like him at all. He's been the best mayor this town has ever had, and Goro says he was in budget meetings that whole day. So unless he hired someone to kill Mr. Kano, he's not the murderer."

I recalled Akiko's house the morning after her father was

found dead. Nothing seemed haphazard or out of place, and the police didn't suspect murder until the autopsy.

"I don't think anyone was hired to kill Mr. Kano. The house wasn't disturbed, and if a stranger had come into the house to kill him, Kano would've fought and there would've been signs of a struggle. Akiko says her father had been sick but was getting better, but not that he was frail or weak or anything. He would have been able to fight."

"So it must have been someone he knew." Kumi nodded as she chewed on the skin around her thumbnail.

"What about Fujita Takahara, the division head of Midori Sankaku? Do you know anything about him?"

She pulled her phone from her pocket. "A few things. He's supposedly the rising star in the company, expanding their reach and increasing profits." She turned her phone to me so I could see a recent article on him. In the photo, he wore an expensive suit and smiled at the camera. "He's another sought-after bachelor in this town."

My skin crawled. "Ugh. I don't know. He was creepy the other night."

"Creepy? How?"

"He followed me home! In the dark! I was walking home after the meeting and he pulled up next to me, got out of his car, and started talking to me. It was weird. I almost called Goro."

She gasped and covered her mouth. "No!"

"Yes. He gave me his business card." I opened my purse and dug through the contents until I found it. I handed it over to Kumi and she examined it on both sides. What was she looking for? A clue? It would be nice if murderers had their own business cards so we could identify them easily. I imagined a scene where a man dressed in black bludgeoned someone else over the head, laid down his business card, and then walked out the door. Surely detectives would no longer be needed if the world came to that.

"Mei," Kumi interrupted my daydream, "did you call this number and ask questions about where he was the day of the murder?"

"No." I blinked my eyes a few times, focusing on the situation. "Is that something I should do?"

"Have you learned nothing from crime TV? I'm brushing up on my English by watching American crime dramas online. Goro thinks I'm crazy, but he watches with me. He wants to be a detective someday, but there's training and an exam and everything."

"I used to pass a school for private detectives in Tokyo every day. I always wanted to go in and see what the place was like."

Kumi laughed. "Whatever you do, don't tell Goro that."

"Okay. Anyway, what should I do?"

Kumi jumped up from the bench and paced back and forth. "I know. Goro said that Takahara was cleared that day because he was in Tokyo at some restaurant opening." She took out her phone again and searched. "Yes, here he is." She showed me a photo of him, dressed up again and flashing his prize-winning smile, shaking hands in a new restaurant. "He's one of the owners. So this is what you do. You call up his office and pretend you found something that belongs to him, like his wallet, and see if his secretary can confirm he was at this opening."

My heart began to race, but I was a good liar when I needed to be. I could handle this.

I took out my phone and dialed.

"Good afternoon. This is the office of Takahara at Midori Sankaku. How can I help you?" The polite voice on the other end of the line sounded practiced and curt.

"Good afternoon. I've been calling around to a dozen Fujita Takaharas for the last week looking for the owner of a wallet I found in Shinjuku on Friday, October the second. Can you tell me if your boss has lost his wallet?"

"Hmmm, I don't think so. He hasn't mentioned it to me."

"Perhaps I've got the wrong Takahara again then. This name seems to be common," I said, giving a little fake laugh.

"Indeed, it may be," she replied.

"Was your boss in Shinjuku on the second? It was dropped near the Starbucks at Shinjuku Station."

"Hmmm," she said, breathing into the phone. "Let me check." She paused for a moment. "No, I don't believe he was. He was in meetings at the corporate headquarters in Yokohama all morning, had lunch in Ginza, and then attended a restaurant opening in the late afternoon in Ueno. He then returned to Saitama prefecture for the evening. None of his stops were anywhere near Shinjuku. I remember this day. He was very busy, and he would have said something if he lost his wallet that day."

"I see. Sounds like it. I'll keep trying."

"I would suggest you return to Shinjuku and drop it off at a koban so the police can find him."

"I will. I don't want to spend anymore time looking for him."

"Have a nice day!" she chimed.

"You too." I swiped my phone to hang up.

"He was busy all day that day," I said, placing my phone back in my purse. "Yokohama, Ginza, and Ueno. I don't believe he was the murderer either. It would have been hard to sneak a trip to Chikata in amongst the other things he was doing."

"I see. Well, I suspected him too. Goro doesn't like him one bit, but I think it may be jealousy. Between Fujita Takahara and your chef, Yasahiro, all the ladies in town have been head-over-heels for the injection of hot men Midori Sankaku has brought in."

I waved my hand at her. "He's not 'my chef' so please don't say that. I challenged him to prove to me that slow food is as tasty as regular food. He must secretly hate me for giving him more work. It's not a date."

"Sure it's not." She said that seriously, but deep down I could tell she believed we'd be a couple in no time. I didn't even know him! He was handsome and could cook, but what else? Maybe he had a schoolgirl fetish or collected train sets. He could've been completely weird. I didn't do weird. I needed normal.

"Who else could have killed Mr. Kano?" I asked, changing the subject.

"Tajima and Takahara are out. Akiko?"

I shook my head. "I really don't think so."

She narrowed her eyes at me.

"I'll get into it later. I just don't think so, okay?"

"What about Tama? He's always been aloof with me."

"And that makes him a killer?" I asked, taken aback.

"No. Just strange. So, not Tama?"

"No." I didn't feel like explaining my feelings on this matter either, so I moved on to the basics. "I'm sure Goro told you he was at school with a solid alibi."

"Right. Right." Kumi nodded her head, defeated, before perking up, her eyes wide. "What about his neighbor?" She snapped her fingers a few times. "Senahara?"

"Old Man Daichi? Why would he kill Kano?" I pictured Senahara as my mom last saw him, pants down in his fields, pissing into the cabbage with a saké bottle in his hand. "He's an angry, old drunk but not a killer."

Kumi glanced at the clock on the wall. "Oops, I said I would unload the soaps and stuff by 15:00. Come into the back with me?"

"Sure." I followed her into the ladies' washroom, averting my eyes from my painting on the wall over the baths. In the center of the wash stations, four giant boxes of liquid soaps, shampoos, and conditioners occupied the washing area's floor space. Kumi sliced each open with a box cutter she pulled from her back pocket.

"The story with Mr. Senahara is that he doesn't want to sell to Midori Sankaku ever. He'd rather go down in flames than ever give up his land." She handed me several bottles of shampoo, and

I stood still with them in my arms. Was I supposed to put these away? "But there were rumors Kano was going to sell."

I flashed back to the day I walked in on Akiko yelling at Tajima and Takahara. Tamjima had said, *"Her father hinted he might be amenable to our plan before he died."* Oh no. He had said that, hadn't he?

"What? If so, that would ruin all of my theories on why the murder happened." If Kano sold before he died, that would have put an undue burden on Akiko. She would have had to facilitate moving her father to a different place of residence, sell the house and land which she loved, and then where would the money go?

My skin slicked with sweat as Kumi took bottles of shampoo from my arms and placed them at each station. Suddenly, my best friend had the perfect motive for killing her own father.

"Senahara and Kano were always fighting. Senahara thought Kano should stay till the bitter end, never sell, and screw those big city bastards that came to ruin our town." Kumi raised her fist into the air in a mock tribute to Senahara. "That old man was constantly screaming about something. He was outside of the Midori Sankaku building protesting when they broke ground, and he and Kano fought at Izakaya Jūshi. My friend, Etsuko, works there. She told me all about it. That's where Kano was heard to say he would sell."

"This changes everything," I whispered, lifting my gaze to my painting at the back of the sentō. I felt like everything I'd ever known was a lie, even my own painting up on the wall. I looked at it and believed someone else painted it, not me. Just like my own best friend could be a killer, or my town was a veneer of deception coated over the truth.

Kumi followed my line of sight to the depiction of Mount Fuji.

"Mom is looking forward to her painting of a pine tree forest. Your mom came by yesterday and said you were in town picking up painting supplies." She reached out and squeezed my forearm, and the sudden contact unfroze me. The warmth of her hand defrosted my thoughts. "I'm glad to hear you'll be painting again. From one artist to another, creating something is a great way to work out your demons. Who knows what you'll find once you start a new project."

I hoped I would find a way out of this for everyone I loved.

CHAPTER
SEVENTEEN

I walked into Sawayaka on Tuesday sleep deprived and anxious. I'd spent all night running through lists of reasons why Akiko could never kill her own father, but the list items reversed in my head and instead she became the perfect murderer. She had motive *and* opportunity, especially if her father planned to sell to Midori Sankaku. Her patients and the nurse service she worked for weren't watching her every move on that Friday, so how could they be sure she didn't sneak away and do the job?

By morning, I felt sick, and my run was jerky and no fun. Still sweaty and upset from my run, I worked in the fields with Mom picking daikon for two hours. She tried to talk to me about our schedule for the next month, but I kept slipping away into my head, watching my best friend suffocate her own father under a pillow. Chills racked my body every time I thought about it.

At 14:00, Sawayaka was almost deserted. I hesitated at the door, thinking it was wrong for me to come here today with everything I had on my mind because I clearly wouldn't be concentrating on the food. I took a deep breath and went in anyway.

Ana smiled again when she saw me, so I snapped out of my

daydreams and came back to the present. "Yasahiro is looking forward to eating with you today," she said, beaming a blinding smile at me. Right. I had almost forgotten I asked him to sit with me.

The usual spot was set for two, and this time I wove around empty tables, their white table clothes absent, and sat facing the kitchen.

"He'll be right out." I watched her return to the front hostess station where she grabbed a coat from the hook near the front door, bundled up and walked out into the daylight. It was warm in the restaurant, so I shrugged off my coat and took my phone from my purse.

I opened the texting app and my thumbs hovered over the keyboard, reading the text I exchanged with Akiko last night. She wrote, *"I'm so sick of Tama. He's going to kick me out of my own house, I know it."*

I responded that she just needed to hang tight until they found her father's killer. I doubted anything could be done until that was worked out. She never wrote back. Did that mean something?

"Hello again, Mei." Yasahiro appeared over me, deftly carrying several plates and bowls along his forearms and in his hands. "I hope you're ready for Day Two of our challenge." His smile eased away some of my anxiety, and I smiled in return, relieved to think of something else for a moment. The scent of freshly chopped cilantro wafted to me, and I inhaled deeply.

He placed a small bowl and a plate in front of me. "Mini bowl of pho and pork bánh mì."

I pulled back from the dishes, surprised. "Are we touring Asia all this week?"

He placed his own bowl and plate across the table. "We can, if you like," he said, chuckling. "I thought you might like a little variety."

"I do." Taking a napkin from the table, I draped it across my lap. His restaurant provided linen napkins which was such a foreign thing to do in Japan unless your place catered to an upscale clientele, which he did. I glanced around the room again and took note of everything, the plaques in the window shouting acclaims of his culinary brilliance, the snippets of five-star reviews, the Michelin star, the low lighting, the uniforms of everyone who worked there. No wonder Mom quickly backed him. Sawayaka was the epitome of high dining.

"I noticed a hesitation there."

I ignored him and sipped the pho. "Mmmm. I've never been a big fan of pho but this is pretty good. What's different about it?"

"The spices. I like to go easy on the Chinese five-spice powder because cinnamon is usually a little too weird for the Japanese palate."

I sipped again, lost in my head. One time, Akiko came to Tokyo to visit me and we went to have Vietnamese in Shinjuku. I didn't enjoy the soup but I did like the rolls.

"Mei." Yasahiro interrupted my thoughts by waving his hand in front of my face. "Are you in there?"

"Yes! Yes, sorry. My brain is preoccupied today." I shook my head to clear it and returned to sipping the soup. "Tell me, Mr. Suga, what kind of restaurant is Sawayaka?"

He blinked a few times before picking up his sandwich. "I thought that was obvious. The name means 'fresh' and the menu is all Japanese traditional slow food."

He bit into his sandwich and nodded at the taste. "Mm, could use more sauce."

I picked mine up and took a bite. The pork, tender and bursting with flavor, had a crisp, vinegar dressing on it. The cucumbers and carrots inside crunched with the tang of cilantro.

"I think it's perfect," I said, from behind my hand. "And this lunch is very tasty, as was yesterday's meal."

I stopped complimenting him to eat, taking a pair of chopsticks and slurping up some of the rice noodles from the bowl.

"But?" I looked up from my meal, and he had ceased eating, inspecting me over the tops of his steepled fingers.

"No buts. It's delicious. It's not something I would eat every day, but I like it."

"I don't believe you." His eyes narrowed, and I sighed, setting down my chopsticks and leaning back into my chair.

"Okay. Okay. It *is* really delicious, but I don't understand why you would serve me Thai yesterday and Vietnamese today, when your *specialty* is *Japanese* slow food."

His face fell. "I, well, I figured you would be sick of Japanese slow food. You do realize that a lot of the dishes I serve here come directly from your mother's kitchen, right?"

I smiled, sweeping my hand over the food. "Exactly. You do realize that until this past week I haven't eaten my mother's food since I was an early teen, right?"

"You're joking around with me, aren't you?" He laughed, picking up his sandwich. "I like this about you. All the other women I know are too serious." Opening his mouth wide, he chewed off a chunk of his sandwich, half of it disappearing straight into his stomach. All men ate like this, I swore it.

I cocked my head to the side, placed my chin on my hand, and blinked at him. "I am dead serious."

He paused for a full second, mouth in mid-chew, and hands holding the last of his sandwich.

"What?"

"You heard me. I'm not lying."

He threw the sandwich down on his plate and jumped up from the table.

"You *can't* be serious. Your mother is a bastion of traditional Japanese food. Chefs worldwide have raved about her techniques. I was honored beyond measure that she took me into her confidence." His hands grasped at his hair, and I worried he was about to have a heart attack before he deflated. "Did you know she gets mail and email almost every day from other chefs that want to learn from her?"

Whoa. I had no idea! I loved my mom, but I never cared about her cooking, so she never bothered me with it. Huh. Was my mom famous? It never occurred to me to Google her.

Yasahiro sat down, calm now, and pushed his plates to the side. Too hungry not to eat, I continued to consume the sandwich.

"You stopped eating your own mother's food when you were a teen?"

I had his full attention now, so I soldiered on with my sad tale of woe.

"I was one of those over-achiever student types. I ate breakfast at home, and I've always loved my mom's breakfasts, but that was the extent of what she cooked for me." I switched to the soup. I would've asked for the recipe, because I did like it, but I would never cook it. "I ate school lunches, went to cram school, and ate convenience store food for dinner. Mom was always asleep by the time I got home. That was when my deep love of convenience store food grew to staggering heights."

I sighed, wistfully, and his eyes grew wide.

"You actually *like* convenience store food?"

"Like? I love it. Adore it."

He twisted his lips to the side.

"Hey, don't be a snob. You can't tell me you don't love hot *oden* from 7-Eleven on a cold winter day."

His mouth dropped open.

"Admit it." I set down my spoon and crossed my arms.

Yasahiro rubbed his face and sat back. "Of course, I do. I'm just, wow. I can't believe you don't eat her food. You're so... different from what I expected."

"Excuse me?" What was that supposed to mean? Has someone been gossiping about me? My eyes darted around the room, certain I was being watched.

"Never mind," he said, waving me off. Ugh. Fine. "Do you eat her food now?"

"Well, yeah, I do now because I'm home." I frowned and he appeared ready to jump up and flip the table in rage. "It's starting to grow on me." I waved him back to calmer levels. "But it's taking time so far. I still go to the convenience store when I can."

We sat at the table, silent while I finished off the soup and picked at the leftover crusts of bread on my plate. "Did you get this bread from the bakery by the train station? It's really good."

"Don't change the subject." His face settled into a stony expression.

I cleared my throat, sipped water, and smoothed out my fine-gauge knit sweater. He drummed his fingers on the table and stared out the front window, past me to the street outside.

"This changes everything," he whispered, and it reminded me of my conversation yesterday with Kumi. Akiko could be the murderer. My face grew cold and my upper lip broke into a sweat.

"Are you all right?" he asked, leaning forward and grasping my arm lightly for a moment. The genuine concern on his face brought back some warmth.

"I was just reminded of Akiko and her father. Did you know Mr. Kano was murdered? The police say he was suffocated."

"No. Really?" He pulled back, shock covering his wide eyes and parted lips. "I heard something was wrong, but I didn't know what."

"I'm worried about Akiko. I've been trying the last week to figure out who murdered her father, but I'm not getting anywhere." Or I'm denying the evidence that's right in front of my eyes, but I can't say that to Yasahiro.

"You're trying to solve the crime? That's very —" he paused, examining my face "— noble of you. Especially to help your friend."

I remembered my suspicions yesterday about him being the killer. "Where were you the morning Mr. Kano was killed?"

He laughed, good-naturedly, and my body relaxed. "I was here, of course. We open the kitchen at 7:00, me and the staff, but most days I don't come in until 8:30 or 9:00. On Fridays and Saturdays, though, we're always busy, so I make it in early to help prep. Want me to call someone over to verify?" He looked towards the kitchen where some of his staff were eating lunch, but I shook my head. No. This was dumb. I didn't know him, but everyone else found him trustworthy. I liked to believe I could tell when people were lying, and he struck me as the honest and open type.

"No. I believe you." I smiled, hoping to ease back into a normal conversation.

"I think your efforts will be helpful, regardless of who you question." He pulled his plates back in front of him and smiled.

I swallowed in a dry throat and grasped the water glass to chug down half of it. "Yeah, well, we'll see how far I get. So far, I haven't managed to do anything but eliminate two of my suspects, and I'm at a loss as to what I should do next."

"I didn't know you had a desire to be a private detective. Your mother said you were out of work right now."

"Oh, she did?" Thanks, Mom. I wanted to say, no, no I have a job. But that would've been a bald faced lie. "Yep. I got fired from my last job almost three weeks ago now. It was my third crappy job in five years. So much for being the over-achieving student, right?" He stared at me, his eyes blank and unbelieving. "Now, I'm back to being a farmer's daughter again, picking potatoes in the morning and falling asleep at 20:00 when the sun goes down."

"There's nothing wrong with being a farmer's daughter," he said, his voice softening. "I'm a farmer's son."

"But you're a successful chef now. Just look at this place." We both turned and looked at the tables, the rustic yet refined decor, and the people reading the menu outside the window. "You have so much to be proud of."

"Aren't you proud of anything?"

I didn't like where the conversation was going. I was a complete failure. I wanted to be a successful businesswoman, a project manager at a high-end ad agency or a design firm. Instead, I had been a low-end sales rep at a string of jobs, my best being a print job manager at the last place that fired me.

I picked up my napkin and dabbed at my lips. "This was a lovely lunch. I think I'm going to declare the challenge over." I stood up from the table and Yasahiro hopped up with me. "Your food is delightful, and I'm sorry I took up so much of your time."

I wanted this to be over. I was in danger of ruining Mom's reputation with someone she obviously admired. The idea of the challenge was fun at first, but now that he was eating with me, talking with me, I had to stop this before it went too far. In my teens, I rebelled in my own ways, and the desire still surfaced, but it was time to be an adult.

I turned to grab my jacket from the chair but he darted forward and grabbed my arm. "Wait," he pleaded. His fingers were warm and firm, and I glanced down at his arms, the same strong arms that took me by surprise at Kano's funeral.

"No. No, you're right. I should have been feeding you the cuisine I specialize in." He let go of my arm and brought his hand to his chest. "The food that's in my heart. Even when I'm far from home, I still love Japanese food the best."

A burst of warmth blossomed in my belly — to hear how he loved the food he cooked crushed me, inspired me. I wished I loved something that much.

"Come back the rest of the week. I'll show you what you've been missing."

CHAPTER
EIGHTEEN

Potatoes, potatoes, and more potatoes. I knew my mom farmed a lot of vegetables every year, but I had no idea it would take so long, nor take up so much space in the barn every harvest. The sweet potatoes were selling, but every day we replaced them with a new crop. So far, I had picked turnips, daikon, three different kinds of potatoes, a couple of different lettuces, carrots, spinach, and beets. My back ached, my hands were rough, and my nails were broken, and each night I fell asleep at the ridiculous hour of 20:00.

Between the hard labor and the road race training, I was beat. Last night, I'd spent time at the computer searching for all the information I could find on Midori Sankaku and Fujita Takahara. I rubbed my eyes to stay awake and look at photos of Takahara attending several exclusive events in high-end suits, each time with a different gorgeous woman on his arm. I'm not sure why but he pinged my guilt radar, like he was guilty of something but I couldn't put my finger on what. He probably had some skeletons in his closet.

I tossed a few potatoes in my basket and moved down the row with Mom by my side.

"What's in your head today, Daydreamer?" Mom asked, elbowing me in the ribs.

"Huh?" I stopped and stretched backwards, grunting at the pain in my back. How long until I acclimated to this lifestyle like Mom? She could harvest a whole row and go on to hauling vegetables to the market, teach cooking classes, and make two or three full meals without so much as a moment of pain. "I'm thinking about our dwindling list of suspects. Mr. Tajima is out. I don't believe he's done anything except his job."

She nodded, poking at the ground with her potato fork. "He's a good man. Always has been."

"Mom," I paused until I had her attention, "Kumi said something the other day, and now... now I suspect Akiko killed her father." I swallowed hard. Saying the words out loud made me sick to my stomach.

"What did Kumi say?"

I brightened a bit, pleased she didn't jump on me and call me a horrible friend.

"She said there were rumors that Mr. Kano was going to sell his land. He was giving in and wanted to be done with it. And if he was going to sell, that would make Akiko the prime suspect, right?"

Mom stared off in the direction of Akiko's house. Her front door and driveway were hidden by a forest of pine trees meant to lessen the effect of autumn typhoons. They surrounded our house as well.

"What makes you think that?"

"He would have had to sell the land, sell all his furniture, and move. And if Akiko wasn't going to get anything from it, I'm sure that would have made her bitter. You should have seen how upset she was with Tajima and Takahara when they came to see her. She was adamant about not selling to them."

"But would her actions rest on whether she was going to get the land or not?"

Hmmm. I hadn't thought of that.

"I'm not sure. If she knew she was going to get the land and wanted to keep it, she could have killed her father to keep it before he sold it. If she didn't know she would inherit the land, it's a burden either way, to keep him alive or kill him."

I sighed and plopped right down in the dirt. "Any way I look at it, it doesn't look good."

Mom kneeled down next to me, her strong hand on my shoulder. "Unless you remember that she is a good, honest, and sweet person. She's devoted her life to taking care of others. We can't forget her character in all of this."

When we were eleven, Akiko had rescued an injured baby deer from her farm fields and nursed him back to health before releasing him to his mother. For two weeks, she fed him by bottle, splinted his leg until he could walk straight, and then waited for his mother to return. She devoted herself to that little creature, and I loved that about her.

We had tons of animals growing up. My mom had cats, dogs, and horses, and so did Akiko's family. Once we were in high school, our families sold off the horses and renovated the barns for storage (and ours for my artist's loft). I figured Akiko would become a vet but she chose people over animals because people can describe what's wrong with them. It always bothered her that animals couldn't detail their pain or symptoms.

"I keep trying to stop by, but I think she's depressed and doesn't want to see me." Across the expanse of land between our two houses, the pine trees swayed in the breeze, and I zipped my hoodie up to my neck. It was edging into late October and getting colder every day.

"She'll come around. In the meantime, we have potatoes to harvest."

"Right." We both stood up, and I stretched my arms and shoulders before moving further down the row.

"So," Mom started after a few minutes of silence, "if it's not Tajima and it's not Takahara —"

"I didn't say it wasn't Takahara."

"Doesn't he have an alibi?" she asked, her hands on her hips.

"Yes. Kind of. I spoke to his assistant and she said he was busy in Tokyo all day. But it wasn't iron clad or anything. I'm not counting him out."

"Okay," she said, not convinced. "And if it wasn't Akiko, who's left?"

"Daichi Senahara. I added him to my list yesterday."

Mom laughed, her head thrown back. "That old man? How could he kill anyone when he's piss drunk all the time?"

I grimaced at her observation because it was true. In all the years I'd known him, he'd been sober maybe three days. Maybe.

"And Tama," I countered. "Tama is the only other suspect right now and the police cleared him."

"Well, if Takahara isn't rock solid then neither is Tama."

I sighed, throwing five more potatoes into our basket. The potatoes were never ending.

"Yes, you're right. If I'm going to spend the time working on everyone else, I should investigate him as well. It's only fair."

And his strange behavior made me suspicious, though he could've been guilty of just about anything, including cheating on Haruka. If I started digging, who knew what I'd find?

Mom waved at me. "Why don't you go inside and rest for a while before lunch?" She winked at me and I rolled my eyes.

"Why is everyone in this town all up in my business?"

Mom raised her hands in surrender. "I'm just glad to see you getting out. I'm sure if you wanted to date Yasahiro, he would be amenable."

"Mom!" She snickered at me. "Don't be a busybody. Besides, Yasahiro is a successful chef and businessman. I wouldn't stand a chance with him."

"Don't you say that," she said, her voice stern. "You have as much chance with him or *any* man you wanted to date."

"Shouldn't that be the other way around?" I raised my chin. "This is 2015, after all."

My contradictory nature rose to the surface. I believed, deep down inside, I was worthless, but by god, I wouldn't throw myself at some guy's feet because I was now a lowly farmer.

"Of course." Her shoulders deflated. "I didn't mean it that way. This is 2015 and..."

"Mom, stop," I said, my voice lowered. "I'm sorry. I didn't want to pick a fight."

I dropped my head and looked at the cold, dense, and unforgiving soil. I needed to learn to love that soil because it was going to feed me as I got older. It was hard to come to grips with the fact that my life had fallen back to farming when I used to get coffee at Starbucks, commute on the subway, and sit in an office all day. If my old coworkers saw me now, they would pity me.

"I just... I didn't expect to be back here, jobless. I worked so hard —" I clutched at my chest "— to make something of myself, and I failed. I feel like life is over for me now."

"Listen to me." Mom shook my shoulder and smacked me upside the head. Ow! I clutched at my temple and rubbed it. I supposed I deserved that. "Your life isn't over. You're twenty-six and this is just the beginning. Consider your time here a sabbatical. I know you don't want to farm for a living. This is a... a detour. Get back in your studio and paint. Work out these feelings until you find your path. You know I'll be happy with whatever you decide."

The upper window of the barn reflected back at me, dark and lonely. I hadn't been up there since I brought home my art supplies last weekend. I'd dumped them there and walked away. I wasn't up to painting yet, but still, I daydreamed about it often, how I would unbox my new supplies and what I might paint first.

My head hurt with all the tossing and turning of emotions I did on an hourly basis.

I pushed my thoughts aside and glanced down at my dirty clothes.

"Thanks. I'm going to go inside and warm up. Maybe I'll take a bath."

"That's a good idea. Go soak away this mood you're in. So sullen lately. *Chi chi,*" Mom chided me harshly. I had only ever heard those sounds from her when I used to sneak out at night or ruin something in the kitchen, so she must have been annoyed with me.

I turned my back on her and stalked away, deciding I would spend the day away from the house and give her a much-needed break.

———

Sawayaka was locked up when I arrived at 14:02 ready for lunch. I knocked on the window, but no one came to the door. The weather had turned cool and rainy after digging for potatoes all morning, so I warmed up in the tub with some scalding hot water, clipped my nails off, stretched my muscles, dressed, and made it to the restaurant only two minutes late. Two minutes. Ana couldn't have waited two more minutes?

I wrapped my wool coat tighter around me, adjusted the scarf over my head, and stood under the overhang of the restaurant, wondering what I should do. Had Yasahiro bailed on me? Was I going to have to walk home in the rain with a box lunch from the convenience store? I supposed I could search for the restaurant's main number online. I dug through my purse and pressed my back against the glass as knuckles rapped against it behind me.

"There you are," Yasahiro exclaimed as he unlocked and opened the door. "I thought you decided not to come."

"I was thinking the same of you." I smiled as I brushed past him and into the warmth of the restaurant. "I knocked on the window, but no one came. Is Ana not working today?"

"She has Wednesdays off. Another woman works in her place but she locks up and leaves immediately at 14:00. She's very strict like that." He gestured to our usual table, and I draped my coat on the chair at my spot. As I removed the scarf from around my head, Yasahiro blinked at me. "Something's different about you today."

"Oh, I didn't straighten my hair." I reached up to my hair and patted it down. In its natural state, my hair was unruly and wavy. When I worked with Mom in the fields, I pulled it back and threw a kerchief over it. When I went out, I straightened it with a hair iron, but I knew that would be a lost cause in the rain. The humidity would have kinked it anyway. So I clipped back my sides and let the hair do its thing. I had no one to impress. I'd thought about getting it cut really short, but the only salon in town was Haruka's place, and I refused to go there on principle.

Yasahiro nodded at me and headed to the kitchen. I panicked, suddenly feeling I should have put in more effort before I left the house. Reaching into my bag, I grabbed my mirror and snuck a quick peek at myself. Nothing seemed out of place. Hmmm. Maybe he just didn't like it.

Well, too bad for him. I wasn't trying to impress him anyway. I squared up my shoulders as he emerged from the kitchen with plates of food.

"Today, I have fresh green beans in a miso dressing. Then tofu I made this morning, octopus rice, and seaweed salad."

I tipped my face over the rice and let the steam waft into my nose. "Mmmm, I haven't had octopus rice in forever. Thank you."

We both said "Itadakimasu!" and started on the green beans. I popped a few in my mouth, and trying to be discreet, I played with my hair again, hoping it would settle down and not attract any more attention. I ate as he stared out the window, not saying anything. He was so reserved, when our last few meals together had been chatty. Maybe my newness had already lost its charm.

"You're quiet today," I said, sipping on the water at the table.

A fleeting smile graced his lips before they fell again. "I was thinking of our conversation yesterday."

"Is that so? What was so interesting that it's still in your head today?"

I figured he was wondering about Akiko's dad's murder or my dig on him about not cooking what he loves.

"Why didn't you tell me you're a painter?"

I coughed and choked on a green bean, the miso dressing sliding straight down my windpipe. Thankfully, after a burst of hacking into the fine napkins Yasahiro's restaurant provided, I pulled myself together.

"Are you okay?" Yasahiro rose from his chair and poured me a new glass of water. I gulped at it and cleared my throat.

"I'm okay. The green beans are fantastic, honestly." My voice cracked as I tried to act normal. "I promise I'm not choking on your food because it's bad."

I kept drinking, hoping he'd forgotten what we were talking about.

"That's good. I'd hate to think I kill people with my cooking."

"I've had enough of murders lately, thank you very much."

I ate another green bean, this time slowly and carefully.

"Anyway, I asked you yesterday if there was anything you were proud of and you didn't say a word. Then I was at Izakaya Jūshi last night, and a woman who works there told me you're an artist and one of your paintings is hanging in Chiyo Hokichi's new bathhouse."

Uh oh. I never intended for him to know anything intimate about me! *Lie, Mei. Lie hard.*

"No, no," I said, waving my hand at him. "I'm not an artist. Please. Not even close. Chiyo bought that painting from my family, but it wasn't mine." Oh my god, that was the worst lie I'd ever told, but he'd never see the painting because it hung on the women's side of the bathhouse. I didn't think I'd ever paint again. One moment I wanted to, and the next I broke into a cold sweat at the thought of it. I'd bought those art supplies over the weekend at Mom's insistence, but I couldn't bring myself to look at them. They were a complete waste of money.

"Huh," he grunted, confusion blanketing his face.

Guilt coated me like an oil spill in the ocean, weighing down my feathers and sinking me to the sandy bottom below. I wished I could take that back. I should've just admitted that the painting was mine. What was wrong with me?

"This woman is a friend of Kumi's and swore it was yours. She said Mrs. Hockichi paid a lot of money for it too."

My face bursted into flames, and I directed my eyes down at the tofu. I was a horrible, lying fool. I needed to stand up and get the heck out of the restaurant. Nothing good could come of this.

I set the napkin aside, took a deep breath to steel myself, and raised my eyes to Yasahiro's.

"This has been really lovely —"

"Stop," he commanded as my butt left the chair a centimeter. I froze in place. "Sit back down."

My inner fighter yelled at me to get up and give him a thorough shake down for commanding me to do anything. But my conscience told me to fess up. I had to stop lying and avoiding the parts of my life that I didn't like.

I returned to my seat. "Fine. Fine." I pushed my plate aside and made eye contact with him. His arms crossed over his chest were tense. "The painting is mine. Yes, I was a painter. I was an artist, but I'm not anymore. I gave it up when I went to college so that I could focus on my studies."

He sighed and rubbed his face, and the guilt covering me became thicker, suffocating. He looked ten times more tired than he did five minutes ago.

"Why... Why would you lie about it?"

"Because you've known me for what? A few days? And suddenly you want to know these things I don't tell *anyone*? That part of my life is over, and it has nothing to do with the life I have to live now." I sighed as I placed my napkin back on my lap. "It's not like my work was any good, anyway. The art teacher I had growing up always said my grasp of depth and light was weak, my form was sloppy, and I should give up."

I closed my eyes and remembered the old man Mom had hired to teach me, Mr. Fukuda. He gave up on me after two years and told my mom I had no talent. I stood in my room and listened to his assessment of my "abilities" and then I pretended like I hadn't heard because I was in the bathroom. Mom never knew. I tried to continue painting after that, but my confidence was sapped dry. The last painting I ever did was the one of Mount Fuji and Tama hated it. He said it was "boring and uninspired." That was when I hid it in the barn under a tarp. Mom must have uncovered it at some point.

"Really? Who says that to a young artist? That's horrible! Young talent should be nurtured, not put down." His jaw locked tight and his eyes unfocused, staring far off, probably remembering all the times his talent was cultivated so it could grow into this wonderful thing he'd created.

"Please. I'm not an artist, and I'm certainly not talented. I love art and I love painting, but I just don't have the knack for it. I figured I would channel my love of art into a career in advertising or graphic design. I wanted to manage big projects and teams of people, but companies kept sticking me in sales jobs. I learned pretty quickly I'm a horrible sales person." My voice caught, so I swallowed to keep it clear. Anymore talk of this and I would break into tears. I was still not strong enough to be okay with my failure.

I picked up my chopsticks and snagged some tofu. It slid between my tongue and teeth, slightly sweet and no aftertaste. "Wow, this is so good. I've never had tofu like this before." I grabbed another mouthful and sighed over it. My mom never made tofu, so I didn't eat much growing up. Yasahiro's was wonderful, and I was grateful for the change in conversation.

"Maybe you're a horrible salesperson because you're actually an artist. The two don't always mix well. That's why I have a business manager, an accountant, and a PR person for the advertising."

"Cooking is an art form all its own, right? I never thought about it like that until now." I looked down at my devastated plates of food. When they arrived on the table, they were worthy of a photograph. And I should have taken one! Cursed me. My Instagram account would be barren now. I took out my phone anyway and snapped a photo of the octopus rice.

Yasahiro laughed. "It's weird when people take photos of my food."

"I'll post it online too. Free advertising!"

He shook his head and chuckled. "I get a lot of that already. Yeah, cooking is like painting. You work with a canvas, brushes, and paints. I work with ingredients, the stove, utensils, and plates."

I nodded my head, turning to the rice. "That would be true if I painted anymore, which I don't."

"Maybe you'll change your mind."

"Or maybe not. Maybe I was never meant to be a painter. Maybe I was meant to be a farmer like my mom. I certainly won't be a chef. Not after I set the kitchen on fire that one time."

He waved his hand in front of his face. "Whatever. I've set my own kitchen on fire a bunch of times."

I shuddered, a wave of tingles crawling up my spine. "Fire is not my friend."

"What?" he smiled, a quirk of his lips goading me. "Did you burn your fingers and never want to cook again? My sister tried that once, but my mom forced her to keep cooking. I'm surprised your mom was so lenient with you."

A geyser of anger erupted up through my chest and I held it back long enough to ask myself one question: how far away did I want to push him?

"No. And stop being a jerk. When I was a kid, I fell into a campfire after some kids pushed me around. So I don't joke around about fire. Ever."

He dropped his chopsticks and his face whitened. "Oh god, what happened to you?"

"I spent a month in the hospital, lost more than half my hair, and I have scars on my back." Actually, scars covered my entire back, but I didn't want to be explicit. I was glad I couldn't see them on a daily basis unless I looked in the mirror. It happened when I was eight, and I'd been afraid of fire ever since. I never saw who pushed me into the flames, and no one ever confessed. My mom almost held me back in school, but I worked hard to keep going. I was advancing in reading and math, and I didn't want to fall behind.

Yasahiro sat on the other side of the table, his eyes on me, and I began to sweat. I flip-flopped between being attracted to him and scared to death of him. Not because I feared he'd be violent or anything. More like, I was sure once he knew what a loser I was, he'd blab it all over town. Not only would I be the failure that got fired from her big Tokyo job and became a farmer again, I'd also be the woman who was turned down by the hottest young chef in town. Everyone wanted him, in some capacity or another. I would bet that, if I looked out the door, I would see young, desperate women circling the restaurant like vultures hunting for a fresh meal.

I needed to put some distance between us because a romance with him, if he even liked me, would be a disaster. I had to make that crystal clear. He could never be interested in someone like me, and I had to avoid falling for him, if only to keep my meager reputation intact.

I couldn't get up and leave. I'd already tried that a few times, and he was watching for signs of flight.

"Are you going to eat?" I gestured to his meal, growing cold. He dragged his hand through his hair, sighed, and started on the green beans. "Wouldn't want you to get too skinny now." I winked at him and laughed. "I'm sure your girlfriend doesn't want you starving."

He barked a laugh. "I don't have a girlfriend. The restaurant keeps me pretty busy."

"Oh, really? Kumi, Chiyo Hokichi's daughter-in-law, you know her, right?" He nodded as he ate his octopus rice. "She was telling me she has a friend who's interested in dating you." He stopped with the chopsticks paused in front of his mouth. "I could have her set you up, if you like."

Message sent. *I'm not the right person for you, Yasahiro.* And it was way too haughty of me to believe he'd be into me anyway.

He leaned across the table to look into my empty bowl and stood up. "No, thanks. How about we leave the matchmaking up to fate, okay? Would you like more octopus rice?"

"Sure. Thanks."

He nodded and took my bowl into the kitchen.

I sucked in a quick breath to halt a flood of tears. I'd tried to light myself on fire and he stomped out the flames before they climbed up my clothes.

Was it wrong to be relieved?

CHAPTER
NINETEEN

The day dawned chilly again, a thick mist of rain coating everything outside in a blanket of water. Mom didn't want to work in this mess, so we took the morning off, but I stood at the house's back door and stared at the barn while drinking my morning coffee.

That barn symbolized so many things for me. It was the place I played when I was a kid with my older brother. It was where we stored our winter vegetables. Mimoji was born in that barn when we had horses. When we renovated the space after we sold the horses, Mom asked me what I wanted, and I wanted a loft, a place to be alone and to create. Back then, I was certain I was going to be an artist someday with my own studio, attending gallery openings, and making enough money to stay home with my kids. Yep, I would have at least three kids and be married to some successful CEO. I sipped on my coffee and sighed.

The barn's loft turned against me some time in my teens. I lost my way with my art, not knowing what to paint or even why I wanted to paint. Then I poisoned the place by bringing Tama around. We would drink saké, get drunk, and have sex whenever we felt like it. I never got pregnant or even got a disease from him so that was good. The barn was cursed, but at least I hadn't completely ruined my life with him.

I set my coffee down, grabbed my rain boots, coat, and the kerosene space heater, and headed into the barn. When I opened the door, a small bird burst past me and out into the rain. It must have been trapped inside yesterday when we were loading in the potatoes. The air inside smelled musty, but as always, the barn floor shined immaculate and clean, the sealed concrete slab well taken care of over the years. The rest of the barn, made of wood and gypsum board, was a step down from a true Japanese storehouse made of timber and clay.

I hung up my coat inside the door, and taking off my rain boots at the foot of the loft's stairs, I climbed up in socks. In the loft, I set the heater down and turned it on, cracking open a window to let out any fumes it may produce, and then I stared out the window for twenty minutes.

What was I doing? I promised myself I would give up painting, get a real job, and get on with my life. When I made that decision over five years ago, I thought it was the best decision I'd ever made. I had made a life long choice that would put me on the right path to success. I couldn't have been more wrong. I'd always had the desire to create, to make something for myself with my name on it. Each job I applied to, I tried to get in on the creative side of the business, but each time, they funneled me into a sales position instead. So I would spend my weekends at museums or at art gallery openings looking at other people's art. If I couldn't make art, at least I would appreciate it.

The barn's loft floor creaked under my feet as I rocked side to side and stared at the blank canvas on the easel. I'd placed the canvas there over the weekend and hadn't looked at it since. I'd had so much fun at Sekaidō, buying the missing supplies I needed. I got excited just seeing all the colors, new brushes, and fresh stretched canvases. I really loved so many things about painting: a fresh paintbrush, a brand-new tube of paint, a clean canvas. Until the canvas was staring me in the face, and I had no idea what to put there.

I wasn't ready to paint Chiyo's pine forest yet, but I needed to do something, anything, to get back in the groove of things or else I'd walk out and never look back. I closed my eyes and the first thing to pop into my head? I shifted my shoulders around, my bra strap rubbing against the damaged skin on my back. The first thing in my head was the campfire I fell into when I was a kid. My head jerked, and my eyes flew open remembering that moment of sheer terror as I dropped onto the hot coals and screamed.

My heart raced into a gallop and my forehead slicked with sweat, but I immediately turned the terror into a challenge. I sank to my knees in front of my three tackle boxes of paint and started digging. Black, green black, and mars black. Burnt orange, ochre, brown black, and burnt umber. A handful of reds from carmine and crimson to alizarin. I lined them up on the floor in hue order, flipping a few around and keeping them in place with the tips of my fingers. I needed to start with black, build up the night sky and ground, then the fire pit, and the flames that danced up into the smoke. Did I even have a black primed canvas? I opened the big plastic bags Mom stored some of my old stretched canvases in and there was one, 50 cm by 40 cm, a decent size. I'd forgotten I had that! And it was still in great shape. Perfect. I placed it on the easel and got to work.

I worked for hours without stopping, layering on the shades of black first, shaping them with my brushes, my fingers, or a palette knife. Whatever I needed, whatever I felt like using. The strokes on the canvas came from deep inside, a memory flowing out my fingers, feeding off the agony and the pain, and turning it into an image in front of me. I was consumed with the energy to push harder, to dig deeper, and to make the shadows speak volumes.

When I backed away from the canvas for the first time, I

drew a shaky breath and looked down at myself. Dabs of paint covered me from my shirt down to my socks. In fact, I'd left little sock prints all over the floor because I didn't put down a drop cloth. *Careless, Mei!*

"Oh no," I breathed out. Mom was going to be pissed with me if I didn't clean it up. I glanced out the windows and the rain was really coming down instead of just spitting mist everywhere. I grabbed a clean towel from the pile next to my supplies, opened the window, and thrust the towel in my hand out into the rain to get it wet. We should've considered installing a sink.

While I waited for the towel to wet, I watched a small car in the distance grow bigger as it got closer. Daichi Senahara, Kano's next door neighbor, slowed down as he drove to his driveway and pulled up to the house. I wondered where he'd been. I had to remember to go by his house with a bottle of alcohol and pump him for information on Kano's supposed plans to sell his house and land to Midori Sankaku.

Thankfully, once the towel was wet, I could clean up my paint spills. I had to take off my socks because they were soaked with paint, and my feet immediately became bricks of ice in the cold barn. Brrr. I needed to go back inside and take a hot bath.

I folded my arms across my chest and stepped away from my painting. The scene, a mess of black, unfolded into the division between land and sky. The eventual resting place of the fire that nearly killed me sat in the center. It was a good start, and amazingly enough, I didn't hate it. Huh.

As I put the caps back on the paints, I thought back on all the things I'd seen on my twisted path to this moment: the fall we ate almost nothing because the crops were devastated with mold, my mother cooking food at the school as a side job so we could eat, the summer festivals in town, Tama's body over mine on the loft couch, the shrine on the mountain where we would pray every New Year's Day, and my boss's face when he fired me. My life had been filled with ups and downs and constant flip-flopping.

Was I heading for rock bottom or was I on a climb to the top of the mountain? I honestly didn't know yet.

I turned off the kerosene heater, reached for the handle to close the window, and stopped when flashing lights caught my attention. I narrowed my eyes at the distant blinks of blue heading out our way, hoping they didn't slow down. *Please, don't slow down!*

But they did and turned straight into Akiko's driveway.

I acted fast, sprinting down the stairs to the barn door, stuffing my bare feet into my rain boots, and grabbing my coat. I ran into the pouring rain, reaching into my pocket and feeling for my phone. My fingers locked around it and let go.

"Mom!" I called out as I raced past the back door. "Mom! Akiko!"

I hoped she heard me because I wasn't stopping to find out. Pumping my legs hard, I crossed the road and headed down her driveway as fast as I could. The two cars in the driveway besides Akiko's were both police cars. I feared one of them was an ambulance. She'd been so down lately, I worried she may be suicidal.

Her front door was open, and I attempted to climb the steps and run inside, but a harsh voice told me to halt.

"Don't come in, Mei!" Goro's partner raised her hand to my face. I wiped the rain from my eyes and tried to peer past her. "Akiko is coming down to the station voluntarily. Don't cause a scene, please."

Inside the house, Goro bent over and whispered into Akiko's ear as she nodded her head and cried.

"I didn't do it, but if coming down to the station for a few days will help, I will." She shook her head side to side. "But it wasn't me. I won't confess to something I didn't do, could never do."

Goro kept his voice low, so I couldn't hear anything. I could only tell Akiko was in far worse circumstances than I imagined her to be. I daydreamed she was exonerated and apologized to, and she went back to her job and her life, her home and family name intact. This? I wasn't prepared for this.

"Mei?" Akiko saw me in the doorway and came forward with Goro's hand on her shoulder. "You know I would never do this, right? There's no way I'd kill my own father."

I glanced between Goro and his partner, knowing full well that neither of them gave a crap what I thought of her. Of course I would back her up. We'd been friends since we were born.

"You know I believe you," I said to her. "And I'll do whatever I can to prove it." I turned to Goro. "What the hell is going on?"

He sighed, probably because he knew he couldn't put me off for long. I'd badger everyone until I got answers.

"I need help," Akiko said, glancing at Goro. "They questioned my patients on the day Dad was killed, and two of them don't remember me being there. But I was, I swear it!" Tears fell down her cheeks. "You know how it is. They'll keep looking for evidence until the prosecutor is satisfied, but it wasn't me. It wasn't."

My brain tried to process this new development as Goro directed her from the house with the help of two other officers. Her workplace had verified everything! How did things change? They headed into the rain, and I followed doggedly behind.

"Wait. There must be some mistake." I pulled on Goro's sleeve, but he shrugged me off, handed Akiko to the other officers, and turned to face me as they helped her into the back of a police car. Raindrops bounced off his officer's cap while my hair plastered to my head.

"Don't make a scene of this. If no one knows we brought her to the station and everything turns out fine, she'll go on with her life, and no one will suspect anything. I know we said we'd wager on this, but we need to stop because I don't want to ruin her life. We can't account for her whereabouts the day of the crime, and Tama says she's been depressed and out of sorts for months now." He glanced left and right.

"She just wouldn't do this." I threw up my hands in exasperation. "What do I have to do to get her cleared?"

"Come by the station later and we can talk about this more. But not here."

"But... I don't want her to go alone!" I yelled at him as he got in his car and pulled away. How could I let my own best friend be carried off by the police? She seemed so terrified and depressed. I couldn't let her deal with this on her own.

Screw it. I wasn't going to let them take her there all by herself.

I ran down the gravel driveway, my feet burning in my rain boots as my bare skin chafed against the unforgiving rubber over and over. I ignored it and kept going. I made it to the gas station on the edge of town before I slowed down to a limping crawl. It'd take me another twenty minutes to walk to the police station. Why had I not run across the street to get Mom's car? Because I was stupid, that's why.

I limped in a daze, remembering Mom's words from the day before. *"Unless you remember that Akiko is a good, honest, and sweet person. She's devoted her life to taking care of others. We can't forget her character in all of this."* Had we been blind? Could Akiko really be a murderer? Or had her character never wavered and this was a ploy to pin the guilt on someone else?

"Mei? Mei!" I came to an abrupt halt on the corner, and Yasahiro stood in front of me with an umbrella in one hand and a bag of garbage in the other. "What..." He scanned me from head to toe, and I wiped the rain from my eyes and realized I was walking the stretch of sidewalk just past his restaurant and its back door. "What happened to you? Are you okay?"

He tossed his garbage into the dumpster and came straight to me. I started to shiver. If I had kept moving, I would have stayed warm, but the rain seeped into every seam of my jeans and coat, poured down my legs, and filled my boots.

"Mei!" Yasahiro put his umbrella over me and bent down to

make eye contact. "Come inside now. You can't stay out here like this."

I couldn't argue despite wanting to bolt and head to the police station. I was in no shape to show up there. So, I nodded and followed him into the kitchen.

CHAPTER
TWENTY

"What were you doing out there?"

I stood in the doorway of the kitchen, dripping a flood of water onto the ceramic tiles. I must've looked like a drowned rat with my hair soaked and coat stuck to me. The kitchen was not as busy as I expected, only a few guys washing dishes and no one at the stoves.

"What time is it?" I hadn't even noticed the time when I ran out of the barn and across the street to Akiko's house. I doubted it was past noon.

Yasahiro worked the buttons of my raincoat and peeled it off my shoulders. "It's almost 14:00. I figured you'd be here in about twenty minutes. Are you going to tell me what happened?"

"I... I don't know." I looked down at my jeans plastered to my legs and sighed. "I'm soaked. I didn't realize it was raining so hard."

Each of the guys in the kitchen threw sidelong glances my way, and I dipped my head to avoid eye contact. I decided I better keep my mouth closed and not broadcast to everyone that I ran through the streets on a cold, rainy day. What had I been thinking? That I could run after the police car, pull Akiko out, and take her home? There were days when I believed I was a smart person. Today was not one of those days.

I grabbed at my raincoat before he took it away. Reaching into the pocket, I groaned as I extracted my soaked phone. The lake's worth of water in my pocket had sent it to its grave, and it wouldn't even turn on.

Yasahiro took my phone from my hands, brushing his long warm fingers against my freezing cold skin. "I'll put this in some rice. Maybe it'll turn on tomorrow."

He set it on the counter, grabbed his chef's coat from the hook next to an office door, and bundled me in it. Then he grabbed a clean kitchen towel. "Here. For your hair."

I flipped my head over and wrapped up my wet locks into a turban.

"I should call Mom and let her know I'm not at home anymore. I kind of ran out without saying goodbye." I had screamed at the house as I ran across the street, but I didn't think she heard me. She may have been napping or in the bath.

"Here." Yasahiro handed me his phone. "Your mom's number is in my address book."

I took the phone with a shaky hand and dialed Mom's mobile.

"Yasahiro, I hope you're well."

"No, Mom. It's Mei."

"Mei, where are you? Are you calling me from the barn on Yasahiro's phone?"

"No," I said, sighing. "I'm actually in town at Sawayaka. I was in the barn, and then I looked out the window and saw police cars pulling up to Akiko's house. They took her in for questioning." Tears started to fall down my face, so I turned my back to Yasahiro. "She says her patients can't remember if she visited them the day her Dad died, and Tama is telling the police all types of lies about her mental state. Why would he do something like that?"

Mom paused on the other end of the phone for a moment.

"Something strange is going on between those two. I think we're going to need to do some digging, and it won't be pretty. They're definitely hiding something. Isn't it pouring rain outside? My car is in the driveway so you must've walked."

I squished back and forth in my soaked boots. "I'm a little wet, but I'll be fine." I turned around and Yasahiro gestured that he'd drive me home. "Yasahiro will drive me home in a little bit. Don't worry, but my phone is soaked and won't turn on. So don't try to call."

"Oh no, Mei. I hope you have a backup." Of course, I didn't have a backup phone. I was too poor for something like that. "We'll talk about this when you get home."

I hung up the phone and gave it back to Yasahiro. The kitchen was now empty, the lunch hour over, and everyone had left for their break before the dinner rush.

"It's a good thing I was making miso soup for lunch today. Come over here and have something to eat before I take you home."

I took two steps in my squishy boots before he placed his hand on my shoulder and stopped me. He directed me to a stool at the kitchen island and sat me on it. Squatting down, he removed each of my boots and looked inside.

"There's a bucket full of water in each of these, and where are your socks?" His fingers trailed up my jeans, stopping at the splats of paint. Taking my right hand in his, he smiled at my blackened fingertips. My face caught fire, burning at this sudden intimate contact. I stared at our hands together, not believing he was touching me. Yesterday, I pushed him away, and today, he was closer than ever. How could I let that happen? I tried to snap my fingers back, but he held them tight between his hands, pressing warmth into them.

"You were painting." He raised his eyebrows at me, and after a moment of strong eye contact, he let my hands go. I held my breath and let it go slowly as he grabbed my boots and dumped the water from both into the sink.

"I was painting, yes."

I smudged the paint on my jeans with my index finger, watching it blend with the rain and spread through the fibers.

"Mei, that's great! I'm so happy for you."

I rolled my eyes at him and sighed.

"What?" His face fell into a frown. "I *am* happy for you. This may be the start of something important for you."

"Please." I injected extra sarcasm into my voice. "It's just painting. It's nothing special." I paused as I gauged how upset he was with me. Judging by the set of his jaw and the way he narrowed his eyes, hugely upset. I wondered if I could dial that up even more. "Honestly, I was going to paint, get cleaned up, come here and never mention it. I guess, I don't see why you even care."

He sighed, setting my boots by the door. "Of course I care. What do you have against me knowing you're an artist?"

He turned his back on me, grabbed a bowl from a stack of clean dishes, spooned miso soup into it, and slid it across the kitchen island to me.

"I'm not an artist. I try, and sometimes I like what I do, like what I make, but everyone always hates it, including me."

"Didn't Mrs. Hokichi buy your painting for 60,000 yen? It seems to me that if she hated the painting, she wouldn't have bought it." He spooned hot steaming rice from a rice cooker into two bowls and set them aside.

I leaned over to smell the soup, letting the steam warm my face. I tried not to be annoyed that he knew all of these details about me that I never told him, but his knowledge of my life slowly chipped away at my patience. Damned small towns. And this was why we couldn't become involved. I needed to build a good reputation if I stayed here for the next year. Already most people suspected I had been fired from my last job, and I was back home, penniless, which was the truth, but something I couldn't admit openly. If we dated and he broke up with me because I'm a loser, which would surely happen, that would be the end for me. Everyone would find out, and I'd be laughed at until I couldn't leave the house.

"Chiyo has never said a bad thing about anybody ever in her life. She bought the painting because she felt bad for me. She knew I needed the money. No other reason."

Yasahiro handed me a spoon, grabbed a stool, and sat down next to me. "You're so hard on yourself. This is a common thing amongst artists. Did you know that?" I tried to ignore him, hoping he'd change the subject, but he went on. "It's common amongst successful people, too. Imposter syndrome. Trust me. I get it all the time. I look at the rave reviews of my restaurant, my work, the stuff I do, and I don't believe any of it. Yet, people come here to eat. They take pictures of my food and put them up online. I receive constant calls to return to France and teach new students the techniques I've been learning. And I keep thinking, 'Why me?'"

I sipped the soup carefully and shivered as the warm broth defrosted me from the inside out. "Because this is the best miso soup I have ever tasted. Wow. It's a lot like Mom's but... There's something else."

"I use two kinds of bonito. Your mom only uses one." He laughed before sipping his own soup.

Imposter syndrome? That sounded about right. I'd felt like an imposter my whole life. I believed my good grades were a fluke and any success I had I didn't deserve. Then I fell into a depression the past few years as I watched all of that come to fruition.

"Do you really feel like an imposter? After all the success you've had?"

He adjusted the kerchief he kept around his neck in the kitchen. "Sure. Every day I stand outside the restaurant and believe it'll be the last day I'm successful. That someone will finally point their finger at me and call me a fraud, and everything I've worked for will be over."

He said this matter-of-factly, like he had always felt this way. Warmth grew inside of me, my earlier resolution to keep him away from me waning. I desperately wanted to reach over and hold his hand and remind him of his talent.

Why was I such a hypocrite? I wanted to do that for him but not let him do that for me.

We shared a moment of silence punctuated by soup slurping, and it felt comfortable and easy. It also felt soaking wet, but only to me. I shouldn't have been so hard on myself, or him.

"I've been so... lost." Confession time. I didn't know Yasahiro that well yet, but he felt familiar, like someone I could trust. He wanted to know more about me, and I could do that without letting it get romantic. I reached down into my gut and pulled up some courage. "I put my painting away years ago, determined to give it up. And then I was eliminated from every job I've had for the last five years." Tears crept into my eyes and my voice cracked. "I'm a complete failure. And now Akiko is in trouble..."

Yasahiro, to his credit, didn't freak out about seeing me cry. The last guy I dated two years ago, the last time I got laid in fact, would stand up and walk away every time I cried. He didn't know how to handle emotions. Yasahiro placed his warm hand over mine on the kitchen island and squeezed.

"You're not a failure. You're only just beginning. I promise. Now, did I hear you say Akiko was arrested?"

"No, they brought her in for more questioning." I shook my head, forcefully, my tears launching every which way. He tugged on the sleeve of his chef's coat I wore and indicated I should use it to dry my eyes. I dabbed at my face with the corner of the cuff.

"She takes care of all these old men and women, in their homes, as a visiting nurse. I'm not surprised they're horrible witnesses what with their bad memories. The police questioned them, and two can't remember her being there. And Tama says she's been depressed the past few months." The last time she came into the city, she was bummed about her Dad, but we had a great time and had talked on the phone and on Skype several times since then. Plus, she always went to work. If she had been depressed, it wasn't debilitating. Lots of people led day-to-day lives while depressed. It didn't mean they were murderers.

"Hmmm," he said, rubbing at his chin before getting up from his seat, opening the oven, and taking out a pan of cooked eel in brown sauce. He must have prepared that earlier and kept it warm for me. He placed the eel on the rice, added bits of seaweed, and served it to me. "I know Tama. I see him most nights at Izakaya Jūshi."

"Really? He was never much of a drinker when I knew him."

"Well, that's not the case now. He always seemed like a pleasant guy to me, and we've talked on a few occasions. He's dating Haruka from the hair salon up the street."

"Yes. I know," I ground out between clenched teeth. Yasahiro eyed me but didn't ask. I relaxed my jaw. "I guess things have changed a lot since I've been gone."

"That may be true of the town." He sat next to me again with his own eel and rice bowl. "But I can tell you one thing. Your spirit has always lived on in your home and your mother's love for you has never wavered. Not one bit."

"What?" The change in conversation startled me enough that my chopsticks rolled out of my hand and hit the floor. Yasahiro calmly got up and retrieved me a new pair.

"I've been here for over a year now, learning from your mom, and opening the restaurant. She would often have me over to your house for cooking lessons, especially during the summer when she was busy on the farm and couldn't come to my place or the community center. She caught me a few times looking at the family pictures on the wall."

I blushed five shades of crimson, knowing the photos on the wall at home: baby pictures of me and my brother, graduation photos when I was still super awkward, and some candid shots Mom had taken over the years.

"Your mom always bragged about you — how smart you are, where you went to school, your jobs and an apartment in the city. She was always happy about how much you had accomplished, showing me photos on her phone or telling me stories about things you did. I probably know you better than you think I do. Sorry." He averted his eyes and stared at his food while I panicked inside. How much did he know? "She never mentioned the painting though. It's as if she knew how you wanted to leave it behind." He shook his head as he ate a bite of rice and eel. "I would never have known if I hadn't met you."

I didn't believe it. "Surely, Mom bragged more about my brother than me. He's the one with the successful business in Osaka, the wife, and kid."

"Nope. You're the only one she talks about."

Tears welled up in my eyes again. I had the best mom on the planet.

I took a deep breath and blew it out slowly. I liked being with Yasahiro, and I both didn't want it to end but felt it would someday soon.

"So, you ran into town with no umbrella, and apparently no socks, to try and rescue Akiko from the police?"

I laughed, mopping up my face again with the sleeve of his coat. "Yep. Some days my brilliance knows no bounds."

He laughed too. "I like your sense of humor. No one ever understood me growing up. It wasn't until I lived in France that I realized I was sarcastic."

"I learned sarcasm from the internet, hours of YouTube videos and some show called *How I Met Your Mother*."

"I love that show!" He backed away from me briefly to scan me from head to toe. This time his gaze was appraising, and I warmed with the attention. "No one here has ever seen it."

"I know." Those hours of alone time in my apartment in

Tokyo in my pajamas with ramen noodles and a pint of ice cream were spent watching tons of internet TV. I didn't have much of a life in Tokyo.

"I heard from the town gossipers that you have a bet with Goro? On which of you can solve the murder first?"

"Yeah, but I'm doing a horrible job of it. I'm sure I'm going to lose."

Yasahiro took my empty miso bowl and refilled it. "Well, if you want, we could go to Izakaya Jūshi tomorrow evening and see if Tama is there. We could casually ask him about what's going on and see if he gives us any information."

Interesting. A night out with Yasahiro? But it wouldn't be a date, it would be an information gathering session. I could be okay with that.

"Okay, yeah. Let's do that. What time do you get off work?"

"23:00. Is that okay?"

I guffawed in an unladylike manner, and he quirked a smile at me. "Yikes. I'm an old timer now, and I go to bed ridiculously early."

He smiled, squeezing my hand again. My heart soared with the contact. Stupid heart. "Take a nap or something. You can meet me here at 22:30 and I'll make you a pre-outing cocktail."

"You mix drinks too?"

He blew on his nails. "I do a lot of things, Mei. You haven't seen anything yet."

"Okay. Deal. I'll be here."

He stabbed his finger into the air. "But don't miss lunch tomorrow! I have something special planned."

I couldn't wait.

CHAPTER
TWENTY-ONE

Being warm and dry again never felt so good. I was back home, and I never wanted to run in wet rain boots again because my feet stung and had acquired blisters. I taped them up, got dressed, and got moving anyway. After telling Mom everything that happened, we drove to the police station, and in true Mom fashion, she walked in and everyone cheered, smiled, and bowed to her. My mom was more popular than I was.

I glanced at the man talking to her, and based on the way he commanded the room, I guessed he was in charge. Good. She went straight for the top. But first came all the pleasantries of how's your family, how's work, how's your health, et cetera, et cetera, and I nodded and smiled the whole time, hoping we would see Goro soon. Goro said we could come by and help out, and I wanted that to be the truth. I wouldn't take no for an answer, and I had Mom to back me up. She'd known everyone in this town for decades, and even babysat plenty of the people in the police force when they were kids. They were unlikely to tell her no unless it'd get them fired.

"Now, we are here to see Akiko Kano. We've known each other for a long time, and I'm sure you can let us in to see her."

Mom folded her hands and waited. People behind the supervisor nodded their heads, but he stood firm, rigid and unable, or unwilling, to help us.

"Mrs. Yamagawa, you know police procedures. We're just questioning her, and she came in voluntarily. If we can clear her and establish her alibi, she'll go home. She *wants* to stay and get this taken care of."

Mom smiled and clapped her hands. "Fantastic. Mei and I will wait out here for Goro. We've been invited to help out, and that's exactly what we're going to do."

"Please sit down and wait. Goro has told us of your bet, Mei. What a ridiculous man!" He laughed. "He'll be out soon."

I grimaced as Mom and I sat down on the bench. Goro had been gossiping, and they were excited to see me run the 3K in my underwear, no doubt. As soon as this rain let up outside, I needed to get out for a run or I could forget about that good reputation I wanted to build. I thought going out with and getting dumped by Yasahiro would do me in. Turned out, I had done a pretty good job of sabotaging myself all on my own.

"Looks like we'll be waiting for a while," Mom said, peering down the hallway through the tiny window in the locked door. "I'm sure they have a lot to talk about."

Great. And here I had no phone to distract me. I could only daydream.

What was the first thing that popped into my head? Yasahiro, of course. I should have been thinking about who killed Akiko's father, and the suspects that we still had to vet, but it'd been ages since anyone flirted with me. Had he flirted with me? Or was he just being kind? I couldn't say since I didn't know him very well. If I'd had more time to observe him, I would have the chance to see if he was like that with everybody. If he was, I would know not to take his little gestures seriously. Maybe he was a touchy-feely kind of guy. I could imagine him walking the streets of Paris and helping little old ladies with their groceries. I saw him drinking coffee at a tiny café and laughing at some person's joke, reaching across to touch them on the arm. I imagined him kissing people on the cheek to say hello or goodbye. That's what they did in Europe. I'd wanted to brush up on my English so I watched American shows online for the last five years. Sometimes the girls kissed each other on the cheek hello, and the guys would shake hands, but that was about it. I should've watched European television, but I sucked at French.

Mom shifted next to me, leaning over to my ear. "Should I ask you what's going on between you and Yasahiro?"

"No."

Mom The Mind-Reader hummed and shook her head but didn't ask me anything more.

My thoughts wandered back to the side of the road when Takahara drove up and creeped me out by following me home. He gave me his business card and seemed sincere about Midori Sankaku's motives for their involvement in Chikata.

"So when do they break ground on this greenhouse Midori Sankaku is building?" I asked Mom.

"I've heard they have enough land to break ground in February. If it gets too cold, then it'll be moved to March. They need to pour a concrete slab and it can't be done in this weather." She waved her hand at the door and the rain falling outside. "But it can't be done in freezing temperatures either. Anyway, if they secured Kano and Senahara's land, they could also build administration buildings there. In the meantime, the people who will run the construction operation will work out of the grocery's main offices and a temporary building about two blocks from here. It's not ideal, but it was the best they could do."

"How do you know all of this?"

Mom tapped her ear with her finger. "I hear all and see all. Don't think I didn't notice the paint on your fingers when Yasahiro dropped you off today." Mom squealed and smiled like a little girl. Embarrassment radiated from my pores as a few people in the front office smiled at her. "I'm so happy to see you painting again."

I dropped my voice. "Don't broadcast it to the whole town, okay?" I lightly punched her on the shoulder. "Hey, how come you never told me how famous you are?"

"Me?" She pulled back in surprise. "You must be joking. I'm not famous. I'm not even online."

"You should be. Yasahiro told me that people write to you all the time looking for help with traditional Japanese food, and that he was honored to work with you."

Mom blushed. I knew where I got that trait from. "Stop. It's nothing. I'm just passing on my knowledge like Grandma did for me."

We sat in silence for another fifteen minutes when movement at the end of the hall caught our attention. Goro left an interview room and headed down the hallway. The door buzzed and he exited into the waiting area.

"Mei, Mrs. Yamagawa, I'm glad you could make it down to talk about Akiko." He gestured to a conference room, off to the opposite side of the hallway he just came from. I took one last glance towards the room Akiko was in, but I couldn't see her. I hoped she knew I would do everything I could to help her out.

Goro poured us each a cup of hot green tea and we sat at the table.

"I'm guessing Mei told you about what's going on with Akiko. First, we called the visiting nurse service she works for, and they said they could verify she saw all her patients because that's what she reported." He sighed, turning his cup in his hand. "But then we went to speak with her patients, and they couldn't remember anything."

"This is so hard to believe." Mom shook her head, her mouth set in a firm line. "We'd like to help in any way we can."

"Hmmm," Goro said, sipping at his tea. "You know it's tradi-tion to allow the community to help with evidence gathering and apprehending criminals, so I'm willing to let the bet go if we can work together."

I breathed a sigh of relief, though I would still participate in that run. I needed something to focus on.

Mom hummed, staring out the window. "I've heard the biggest sticking points are that Akiko's whereabouts during the day of the crime can't be verified, and that she was feeling down for the last few months. While I can't account for her state of mind, I'm sure the people she saw every day could speak to her upbeat and happy attitude. Her father's health had been failing this last year and she was doing everything she could to help him feel better. He spoke to me about it on several occasions."

"I was thinking," I said, leaning forward, "I'd be happy to go visit the elderly patients she was supposed to be taking care of on the day of the murder. Perhaps with some baked goods and tea, we could smooth over their worries and help bring back the events of the day?"

Goro took out a notepad and began to jot something down. "We should do it together. Mrs. Yamagawa, you probably know some of her patients?"

"I do," Mom replied. "I'm not sure if I know the ones she was supposed to see that day, but it may be that I do."

"All right then." Goro closed his notepad. "I'm busy all day tomorrow, so would you be willing to visit these people on Saturday? Kumi hates it when I work on the weekends, but I'd like to get going on this case as soon as possible, so we can send Akiko home. She won't leave until she's completely cleared."

I smiled at Akiko's need to be vindicated. She always had a keen sense of justice.

Mom nodded, satisfied. "Akiko could never hurt another person. If she did, I would suspect she had been possessed by a fox."

Goro laughed and rolled his eyes. "I've heard that defense

more than once around here. Daichi Senahara loves to blame everything he does while drunk on foxes."

"I have an idea," Mom said, finishing her tea. "Let's visit these patients early in the morning, no later than 11:00. Often, with older people going through dementia or Alzheimer's, they're more lucid in the morning. This is why the majority of my cooking classes are in the morning."

"A good idea. I hadn't thought of that. I believe we visited them in the evenings." Goro's face scrunched as he flipped back in his notebook. "Yes, we did. Just before dinner. Maybe that's it. Okay, I'll be in touch tomorrow to make definite plans. I'm sure we can get this worked out. Let's remember to keep this from being spread around town. We usually don't like to make arrests until the prefecture prosecutor is satisfied with the evidence and we have a verified confession. Akiko is here to help, and we don't want anyone getting the wrong idea about her."

We rose from the table, and for the first time in a week, I felt like we were actually getting somewhere. If we could verify her alibi, everything would be okay.

But if we did that, then who was the real killer?

———

IF AKIKO DIDN'T COMMIT THE CRIME, AND I HONESTLY believed she didn't, then I needed to figure out who did. The Japanese criminal justice system almost exclusively relied on confessions, and the conviction rate neared ninety-nine percent because the prosecutors didn't bother to bring someone to court unless they confessed. Confessions in Japan were made of gold, but only if the suspect could provide details about the murder no one else knew about. I had grown up reading detective novels and watching the TV Asahi drama, *Aibō*, that portrayed detectives in Tokyo, but then I started watching *CSI* and *Law & Order* a few years ago and saw what the legal system was like in America.

They were so different from us. We didn't even have jury trials in Japan, so their system was almost made for dramas. I was glued to my computer every day for a solid year.

After dinner at home, Mom and I grabbed a bottle of saké and walked across the road to see if Daichi Senahara was home. He was the only other suspect I could think of, so we needed to make sure he wasn't the actual killer.

I rang the bell as the sun set and prayed he was still at home. Maybe he'd already left for Izakaya Jūshi for the evening, but his car sat in the driveway and lights warmed the windows of his house. Perhaps he'd walked into town and left the lights on? I didn't think so.

The door opened and answered all of my questions.

"Mei? Tsukiko? What are you doing here?" He smiled and stepped to the side to let us in. "Mei, I heard you were home, but I haven't seen you around. How are you?"

"I'm good, Mr. Senahara." I stepped into his house with Mom behind me and felt relieved to find it in pretty good order. He'd always been the type that bordered on hoarding with his collection of old appliances and newspapers stacked up against the walls, but it looked like he'd kept them under control the past few years. His usual belongings stood in their rightful spots, his favorite scroll up on the wall and his *katana*, a samurai sword, below it. The house smelled musty but didn't appear different from the times I visited him as a kid, excepting the brand-new flat screen TV blasting NHK from the living room. He was probably half deaf.

"We brought a bottle of saké and thought we could catch up." I smiled as I raised the saké in my hand. "Do you have the time?"

"Sure, sure. It's good of you to bring something by!" He shuffled off to his kitchen, and Mom and I sat down at his kotatsu and tried to get comfortable. I had never been good friends with the old man because his own sons were five years older than me. But Mom had always liked him, so it was good to have her around.

"Start with the pleasantries, Mei," Mom whispered at me, and I nodded back to her.

Senahara brought out three saké cups and a package of rice crackers, and set them on the kotatsu. I cracked open the bottle and poured for him and Mom. Mom poured for me. We raised our cups, said "Kampai," and drank.

I started with the pleasantries as Mom suggested, how's your health, how's your family, how's your farm, and we go on and on, to the point where my eyes cross and my insides dissolve to dust.

"Akira is doing well. His wife just had their second child, too. Oh, let me get the photos. He sent them to me in the mail since I'm so bad at this whole smart phone thing."

I rolled my eyes at Mom as he turned away and grabbed photos of his grandkids to show us. I admitted they were cute, and I smiled genuinely at their happy faces.

"They're adorable. You must be so proud."

"I am," he said, returning the photos to his pile next to the kotatsu. "He was always a good kid. I'm grateful."

"I'm grateful my Mei has returned home." Mom squeezed my hand and I dropped eye contact, embarrassed by her praise and the shame I felt. I still hoped every day I would find some reason to return to the city, that my life as a farmer's daughter was not set in stone. But each day it faded little by little, and it was replaced with... acceptance? I couldn't be sure. I wasn't there yet. It hadn't even been three weeks. I figured I'd be back in Tokyo by the spring.

"It's been a crazy few weeks, that's for sure." I squeezed Mom's hand and turned to Senahara. "I suppose you heard about Mr. Kano? I saw you at the funeral, and I'm sorry we didn't get a chance to talk then."

"I heard a rumor he was killed, but I didn't believe it. Who would kill him?" He shook his head and scratched his hairy ear. "He was a good man. A good a friend as any could ever have. We used to drink together all the time." He threw back another cup of saké and I refilled it. "Who do you think could've done it?"

"We're not sure," Mom said, sighing and sipping at her saké. "We were hoping you had some insight?"

"Me? Why me?" He pulled back with his hand to his chest.

"For the reasons you just said," I interrupted. "You were a friend to him for a long time and knew him well. I'm surprised no one has asked you about him yet."

"Hmmm, I suppose so. He was a good man."

"He was." I paused and filled up the cups. "Did he ever speak to you about selling to Midori Sankaku? It seems to me that the Midori Sankaku business might be at the center of these problems."

He shook his head a few times, his mouth turning to a frown. "Ever since they came to town, our lives have been in upheaval. I wish they had never come."

"Come now," Mom crooned at him, touching his arm. "They seem like good people, willing to invest in our town and see it grow. It's been hard to watch the land around us turn wild."

"That it has. I wish the transition had been easier. I've been considering selling. My daughter-in-law said she'd feel better if I moved in with them." He paused for a long moment, looking at the TV blaring out news programs at the other end of the room, but not really watching it. "But it would be hard to leave here."

"Do you think Mr. Kano would have sold to Midori Sankaku?" I sipped from the saké cup, hoping to calm my nerves with the alcohol.

"Shinzo Kano? No. No, he would never. He was saving that land for Akiko."

My heart beat swiftly at this news.

"He was so pleased with her. She saved him from suffering so many times, always diagnosing his ailments and getting the right treatment for him. He was going to leave her the estate."

"Really?" Mom sat forward, engaged in everything Senahara had to say.

"He had an appointment with an estate lawyer at the end of the month." He shook his head, regretful. "He never did make it. Hopefully Akiko has no problem with that."

My stomach plummeted, straight to the soil below the house. I doubted she'd ever know how much her father appreciated her.

"Might I ask, do you know why or how he was sick?" This was a tough question to ask when so many people don't want to say, "I was puking my guts out all night," or "I was on the toilet every day for several weeks," or other such things deemed "too much information."

But I had to know. So many people had said he was sick for a long time, and Akiko struggled with his health on a daily basis, but she never said what was wrong with him. Just that he was "sick."

I filled up Senahara's cup again, hoping the saké would loosen his tongue. "He said his stomach hurt all the time and he had troubles eating and keeping food down. He lost a lot of weight, but recently, he was feeling better and gaining everything back. Akiko was pleased."

This sounded like the perfect daughter, the best friend I'd always had.

"So she never said what was wrong with him?" Mom asked, prodding him one more time. Her face burned bright red. Even though Mom was a skilled drinker, any alcohol sent her skin to flames.

"No. Just that he was feeling better, and I was relieved, so I didn't ask. Maybe I should have?"

"It's okay. It probably wasn't anything severe," Mom assured him.

But I wasn't so sure. Everyone had mentioned he was sick the past year and he was recently feeling better. Then he was killed? It felt too coincidental.

"Had anyone been giving him any problems lately? Did he mention anything when you two were together?"

Senahara leaned back in his floor chair, stroking his wrinkled and stubbled chin. Only a week ago, I wondered if he killed Kano in a fit of rage because Kano planned to sell his land. But sitting with him now, I could picture him with Kano, laughing and drinking, having a grand old time, like they'd always had for the last twenty years. Best friends didn't up and kill each other. At least, I couldn't imagine that happening.

"I probably shouldn't mention this..." Senahara whispered, and I focused on the conversation, picked up the saké bottle, and refilled everyone's cups again. "Thank you, Mei." He sipped from his cup and set it down to wring his hands. "I often saw Tama come over to the house during the day, when he was supposed to be at school teaching, and I could hear them yelling at each other from over here. Shinzo always brushed it off. He said Tama was giving him a hard time. He never spoke of what they were fighting about, and my hearing is going, so I couldn't make out what they were shouting."

Mom and I glanced at each other. Akiko had never mentioned Tama came by during the day to see their father. But maybe she'd never known. If I were to hide things from my sister, I would be sure she wasn't around before I did those things. Kano had been a quiet man, and many people in town would've called him a model citizen. Tama appeared to have problems with his own father, but none of us ever saw any issues with the family.

That's not to say that there weren't problems, just that they did an exceptional job of hiding them.

CHAPTER
TWENTY-TWO

"Itadakimasu!" Yasahiro and I pressed our hands together in prayer position and bowed to our food.

"I hope you enjoy lunch today. This is my family's secret curry recipe. If you can guess what's in it, I have a special dessert set aside for today." Yasahiro smiled at me as he lifted his spoon and ladled a serving of rice and curry into his mouth. I watched it go past his lips and wondered what it would be like to kiss him. I got a flash in my brain of a dark night full of laughter and kissing on the sidewalk in a secluded spot. I'd never done that before, and I drew in a quick breath to halt my heart from galloping away.

At Yasahiro's request, I arrived at Sawayaka a little earlier today, catching the end of the lunch hour because he wanted to train a new sous chef this afternoon. With the new sous chef in the rotation, he could have a few more hours off per week. He was excited to finally get to this point in his business because it meant he could relax and think about his next venture.

I picked up my spoon and prepared to be dazzled by his newest dish. When the rice and curry hit my palate, I was immediately won over.

"Mmmm. This is delicious! I've never had curry like this before. I think it has... A little bit of sweetness to it."

"Very good," he said, his eyebrows raised. "What do you think is the secret ingredient?"

I tasted the curry again, letting the flavors slip over my tongue and down my throat. This was so different from the fast food curry I ate often. It was refined yet had the essence of home cooking with large chunks of vegetables and meat.

"Honey? Maybe?" Honey wasn't a usual ingredient in Japanese food, so that was a wild guess.

Yasahiro shook his head and laughed. "No. Try again."

One of the tables near the front of the restaurant burst into laughter. I turned to glance at them, but no one facing me looked familiar. I tasted the curry one more time and pondered the complex flavors.

"Maybe it's the kind of pork you're using? I don't know. I'm terrible at this," I said, laughing behind my hand covering my mouth.

"I do love the local pork we get. The farmer takes good care of his pigs, and the meat has a certain sweetness about it. But that's not the secret ingredient."

"I give up!" I threw my hands up in the air, before reaching for a glass of wine he had put on the table. This was the first time I'd had alcohol at lunch this week, and the crisp white wine perfectly matched the spicy curry. "You'll have to tell me."

"Okay. I made you try to guess at least twice, so I'm willing to give away the secret." He leaned across the table and whispered, "Apples."

"Really?" I would never have thought to add apples to curry. I'd heard of people adding honey or maple syrup but not apples. But then again I wasn't up to date on cooking trends.

"And I'll admit, I slipped in eggplant." His eyes twinkled with mischief, knowing I told him that I hate eggplant.

I looked down at the curry and laughed. I laughed so hard I

could barely catch my breath. Yasahiro laughed too, and how could he not? He'd pulled one over on me.

"I can't believe you slipped in eggplant!" I pushed the curry around with the back of my spoon but I didn't see any in there.

"It dissolves in the sauce and adds some depth of flavor to the dish. You won't find any chunks."

"Mei Yamagawa, how are you doing?" I blinked as I looked up to find Fujita Takahara standing over us at our corner table. I dropped my spoon on the bowl, and it clanged and startled me.

Yasahiro, seeing my clumsiness for the tenth time now, reached over and retrieved my spoon from the floor. "Let me get you a new one."

I cleared my throat as he stood up and headed into the kitchen.

"Mr. Takahara, I didn't know you were here." I turned around to see most of the men at the rowdy table standing up and slipping their coats back on.

"I was here with the Midori Sankaku staff. They'll all be working in Chikata on the new greenhouse." He slipped his hands in his pockets and flashed a winning smile at me. My insides squirmed, uncomfortable that he was talking to me or acknowledging me at all, considering I saw him last on the side of the road when he followed me home. I suppressed a shudder.

"That's nice." I cleared my throat again. "I hope they enjoy working in Chikata."

"Many of them are moving here in the next few months. I expect business to be booming in no time."

Yasahiro arrived back at the table and brushed past Takahara. "Excuse me. Here, Mei." He slid a new spoon onto the table next to my bowl and sat down.

"It's good to hear business is expected to pick up," Yasahiro chimed in, turning his face up to Takahara. "My restaurant can always use more customers."

"You make excellent food, Mr. Suga." Takahara bowed to

Yasahiro and he nodded back. A frosty wind from the front door curled around my legs under the table.

Takahara cleared his throat and ran his hand through his hair. "So, Mei, I was hoping to meet you for drinks sometime soon. I'd love to discuss the greenhouse and anything else you may have concerns about. We could even go out for dinner, if you like."

All the blood left my head as both men looked straight at me. What the...? Was Takahara asking me out... on a date? Yasahiro's eyes narrowed. I could tell he certainly thought so.

"Uh, wow, that's generous of you, Mr. Takahara," I squeaked out, wishing I could gulp down the wine on the table. "I think, though, I have all the information I need right now. But, um, I'll keep your offer in mind." I hoped that didn't sound too committed nor too bitchy.

He bowed, graciously. "You have my number. Call me anytime. Have a good lunch." Nodding to us both, he stepped to his table, grabbed his coat and large scarf, bundled up, and left without looking back at me.

I turned around and Yasahiro was watching me, his elbows on the table and hands clasped together.

"Looks like you have an admirer," he said, and I winced from the slight tone of hurt in his voice. Everyone in town knew what a player Takahara was, a wealthy and handsome player, but a player none the less.

I sipped the wine and composed myself. "Takahara is trying to butter me up so I'll stop giving him a hard time about Akiko's land. It's nothing." I waved at him, but he didn't relent his stare.

"It didn't look like nothing to me. He wants to go on a date."

Did I detect a note of jealousy? I wasn't sure. Maybe he was just acting like a big brother would.

"Well, I'm sorry, but I don't really like him all that much. Honestly, I think he's arrogant. I've googled him and seen the flashy women he dates. Anyone who goes out with gorgeous, famous women for arm candy is a bit too big-headed for me." I nodded my head, confident that I'd put that issue to rest. See, Yasahiro? I wasn't into guys like that.

"I see," he mumbled, returning to his curry.

I opened my mouth to further assure him but stopped. Something had changed about his mood, and I couldn't put my finger on it. He went from jealous to sullen so quickly I had whiplash. What did I say?

"Do I still get dessert?" I asked, and he burst into a short laugh. "I didn't answer your challenge correctly, but I love desserts, and I picked winter squash and ran 3k this morning. I could eat this and probably everything left in the kitchen."

"Of course, Mei. I would never deny you dessert." He relaxed a little, his shoulders falling. Good. I said the right thing. He took a deep breath and sighed. "Don't forget about tonight. Cocktails here and then over to Izakaya Jūshi for a little sleuthing of our own."

"I wouldn't miss it," I said, raising my glass. He raised his and we clinked them together, but his mood wavered the rest of lunch.

I left the restaurant doubting everything.

———

I WOKE UP FROM A NAP, DROWSY AND WARM IN BED, unwilling to leave. Mimoji slept against my hip, purring away, and I wanted to go back to sleep for a while if it wasn't too late already. I reached to the side of the bed for my phone to check the time and my hand rubbed against the tatami mat, nothing near my fingertips. Right. My phone was still in rice at Yasahiro's restaurant. I wondered if it would ever turn on again, and if it didn't, would Mom buy me a new one? I hated that I was at this stage in my life, twenty-six years old, and I was living at home, getting an allowance from my mother.

I pulled the covers up over my head and tried to daydream

myself back to Tokyo. Only, it didn't stick. I concentrated hard
to remember my apartment, my coworkers, and the convenience stores I went to all the time, but they remained fuzzy
and indistinct. I'd been away from the city for less than a
month and it was already a distant memory for me? How did
that happen?

I threw down the covers, rolled over, and grabbed my laptop,
disturbing Mimoji in the process and ousting him from the bed.
He slunk off with his tail held high.

Opening the computer, I saw that it was just after 17:00. The
sweet smell of onions cooking invaded my room as my door slid
open at Mimoji's insistence. Mom must have been making
dinner. I had some time to relax before we ate, so I went to my
Documents folder and opened the file where I kept my notes on
Akiko's investigation. I went back and forth between my paper
notebook and my computer as I added details about each person
copied from news articles I found online or photos I snagged off
Google Images.

"*Tama Kano: Son of the deceased. Was bitter and angry last
time I saw him. Wants to sell land to Midori Sankaku. Was at
school all day when father was killed.*" I erased the last statement
and added, "*Have Goro double-check Tama was at school the day
Kano was killed.*" Because if Senahara said Tama came to see his
father often during the day, then how had the school never
complained about his absences from classes? It didn't add up. But
he still didn't have much of a motive besides not liking his father.
It wasn't as if Tama had to live with him or anything. Tama also
had a job and a fiancée. He could easily have waited out his
father's death.

"*Shin Tajima: Mayor. Wants what's best for Chikata. Will be
voted out if he doesn't get the job done. Possible kick-backs from
Midori Sankaku?*" I crossed this off the list. Tajima couldn't do
anything harmful to Chikata. He loved this town like he did a
family member.

"Daichi Senahara: Neighbor. Thought he would kill to protect his land but no. He's as innocent as anyone."

The visit we made to him the previous night replayed in my head. He'd always loved Kano.

"Fujita Takahara: Midori Sankaku Regional Manager. Wants land for the greenhouse and administrative buildings. Will probably get a raise and accolades if he gets what he wants. Secretary accounts for his whereabouts the day of the crime. Doesn't seem like the killer type."

I stared hard at Takahara's line in my document and remembered his proposal today. I couldn't believe he asked me out right in front of Yasahiro! Who did that? But perhaps I'd done a good job of telling the whole town, through all the gossip channels, that I wasn't interested in Yasahiro. That we weren't dating. We were just having lunch.

I opened up my browser and headed to Google. A search for Fujita Takahara showed he attended some movie premiere earlier this week with new arm candy. His smile shined like a million yen and the woman with him was dressed in a slinky, gorgeous silver dress. How did he date these women? They all looked way too good for him. But further digging showed that he came from a prosperous family. His mother earned her fame as a moderately famous fashion designer and his father was a banker. That explained a lot. Money followed money.

Hmmm, I remembered Yasahiro saying he was a farmer's son. I wondered what his family was like. I typed in his name and hit enter.

The screen filled with photos and my jaw dropped. Oh. My. God. I squinted and leaned into the screen, rubbing my eyes to make sure I wasn't hallucinating. The page displayed photo after photo of Yasahiro standing on red carpets with a knock-me-over gorgeous woman on *his* arm. She smiled for the cameras, her hair cascading in waves down her side, her hip jutted out, accentuating her curves. I swallowed, trying to keep the bile in my stomach where it belonged. My hand shook as I clicked one of the photos, and I was taken to a French entertainment website. I couldn't read this! I copy-and-pasted the URL into Google Translate and read, *"Amanda Cheung and boyfriend, Yasahiro Suga, attend the Cannes Film Awards, 2013."*

"What the...?" I began frantically clicking on anything I could find on them. They had been dating for four years in Paris where Yasahiro was an up-and-coming chef and she was a B film star. She spoke four languages and knew *karate* and *tai chi*. She was working on her first novel about the Chinese-American experience and had three apartments in New York, Los Angeles, and Paris. Now, she was filming action movies in Hollywood, and he'd opened his own restaurant in Saitama prefecture, just outside of Tokyo. Amanda and Yasahiro had been engaged to be married, but he called it off when she didn't want to move to Tokyo. The tabloids said they were both single but had been spotted together six months ago in Hong Kong.

Sickness overcame me and the world spun around my head on a tilted axis. In all my daydreams of him living in Paris, I hadn't expected this. I never saw him with a girlfriend. I never even dreamed he'd have been dating anyone, let alone someone famous — someone talented, well-traveled, and gorgeous. I covered my mouth as I retched and the wave of nausea receded. Deep down, I suspected that he had dated before, of course. I expected him to have exes. But I figured they were ordinary women. No one I'd ever feel like a tiny ant next to. Ugh.

I groaned and bent forward as I remembered what I said at lunch. *"Anyone who goes out with gorgeous, famous women for arm candy is a bit too big-headed for me."* I pounded the bed several times with my fist, picked up my pillow, and screamed into it.

Mei! What were you thinking?

I hadn't been thinking, obviously. And his reaction to my statement, the way he mumbled into his curry? Suddenly it made perfect sense. I flat-out told him I didn't date guys like him. I inferred that he was big headed and arrogant. If I ever thought that maybe, just maybe, I'd had a chance with him, I completely blew it.

I glanced at the screen again and flipped through the photos of them together, posing at movie premieres, on the beach in Ibiza, eating at a café in Paris, shopping in Venice, Amanda showing off the gorgeous engagement ring. This was way beyond me. Way. We couldn't have a relationship because he would measure me next to Amanda, and let's face it, I was nobody compared to her. The more I thought about it, I became sure I never had a chance anyway. He couldn't look at me, scrawny, dirt-under-my-fingernails, and crazy-haired Mei, and find me attractive after he dated her. He probably thought of me as a good friend and was disappointed when I inadvertently criticized him.

Not only had I been reading into every one of his kind gestures and thinking they were romantic, but I also possibly killed our friendship. Stupid, stupid, stupid.

I needed to salvage our friendship somehow and tell him I still liked him for who he was, despite my comments about Taka-hara. I didn't know how I would bring it up, but I should.

"Mei! Dinner's ready!" Mom called from the kitchen.

"Coming!" I yelled back, slamming my computer closed.

Too bad the photos of Yasahiro and his ex-girlfriend had burned into my retinas. There'd be no shaking those images now.

CHAPTER
TWENTY-THREE

I changed my outfit twice before heading out to Sawayaka. First, I put on a slinky black dress, did my hair for real with my favorite sleek and shiny hair products, taming the frizz to the maximum level possible, and applying a generous layer of makeup. Then I looked in the mirror and freaked out. I wasn't in Tokyo anymore. I was in tiny little Chikata, and a dress and makeup like this would attract a dumb amount of attention. I ripped off my dress and added it to the pile of clothes in my room, popped open a moving box, and dug deep for my skinny jeans. All my other jeans were now farming clothes, but I saved my dark-wash skinny jeans for when I didn't want to look like I'd been wallowing in the dirt for the past year.

Pulling them on, I went to snap them closed and I had a few centimeters clearance all around my waist. Huh. Looked like the hard labor paid off, even with the rich lunches Yasahiro had been feeding me. I added a loose, long-sleeved, black t-shirt, and bangle bracelets to the mix and retrieved a belt from my closet. In the bathroom, I wiped off most of the makeup and clipped back my hair to give it a more casual appearance. There. Much better. I may not have been as pretty as Amanda, but at least I'd fit in around here.

I immediately hated myself, closed my eyes, and counted to ten. I couldn't get her out of my head. Now that I knew she existed, I couldn't go back to my daydreams of Yasahiro helping little old ladies in Paris. Instead, he and Amanda made out under the Eiffel Tower, and I wanted to puke. I tried to imagine myself in her place, and I couldn't. I sat down on the toilet and talked myself out of crying before I left the bathroom. I could have handled any kind of ex but the famous *and* gorgeous kind. Why did I keep stepping in bad luck over and over?

Mom was already asleep when I headed out the door, so I grabbed the keys to her car and drove into town. I parked in the municipal lot not far from the community center where I could pick it up tomorrow since I never drive drunk. Walking to Sawayaka and breathing deep, I repeated my mantra over and over. *"Everything's fine. Nothing's wrong. Everything's fine. Nothing's wrong."*

The night, crisp and cold, wrapped around me, and my breath fogged in the air as I approached the restaurant. I knocked on the window and waited, peering into the main room, the tables empty and chairs overturned onto each. Slipping my hands into the pockets of my wool coat, I hopped back and forth, trying to keep warm. I hated waiting, especially in a public place all by myself. I always wondered if people thought I was a delinquent. A couple passed me on the sidewalk, eyeing me and the darkened restaurant, probably wondering what I was doing. I knocked on the window again and cursed my stupid waterlogged phone. If it had worked, I could have called Yasahiro on the restaurant's main line.

"Coming!" He shouted from inside, and I sighed in relief. He opened the door and I darted past him to the warmth of the restaurant. "Sorry. I knew you'd be here soon, so I figured I'd get my cocktail mixers ready."

He smiled at me, and my stomach turned over, noticing it was the same smile in all the photographs I looked at this afternoon.

"Are you all right?" he asked, and I snapped my lips back into a smile.

"I'm fine. Just a little tired." This was the only lie I could tell honestly enough.

I followed him into the neat and clean kitchen, the stainless steel counters and floor shining and spotless.

"I have something for you," he said, as he took my coat. A chill ran up my back without the extra warmth. At least had long-sleeves on. My eyes drank in him as he hung up my coat next to his chef's coat. He wore jeans and a button-down shirt with a black sweater over it. Very European. I think I saw him wear something like this when he was with Amanda in Italy.

"Here you go." He set my phone on the table in front of me, knocking me out of my visions of him proposing to Amanda and her squealing with delight. "It turns on even. You're saved!"

"Oh, thank goodness," I said, sweeping the phone up into my hands and pressing it to my chest. "I thought I was going to have to buy a new one, and I'm totally without funds right now."

Yasahiro's eyebrows pulled together. "Really? Not even to replace a phone?"

I laughed. "I don't even have enough to pay for dinner. I have enough to buy two beers tonight, and that's it."

He frowned. "I'm buying tonight then."

"No way," I said, waving my hands in front of him. "I always pay my own way, which is why I stay home most of the time now actually." I shrugged my shoulders as I powered my phone on and watched the screen light up. Relief filled me from my toes to my nose. This was the one thing I didn't want to ask Mom for since she already paid all my bills. A few texts popped up from Kumi. Nothing urgent. She was just fishing for gossip or wondering what I was doing. I texted her back that my phone had died but lived once more, and that we should get together soon.

A loud *ka-cha-ka-cha* sound echoed in the room. I glanced up to find Yasahiro's eyes on his phone, a drink recipe displayed on it, while he worked a metal cocktail shaker in the air. His forearms were tight, and my mouth went dry. I tried to imagine running my hands all over him, but instead, he pulled Amanda into a deep kiss. My heart ached like one of the kitchen knives next to the sink had been plunged straight into it.

Why? Oh, why had such a handsome man landed right in front of me, and then I googled him like an idiot?

That was okay, though. We weren't dating, so it didn't matter.

It was interesting what I told myself to make things better.

"Here's a classic rum drink. A daiquiri. I think you'll like it." He poured for both of us, and I tried not to stand too close to him as I raised the martini glass and looked him in the eyes when we said, "Kampai."

A jolt sparked through me, and I ended up gulping my first few pulls from the glass. The drink, both sweet and sour but not bitter, went down a little too easily. I loved citrus.

"Mmmm, delicious. I'm sure my face will be red in no time." I pressed my cool hand to my cheek to keep the flush away as long as possible.

"I noticed that about you. I like it. It never happens to me." My face blushed, and not due to alcohol. I sipped again. "So, what are we hoping to accomplish tonight?"

I paused with the drink in my hand, refreshing my brain to what we agreed upon yesterday. "We're going to casually sit and have a few drinks and hope Tama shows up. If he does, I'm going to find some way of asking about Akiko and what he's been telling the police. If he doesn't show up?" I shrugged my shoulders, the drink perched in my right hand. "Well, then, we enjoy our beers and go home? Unfortunately, I can't afford to do this kind of sleuthing every night, unless I was being paid to do it." Hmmm, I wondered if I could parlay detective work into a career for me.

Probably not. It required a lot more schooling, which I couldn't afford.

"I see the wheels turning in your head." Yasahiro sipped his drink as well. "Maybe you should concentrate on the painting. I bet you could sell them if you kept at it."

"What's with you and my painting?" This came out of my mouth more adversarial than I intended it to, so I tried to soften my question with a laugh. "Even my own mother doesn't nag me this much about it."

"I enjoy being creative and being around creative people. Being with creative people fuels my own need to create, to inspire." He tilted his head to the side, his fingers rolling the stem of the martini glass back and forth. "I can tell you have an artist trapped beneath the surface, like fish under the ice during the winter."

I took another swig of my drink and reached the cherry at the bottom. Oops. That went fast.

"Well, I, uh, do love to paint." I forced the words from my throat like pushing through a crowded subway car to the wide-open platform during Tokyo rush hour. "And I want to do it more often, but I need to find a job so I'm not dirt poor. And I do mean dirt poor because I'm covered in dirt from working the fields every day." I examined my fingernails, what was left of them, and they were clean, thankfully. "I should spend my spare time looking for work I can do."

"And that's the hard part?" he asked. I cringed because he'd only known me a week and he already understood that I had few actual skills.

"Yeah. Should we get going?" I pushed my empty glass across the stainless steel counter, and his hand came down on mine.

"Look, I'm not one to say I can read minds or anything..." He squeezed my hand and my heart beat faster. "But maybe you just don't know *what* you want to do, not that you can't do anything. I can see it on your face, in your eyes, that you doubt yourself. Don't doubt. Listen to your heart."

I tipped my face up so I could let him see those doubtful eyes. I doubted myself. I doubted him. I doubted life. I didn't doubt that I was in major trouble when it came to this man.

"We should go." I pulled my hand out from under his and headed for our coats. Handing him his, he swung it over his shoulders and buttoned up, pulling a set of keys from his pocket. I slipped into my coat and he handed me his scarf.

"Here. It's cold out tonight."

"Thanks," I mumbled as I wrapped it around my neck up to my chin. I inhaled and got a strong scent of sandalwood. This must've been his scent, not that I'd ever been close enough to tell.

Outside, we approached a Toyota hatchback, and he powered it up with a remote start.

"Nice," I said, nodding at the dark silver lines and hybrid logo on the back. "New?"

"Yeah, I bought it earlier this year."

I smiled as I climbed into the passenger side and admired the interior. Yasahiro looked between me and the car.

"Do you want me to leave you two alone?" He laughed.

"Do you mind?" I purred and rubbed my hands over the dashboard. "It's not an Audi or a Tesla, but I like a hybrid."

"A car girl. I can be okay with that." He nodded as he buckled in and pulled into the street. "What do you drive?"

"Me? Own a car?" I snorted laughing. "I drive my mom's. She has a Toyota too, though it's about ten years old at this point. I parked it in the municipal lot so I can run tomorrow morning and come get it."

"Right. I suppose you didn't have much need for one living in the city."

My teeth began to chatter as we waited for the heat to come on. Didn't matter though because we weren't far from the izakaya. I'm not sure why we drove anyway.

"No. No need. I took the subway everywhere."

"If you could have a car, what would you own?" We passed Izakaya Jūshi and my head turned to watch it go. "Oh, I live up here one more block. I'm going to park my car at home and we'll walk."

"No wonder you go there often. If I could have anything, I'd just make sure it was a V6. I like a big engine."

Yasahiro raised his eyebrows at me as he pulled into a tiny parking spot next to a two-story building. I guessed that last statement was incredibly dirty if you added "that's what she said."

Out on the sidewalk, he pointed up at the second floor of the building. "That floor with the lights on? That's mine."

I tripped on a crack in the pavement as I took in the size of his place. "Wow. The whole floor?"

"Yeah. I own the whole building but I live on the second floor. It used to be a warehouse, for the retail space below. I had it renovated at the same time as the restaurant. Got the space for a bargain because it had been empty for ten years."

His hand on my elbow directed me away from his place and towards the izakaya. "I can't even imagine having all that space to myself. My apartment in the city was a shoebox."

"I'm sure it wasn't that bad."

"Please, Yasahiro, my shower and toilet were next to the kitchen, practically in the kitchen. I didn't even have a genkan. The door hit my bed when you opened it."

He winced. "Ouch. Yeah. That's pretty small."

Inside, Izakaya Jūshi was smoky from both the grill and people lighting cigarettes, visibility down to a meter or two, tops.

I waved in front of my face. "Hey, is your restaurant smoke free?"

"Yep," he said, nodding and ushering me to the end of an open table. "I can't stand too much smoke. Paris was awful that way. So I decided when I opened my own place, I'd make it smoke free. I thought I might lose business, but it didn't make a

difference. And that's why I only come here twice a week now."
We sat down across from each other. "I like it here, though. It
reminds me of a place we went to all the time in Chichibu."

He gestured to a young woman filling beers at the bar, and
she smiled and waved. This must have been Kumi's friend.

"So, whatever made you want to move here? To tiny
Chikata?"

He shrugged his shoulders. "After Paris, I wanted a small
town experience. When I heard about all the developments here,
I figured it would be a good place to settle down."

I thought back on what I read earlier about him. He broke off
his engagement with Amanda when she wouldn't move to Tokyo,
but he saw her six months ago in Hong Kong.

"Besides, I get to travel a few times per year for work, so it's
comforting to have some place small and stable to come back to."

"Yasahiro! It's good to see you. How's business?" Kumi's
friend interrupted us and I sat back to look at her. She seemed
familiar.

"Mei? Hi! Wow, I haven't seen you in years. Kumi said you
were back in town. How are you?" She was a bubble of happiness, the perfect person to work at an izakaya. Her name popped
into my head.

"Etsuko, you were in the same year as Kumi at school, right?"

"Yes I was! Thank you for remembering," she said, bowing to
me. She was always a polite girl. "I work here with my brother
and parents." She waved to the grill where a young man helped
an older man flip chicken over the coals. They must have been
father and son, the resemblance was so striking. "Let me get you
both something to drink and then I'll come back for more of a
chat."

"Beer," both Yasahiro and I said at the same time. We all
laughed at the synchronicity.

"She's super nice. If she didn't work here, I'd ask her to come
work for me," he said, as she walked away.

"How old are you?" I asked him, unable to pin his age properly. Sometimes he seemed so young, but I knew he wasn't. With a five year relationship and an almost marriage under his belt, he might be in his thirties.

He laughed, running his hand through his hair. "Twenty-nine. I'll be thirty next September. You?"

"Twenty-six. I'll be twenty-seven next July. You've achieved quite a lot for not even thirty years old yet. I'm impressed."

"It's nothing," he said, brushing off my compliment.

"No. It's definitely something. Be proud."

Two large mugs of beer hit the table and Etsuko sat down next to us. "Please," she said, waving to our drinks. Yasahiro and I clicked mugs and toasted before sipping. "So, Mei, I remember you being good friends with Akiko..."

Perfect. I had a feeling I wouldn't have to make any weird initial conversations.

"I still am."

"Is everything okay with her?" She placed her hand on my arm and squeezed. Yasahiro hid a smile behind his mug. "I've heard crazy things."

"Definitely don't believe everything you hear. She's fine. She's upset about her dad, but that's about it."

Etsuko glanced around. "I've heard she's at the police station, in custody."

"No," I said, shaking my head. "Not in custody. She's helping them out. You heard her father was murdered, right?" I kept my voice as low as possible in the crowded room. Etsuko nodded. "They've been looking for evidence, and she's trying to help them out."

"I see, I see..." Etsuko's voice drifted off. "I don't suppose Tama's been helping out has he?"

Yasahiro and I made quick eye contact. "Not that I know of. Why?"

"Oh, he's just never around anymore, you know?"

"I didn't know." My scalp prickled. There was so much I thought I knew about Tama, but I may have known nothing at all. "I thought he was still teaching at the high school."

"He is," Etsuko said, leaning towards us. "But he's been visiting Chiba a lot lately on the weekends. He knows a man who owns a craft beer distributor there. They became friends last year — met right here at the bar. So I can't imagine he's been much help to his poor father and sister."

"I guess not."

This new friendship probably explained why Tama was suddenly a drinker, when he didn't used to be.

"This is their beer!" She gestured to the mug, and I picked it up and held it up to peer through it. The wheat beer was light and mellow, nothing too strong.

"I like it a lot." Yasahiro shrugged his shoulders as he took a gulp. I drank a few gulps all at once, too. I loved beer. "I was thinking about carrying it in the restaurant."

"You should," Etsuko said, standing up. "They have steep discounts. Mei, I'm so glad to hear Akiko is okay. I've asked Tama, and he just brushed me off. I was worried. Hey, let's hang out together sometime soon! My boyfriend, Hisashi, will be in town next week. He and Yasahiro are friends so they can talk baseball while you and I drink."

"Sounds great," I replied, excited about meeting new friends.

She headed to the bar, and I drummed my fingers on the table. Yasahiro leaned back and folded his arms over his chest.

"Are you thinking what I'm thinking?" he asked.

"Maybe. Are you thinking Tama has some involvement in this brewery?"

He nodded, turning to the door as it opened, and in walked the man himself. Tama sidled in, made eye contact with Etsuko and her brother at the bar, and sat in an open seat. He never even looked my way.

I wondered if I should go greet him when Etsuko gestured in our direction, obviously trying to inform him that we were there. He turned around, saw me, and his face, which I expected to break into a smile, instead stayed stone cold. I rubbed my suddenly frozen hands together.

"Should we leave, Mei? You look pale." Yasahiro asked as Tama approached.

"Look at the two of you, out on a date?" Tama smiled but his eyes were frosty.

"Nope," I said, sipping my beer. Yasahiro sipped his as well, keeping his eyes on me over the lip of his mug. "Just having a drink together. How are you, Tama? I haven't seen you since the funeral."

"May I?" He gestured to the seat next to Yasahiro and sat at the same time, not waiting for an affirmative answer. "I've been good. And you?"

"I've been fine, thanks. Mom's good. The farm is good. Yasahiro and I have been eating lunch together during the week. Things are great." I smiled at him, convincing him I had no other motives other than to point out my happiness. "I had drinks with Daichi Senahara last night and we were talking about your dad. He said your dad was sick for a long time." I sipped on my beer, trying to be casual. "Do you know what was wrong with him?"

"Haven't got a clue." He shook his head side to side but didn't make eye contact with me. The lie detector in my brain pinged. "Old men get sick, and then they get better. What can you do?"

"I suppose so. Anyway, what have you been up to?"

Yasahiro stayed quiet while I questioned Tama.

"Been busy with work and seeing Haruka. I'm trying to stay positive, and I'm doing a better job of that than Akiko." He paused to gauge my reaction. "She's been so down since Dad's death. I've been worried about her mental state."

"Is that so? Maybe you shouldn't fight with her over the land then. I'm sure most of her worries have to do with not having a home in the months ahead."

Tama's shoulders tightened. I'd hit a nerve. I chugged some more of my beer for courage, though between Yasahiro's cocktail, this beer, and the fact that dinner was four hours ago, I edged on dangerous truth-telling territory.

"She'll have to earn her way in the world, like the rest of us, I suppose. Midori Sankaku is prepared to give me a fair amount for the property. I think I'll be selling." He rose from his seat, probably hoping to have the last word.

I leaned forward. "And what would a teacher like you need all that money for?" My back started to sweat, the straps of my bra digging into my damaged skin as my chest heaved with deep breaths.

"That's none of your business," he snapped, looking around to make sure no one heard him. Sitting himself back down at the table, he lowered his voice. "You were always such a nosey bitch, Mei. You should stick to digging in the dirt."

"Hey," Yasahiro interrupted, his face a mask of hostility I'd never seen before. "Don't you dare talk to her like that."

"Well, well. You two *must* be dating for you to defend her *honor* like this. Though she doesn't have much left. Are you sleeping with her?" Sickness roiled in my belly as he forged on. "You must have more of a tolerance for ugliness than I do. I could barely look at the scars on her back without feeling ill." He shrugged his shoulders as he stood up. "I could only sleep with her for a few months before I was done with her. Good luck to you."

As Tama turned to go, all the color left Yasahiro's face and his hands balled into fists. I didn't think confronting Tama would be bad, but I was dead wrong. It was a thousand times worse than what I imagined would happen tonight. I never thought he'd even admit to dating me, much less make me out to be some kind of leper. This was a disaster.

I grabbed my coat and Yasahiro's scarf and launched from the table, hoping to distract him from a fist fight.

If he followed me. And I couldn't even guarantee that anymore.

CHAPTER
TWENTY-FOUR

"Wait, Mei!" I glanced back at Yasahiro as I reached the door. He pulled out his wallet and threw a pile of yen on the table, but I was too far ahead of him to care about paying my share.

Outside, I looked left and right, orienting myself. Should I try to walk home from here? Or should I force Yasahiro to drive me? I doubted he was in worse shape than me. He stopped drinking as soon as Tama started talking.

I chose his car and headed in the direction of his house.

"Wait," he called from behind, his steps hastening.

"Shhh," I said, turning around and shushing him. "Be quiet. I need a moment to think."

I had been so willing to let Tama slide the last week, not even considering him to be a suspect, because I remembered the sweet boy I was in love with eight years ago. I didn't believe he could ever be cruel or do anything wrong. He approached me to date, he told me he loved me first, and he was gentle and kind when we slept together. He did cheat on me, but I considered it a fault of being young and stupid, not malicious. How could I reconcile that boy with this awful man?

A car bleeped and an engine starting caught my attention. I focused on Yasahiro's hatchback running a few meters in front of me.

"Get in," he said from behind. I opened the door and slid into my seat, buckling my seatbelt and waiting for him.

He got behind the wheel and gripped it with his hands until his knuckles turned white, his breathing labored. I wasn't sure what was going through his mind, but he was definitely angry.

"Are you okay to drive?" I asked, breaking the silence.

"Yeah. Yeah, I'm fine." He loosened his hands and shoulders, shifted the car into gear, and headed in the direction of my house.

We sat in silence again, the only sound the car's gears changing, until we were one light from home.

"I guess you and Tama used to be a couple."

I sighed, my breath fogging up the windshield. He leaned forward and wiped it off.

"It was a long time ago — eight years ago — and I didn't think it made a difference with anything. He cheated on me, so it's not like I held out hope we'd get back together. It's hard enough being in the same room with him most of the time. Now I never want to see him again."

"Why didn't you tell me?" he asked, pulling into my driveway and turning out the lights on the car.

"We're not dating as far as I can tell." He opened his mouth, but I cut him off. "Why didn't you tell me about Amanda?" He groaned, closing his eyes. "Because it seems to me, an old boyfriend of mine, eight years in my past, is nothing compared to a drop-dead gorgeous and famous movie star that you've seen as recently as six months ago, *and* you were engaged to."

I waited, watching him, hoping he'd turn to me and say he was sorry or deny it or something. But he kept his eyes closed.

I grabbed my purse from the floor of the car. "And that's what I get for googling."

"Wait..." He started but I stopped him with my raised hand.

"Don't worry about it, Yasahiro. It doesn't matter. *We're* not dating." I gestured between us and he narrowed his eyes at me. "Being friends with me won't ruin your reputation or anything. Most people in this town felt bad for me because he cheated on me. Dammit, he was there when I fell into the fire pit and never gave a care about my burn scars before." My voice cracked, the truth pouring from my mouth before tears appeared. "Or at least, he didn't seem to. He's obviously a skilled actor and liar. I never had a clue."

I opened the door to leave the car, but Yasahiro opened his door too, ran around the car, and blocked my path to the house.

"I didn't tell you about Amanda because..." He sighed, a plume of cold air billowing between us. "Because you walked into my restaurant and you didn't know who I was, didn't care what I cooked, or how much money I made. You made fun of me and then you challenged me." He laughed. "Most women try to flatter me. That's what Amanda did. She sucked me in with her good looks, money, and charm. I didn't realize just how empty she was until much later."

What did I believe? Did I believe the photos and news stories about how they were perfect for each other and so in love? Or did I believe the man in front of me who had been honest with me so far?

"She doesn't matter anymore either." He reached over and grasped my fingers in his. "She's not the one I want to be dating. You are."

"Me? Why me?" The incredulity in my voice surprised even me.

"Why not?" His anger surfaced again. "You're funny and honest, and you remind me of my friends in France, but you're still Japanese. You understand what it's like to come from a place like this." He swept his hand towards the fields on the side of the house. "Just like me. I may be doing all right for myself now, but I'm the son of a soy farmer. I know this life. I get it."

"I could never compete with Amanda."

"I'm not asking you to. That's over. She's Amanda, and you're you. Two totally different people. And I like it that way."

Silence brewed around us. I stared at his hand holding mine, and the two sides of my brain warred against each other. I desperately wanted to hear how he thought we were alike, and yet I believed he was a liar to think we could be the same. I wanted more details as to why he would want to date me, and yet I couldn't handle the shame of hearing my positive traits out loud. I wanted him, but I wanted to be left alone.

"We never spoke about *what* I would win if I won the slow food haute cuisine challenge," he whispered, and I broke into a laugh, my words on his lips.

"What? What kind of prize are you looking for?"

He squeezed my fingers. "A kiss."

I tried to hold back a smile as my heart thumped erratically in my chest. "A kiss?"

"Not just any kiss — a real kiss — from a woman I want to be dating."

"Like this?" I dropped my purse on the gravel driveway, put my arms around his neck, and connected my lips to his. I didn't make it platonic. I made the kiss intimate. I kissed like I hadn't done in years. I plucked from every daydream I'd had about being this close to him and channelled all my hopes, fears, and anxieties into my lips on his. His surprise lasted only a moment before his hands pulled me in and pressed me to him. Mmmm, he tasted like curry, lime, and beer, and the scent of sandalwood melted me so that our mouths opened and the kiss went even deeper, digging out any last denial I had of wanting to date him. I thought I couldn't date him because I didn't want to be humiliated. Now, I understood that he already knew me, knew my family, and knew my life. I thought I couldn't date him because of Amanda. Now, she was a challenge to overcome.

Forgetting my earlier resolution not to get involved, I changed my mind about everything. I wanted the dates and the kissing and more. I was ready to prove to Mom, to him, to the whole town, that I could make something of myself.

I tilted my head, got one last real connection between our lips, held the feeling in my head and body, and then pulled away. He stumbled forward, his lips trying to seek me out, but I covered mine with my hand and laughed.

"There. There's your prize. If you want more, you're going to have to woo me. I'm not some poor farm girl that goes out with just any guy." I shook my head at him as he tried to come close again. "I may be broke and jobless, but I know my worth."

He pulled himself together and upright. "God, I love that about you."

"What?" I asked, picking up my bag.

"Your directness."

I flipped my hair and smiled. "I was born without the coy gene."

He laughed. "Wooing? You want to be wooed?"

"I do. I've never been wooed, and it looks like fun."

"Challenge accepted," he said, folding his arms over his chest. "I happen to be very good at wooing."

"We shall see."

I walked past him and waved when I reached the door. "Good night, Yasahiro."

CHAPTER
TWENTY-FIVE

On Saturday morning, I couldn't pull myself out of my head to concentrate on the tasks in front of me. Mom made eggs and rice for breakfast with seaweed and I only stared into space. I relived the kiss over and over in my head, until my insides squirmed so much, I had to stand up and walk around to return to normal.

"What is with you today?" Mom asked, eyeing me as I walked back and forth in the dining area. "Are you sick?"

I took a deep cleansing breath and sat back down at the table. "Maybe a little love sick. Actually a lot love sick."

Mom set down her chopsticks.

"Yasahiro asked me to date him last night." My face broke into an uncontrolled smile. If I had more sense, I would've acted like it was no big deal, but it so was.

Mom squealed, clapping her hands together. "Oh, I hoped for this from the beginning! He used to ask all types of questions about you, always looking at your photos." She glanced over her shoulder at the wall that separated the living space from the kitchen, covered in framed photos, her prized possessions. "I didn't want to tell you about him in case I jinxed it."

I slipped back in time and remembered all of my conversations with Yasahiro, all the little mentions of how he knew this or that about me. Huh. I was set up! And I didn't even see it coming. It's possible he had been planning to woo me from the beginning and I played right into it with the challenge. Wow. I never saw it coming.

She smacked my arm, regaining my attention. "And what a gentleman! Asking to date you. I'm glad he didn't turn into one of those awful Western men."

I rolled my eyes at Mom, shoveling some food in my mouth. I'd watched enough American TV shows to know that Japanese dating practices were strange in comparison. Here, men or women declared their love first and then asked to date. In the U.S., it was the opposite. I never understood that. How could you go on dates without saying you liked the other person first? It didn't make sense.

Of course, I'd jumped way ahead of the game by kissing him last night, but that was necessary. He'd won the bet after all, and I never went back on my word.

I didn't tell Mom, though. She'd probably faint.

"He's a gentleman. I'm sure I won't step into his apartment for another few months." Though I wanted to because I was curious about the space. That side of town had the most gorgeous buildings and bordered on the park. I used to stare at them all the time growing up.

"Great. Then you must invite him here. All the time. No use playing coy, Mei. You're already twenty-six. Time is ticking."

"Thanks, Mom. That's just what I need, a reminder of my fading youth. And I don't play coy ever." I smiled, remembering how I said the same thing to Yasahiro last night.

"Text him now and ask him over tomorrow." Mom pushed my phone at me across the table.

"Mom," I said, warning in my voice. "Don't meddle."

"Meddling is my way, and as long as you're living at home, you'll do what I tell you to do."

I grumbled, knowing she was right. No one gave their mother a hard time when they were living at home. She paid my bills and gave me a weekly salary for working around the farm, so there was only so much leeway I had.

I swiped my phone on and realized I'd never called him or texted him. Hmmm, our dating life was not off to the best start.

"I don't have his number." I turned off my phone and set it down, hoping this would put Mom off. She pulled her own phone out of her kimono and turned it on, though. Damn.

"I have it. Here you go."

I sighed as I put the number in my phone and dialed, figuring I should call the first time. The phone rang, and he answered, his voice hesitant.

"Hello?"

"Yasahiro, hi. It's Mei." My face burst into flames with Mom's attention on me one hundred percent.

"Mei, hi! I just realized I don't have your number in my phone. How did that happen?"

I giggled, and then hated myself for being so girlie. *Pull yourself together, Mei!*

"I'm just glad the stupid thing works after it took a bath. I, uh, wanted to make sure you have my number so you can, you know, get a hold of me or text or whatever." I stammered all over the place, like, suddenly, my brain was unsure anything happened yesterday, and I would look like a fool.

He laughed. "Do you miss me already?"

My face burned so hot I feared it would melt off. "Maybe."

I turned to Mom and her eyes were wide and starry. She looked more in love than I did. I waved at her to leave me alone, but she whispered that I should invite him over.

I cleared my throat. "Anyway, my mom is sitting *right here*, and she suggests you come over tomorrow. If you want to —"

"I'd love to! How about I bring something for lunch?"

I covered the mouthpiece and whispered that to Mom. "No!" She blurted out. "I'll cook lunch. He cooks enough."

He laughed again and the sound coated my brain in stupidity. Had I mentioned that I become inane and dumb when I'm gone for someone? Well, it was the truth.

"I heard her. I'll come around noon. Okay?"

"Okay. That sounds perfect." I closed my eyes and pulled myself together. "Great! We'll see you tomorrow."

"Wouldn't miss it."

We hung up the phone at the same time, and I breathed a sigh of relief. I anticipated calling him and him denying last night ever happened. It wouldn't be the first time.

My phoned buzzed with a text from him. *"I'm glad I can text you now. I don't need to be at Sawayaka until 16:00 tomorrow, so I can come for a while."*

"I'm already looking forward to it," I texted back, trying for honesty and directness, which he liked.

"Me too."

I put his number in my address book and turned it off.

"Mmm, mmm, Mei. You have it bad." She rubbed her hands together in glee. "I'm so happy!"

"Don't plan the wedding yet, Mom. I've only known him a whole week."

After breakfast, we piled into the car and headed out. Mom had hitched a ride with Senahara at 8:00 and retrieved the car from the town lot since I was in no condition to run. My brain was too clouded with visions of kissing and hand holding and the possibility of sex. It had been too long since I had romance in my life, and it made me clumsy and awkward.

Autumn grew colder every day and spending time outside got more difficult as the winter approached. We hadn't had a hard frost yet, so the farm still required a lot of work until that happened.

We met up with Goro outside the house of the first person on our list, a woman named Shika Hachiman.

"I don't know this woman, unfortunately," Mom said, blowing warm air into her hands.

As we approached the door, I scanned the surroundings. The building, a one-family home, occupied a small plot of land. Even though it was freezing outside, a line of laundry hung on the upstairs balcony and a cat sat there, staring down at us. No car, but there was a bicycle. Whoever lived here could get up and down the stairs and take care of the property.

Goro rang the bell, and we all stood together and waited.

"Hello?" An old woman cracked the door a small amount, saw Goro in his uniform at the front of us, and opened it further. "Is there a problem, officer?"

Goro smiled, immediately putting her at ease. "None at all. My friends and I have a few questions for you about your visiting nurse service, and we wondered if we could come in and talk to you for a bit."

"Of course, of course," she said, nodding and opening the door to us. We entered, slipping off our shoes in the genkan. I took a deep breath and smelled rice, but nothing else. She kept the place neat, no piles of anything stacked against walls like in Senahara's house. We walked past the bathroom and kitchen to an informal living area with a kotatsu and TV on but muted. "Please sit. Can I get you some tea?"

"Thank you," I said, bowing.

"Please let me help you," Mom said, following the old woman into her kitchen.

Goro and I sat at the kotatsu, and I placed the box of sweet bread we brought on the table.

In the open kitchen, Mom and Hachiman spoke to each other.

"I think I know you," Hachiman said. "Have I seen you at the market?"

"Yes, perhaps you have. I own a farm out on 529 and sell my vegetables at the market on 72."

Hachiman hummed as they loaded tea and mugs onto a tray. "I've seen you there then."

They brought in the tea and sat down at the table, dispersing the mugs to each of us.

"My mom and I brought some sweet breads, if you're interested —" But she waved at me, cutting me off.

"I'm diabetic and unable to eat them, but thank you for your hospitality." She bowed to us, and Goro opened his notebook.

"Is this what Miss Kano helps you with?" I looked over Goro's shoulder and saw him write "diabetic" in his notebook.

She sipped her tea, setting the cup down lightly. "Yes, indeed. Miss Kano is most helpful. She brings me new insulin, checks my heart and blood pressure, and she also makes sure I can get around. Diabetes can cause sores, too, so she checks me to make sure I'm healthy."

I puffed with pride, hearing how Akiko takes good care of these people. "She sounds like an excellent nurse."

"One of the best they have. I didn't like the woman they sent yesterday. Where is Miss Kano?"

Goro cleared his throat. "She's under the weather and hopes to be back next week. Can you tell us if you remember her being here three weeks ago Friday?"

"Three weeks? I barely remember what happened yesterday."

Goro frowned at his notebook. "Do you recall an officer stopping by to see you three weeks ago Saturday?" He double-checked his notes. "Around 19:00?"

She shook her head. "My son is here in the evenings because I tend to forget things like taking my insulin. He checks my blood sugar levels and administers it for me, then cooks dinner."

Goro flipped back and forth between two pieces of paper.

"The officer said that he spoke to your son and you told him no one visits you."

"I did? I'm sorry. I don't remember." The woman's face scrunched as she concentrated hard on recalling the day. She sighed, her body deflating to half its size. "My memory has really changed the last few years. I'm so forgetful."

I glanced at Goro's notes again and then back at the old woman. "Do you happen to keep a diary of your medication?"

"Ah! I do!" She stood up and crossed the room to a closet behind a sliding door. "I keep my medication in here." She grabbed a small notebook from the shelf and brought it to us. "I should have thought of this. I write down my blood sugar checks and how much insulin I take, plus the readings from Miss Kano when she comes here. This way I can show the doctor I'm taking care of myself."

She handed me her notebook and I flipped back three weeks to find the information from when Akiko was here.

"It's not really evidence because it's not in her handwriting, but it's not as if Mrs. Hachiman could get these readings without Akiko being here," I said, turning the notebook over to Goro.

"Hmmm," he said, stroking his chin. "Mrs. Hachiman, do you ever remember a Friday when Miss Kano did *not* come? When *no one* showed up?"

"Someone always comes no matter what. I have never had to call and complain."

Goro nodded, satisfied. "That's good to hear. Well, we won't take up any more of your time. Thank you for speaking with us."

She smiled as we all stood up. "Anytime I can help, please don't hesitate to ask."

Our second patient of the day wouldn't even open the door to us.

"Please leave me alone. I already spoke to an officer about this weeks ago," she said, from the crack in her doorway.

"I understand," Goro said, trying to look inside. "And we're not here to give you any problems. We only want to make sure that Miss Kano is not falsely accused of skipping work on the day she was supposed to be here. At 18:00 on the Saturday after she was supposed to be here, you told the police she never showed up to your house. Is that correct?"

Goro did his best to ask questions while we smiled behind him in the freezing cold.

"That's right." I detected a head nod from my blocked view but I couldn't see her face. Regardless, her voice sounded agitated and unnerved, cracking and short.

"Why didn't you call the nursing service the day of to complain? They have no record of a call from you."

"I... I forgot about it. My memory is bad. Can you come back some other time? I'm busy right now."

"Of course," Goro said, bowing and pulling a business card from his pocket. "Please take my card and call me if you remember anything."

She didn't open the door to accept the card so he slipped it underneath. Back out on the sidewalk, Goro sighed and gestured to a café next door. This was a busier street than Hachiman's residential address five blocks to the south. Only a few residences were sandwiched among the local businesses: the café, a pharmacy, a saké shop, and a bank on the corner. Inside the café, we all bought coffees to warm ourselves up.

"Is it just me or did she seem scared?" Mom asked, as we sat down.

"It wasn't just you."

"I visit people's houses all the time," Goro said, pressing into his chair, "and that's the first time I've ever been turned away at the door like that."

We stared out the window at the block, the people walking bundled up against the cold, and the doors opening and closing at the pharmacy. Inside the pharmacy, the lights blazed.

"Oh, Mom wanted to let you know that she's holding an opening night party at the bathhouse on Wednesday night. 19:00. Yasahiro from Sawayaka is going to be catering the whole thing. Hey, aren't you still having lunch with him during the week? Kumi couldn't stop talking about it."

I piped cool thoughts of winter with two meters of snow on the ground to my brain and shook my head.

"We stopped yesterday."

Mom kicked my foot under the table, and I narrowed my eyes at her. I wasn't saying anything.

I went back to staring out the window and the flash of a TV in the pharmacy caught my eye.

"Goro," I said, touching his arm and pointing across the street, "do you think maybe the security cameras in any of these businesses have views of the street?"

He sat up in his chair and peered out the window. "Hmmm, I'm not sure about the pharmacy, but..." He angled his head to look farther up the street. "That bank would definitely have them. It's worth a shot to ask."

"Good thinking, Mei," Mom whispered to me.

"But it's the weekend. I'm sure I can go in and ask the pharmacy, but the bank will have to wait till Monday. And it may take a day. Then if we find anything, we'll still need to run it by the prosecutor." He sipped his coffee again, glancing around the café. "I'm going to question the people here too. Maybe one of them saw something. In the meantime, I don't feel comfortable holding Akiko at the station, even if she's there of her own free will. I'm going to call and have my partner drive her home."

"Yay!" I pumped my fist at my side.

"I honestly don't believe she did it, but something else is amiss here. We have more work to do."

I opened my mouth to tell him about Tama and his weird behavior but sat back instead. If I told him, I'd have to tell him I was out with Yasahiro and that Tama made comments about my body. And though he knew of my scars too because Chiyo and Mom had been friends for ages, I wasn't sure if Yasahiro wanted to broadcast our new "relationship," if that's even what it was.

I was going to have to look into Tama myself.

CHAPTER
TWENTY-SIX

I stood at the door and watched Yasahiro emerge from his car, arrange his coat, and walk to the house with a bag in his hand. I was more nervous than I'd ever been in my life, my stomach so upset I wanted to run to the bathroom. Up until now, we were barely friends, meeting every day for lunch because I was an ass and challenged him to cook for me. Now, we were dating. It could all go sour tomorrow, but during this moment, he was here to see me because he was interested in me. At least I hoped he was. I had so many doubts. I doubted I could make a life in the country work. I doubted I'd ever paint again. I doubted I'd solve Kano's murder. And I especially doubted that a handsome, professional, and successful guy like Yasahiro could ever fall for me.

"Hi there," he said, stepping up on the porch and coming through the door I held open for him. "Did you have a good Saturday?"

I took his coat and waited while he removed his shoes, set down his bag, and stepped into house slippers. "We were out all day with Goro, and it was freezing. It took a forty minute bath for me to warm up when we got back."

"The weather is warmer today. We should take a walk later."

"Sure," I said, shrugging my shoulders. "Oh, and Akiko is back home." I pointed to her house where the lights were on and smoke streamed from the chimney. "She texted me last night."

"Huh. I didn't realize she lived across the street from you. Anyway, that's good news," he said, a smile widening between his reddened cheeks. He removed his glasses and wiped the fog off of them. "I hate wearing glasses in the winter."

"You wear contacts, too, right? I noticed you weren't wearing glasses the other day."

"Yeah, but I like to give my eyes a break now and then." He reached for my hand, and I had the urge to pull my fingers from his because I wasn't used to it. But the sheer cold of his hands caused me to hold tighter.

"Oh no. You're freezing." I stepped a little closer and pressed his hand between both of mine, looking down at how small my hands were compared to his. I was embarrassed by my short, naked fingernails and dry cuticles, but his hands were much worse than mine.

I picked up his right hand and held it in front of my face. "What happened?" I pointed to a red, hot scar on the back. Tipping his hand side to side, a dozen scars became more apparent. I took his other hand too, and it was the same.

He smiled as he shook his head. "Don't worry. It's a hazard of the business. I burn myself all the time. Sometimes I work so fast in the kitchen, I forget that a pan is fresh out of the oven."

"Mei, is Yasahiro here?" Mom called from the kitchen, and I dropped Yasahiro's hand as if it would burn me, jumping away from him.

He chuckled softly. "Can I get you to come a little closer?" He leaned forward and whispered in my ear. "I like being close to you. It's been absolute agony having to sit across from you all week."

I dipped my head. I said I wasn't coy but... "When my mom isn't around, okay?"

"I understand," he said, and I could tell by his little head nods that he did. Respect to our elders was the way we lived and breathed in our society. Unless we were alone, we kept things platonic. No outward signs of affection, though I believed Yasahiro's years in Paris, the city of love, would make this somewhat difficult. I'd seen the photos. People there held hands and even kissed in public. We might have been able to get away with that in the city or maybe even in town amongst friends, but certainly not in front of my mom or anyone of her generation. It just wasn't done.

"What's in the bag?"

"Saké for lunch and a rosemary plant."

"A rosemary plant? I can't keep anything alive."

He laughed, walking past me into the house. "The plant is for your mom."

Mimoji came out from the back room, meowing at Yasahiro. He bent down and picked the cat up in his arms, making his way into the kitchen. I stood, frozen in shock. How many times had he been here before I moved home? Had he seen my room? Oh no, my room was a mess! I hoped he didn't expect to see it today. I hesitated between running to my room to clean it and heading to the kitchen when he popped his head back out and looked for me.

"Are you coming?"

"Yeah." No time. I'd have to keep him from my room as much as possible, and clean it, as well.

In the kitchen, Mom fussed over the plant Yasahiro gave her, pausing only to stir the pots on the stove. The two had an easy demeanor, like they'd known each other for years.

I perched myself on the stool while they hummed and tasted whatever Mom was cooking.

"Is this a miso soup?" Yasahiro asked, bent over the clay pot bubbling away.

"Miso, dashi, and mirin." She sliced salmon on the island into two-centimeter thick chunks.

I tried not to roll my eyes. Another home cooked dish today when I'd rather eat oden from the convenience store. But I cleared my throat and sat up to gird myself for what was to come. If I was going to date Yasahiro, I'd have to like this stuff.

"You look sick," Yasahiro said, smiling at me.

"Mei hated my salmon hot pot noodles growing up. I'm determined to get her to like them again." Mom added the salmon to the bubbling pot and pushed the slices down into the soup with her chopsticks.

I should have fought for my love of everything convenient and tasty, but it was no use. Eventually, I wouldn't be able to avoid it anymore. And with this being Yasahiro's life, if we actually lasted, there'd be no getting away from the slow food haute cuisine.

"Yasahiro brought saké," I said, changing the subject. I left my seat, grabbed the bottle from the bag, and some cups. "Want to get started?" I asked him, wiggling the cups in his direction. It was just past 12:00 but that never stopped me from drinking before.

"Sure," he said, following me into the dining room.

We sat at the kotatsu, already set with chopsticks and bowls, our legs under the table, enveloped in warmth. I loved this kotatsu. Mom upgraded to the deluxe version two years ago with the comfortable cushions that you can nap on. I filled up the cups and we clinked them together, chanting, "Kampai!" before throwing back the saké.

He glanced up at the wall and stared at my painting of rice fields at daybreak, his face blank for several seconds before recognition washed over him. I hastily directed my eyes to the table and the saké bottle, but I couldn't hide my blush. This was why I wouldn't succeed as a painter. I could never handle a showing. I'd puke in the bathroom the whole time or stand in a corner with my eyes closed.

Yasahiro blew out a long breath. "You have no idea how long or how many times I've stared at that painting and wondered about it. I looked for a signature but didn't find one."

"I never signed my own paintings. Just put my *hanko* stamp on the back."

"Why? You should take credit for your creations."

I filled our cups again. "I didn't want the attention. What if people hated it? Then they'd know it was me."

"What if they loved it and wanted to tell you, or buy it?" His question was sincere, not a hint of anger.

I shrugged my shoulders. I assumed everyone would hate my work like my teacher did. *"Her grasp of depth and light is weak and her form is sloppy. She should give up. No amount of teaching from me will save her now."* I remembered crying in my room while he said those things to my mom, and how much it hurt. After every lesson, I cried as he criticized my work, and he walked away from me disgusted the last time he had come to teach me. Tama made it worse when I got older. He was sweet on the surface, but when he critiqued my paintings, his honest opinion cut me till I bled. I could never shake it.

"Let's talk about something else... Please..."

Yasahiro rubbed his socked feet against mine under the table and asked me about our trip out yesterday. I was grateful for the change in conversation so I filled him in on everything we learned.

"So Goro is going to get the videos this week and hopefully we'll learn more."

"If Akiko didn't do it, then who do you think did?" Yasahiro filled up my cup again.

I drummed my fingers on the table for a minute, avoiding eye contact with him.

"I have an idea..." Yasahiro said, as Mom entered the room carrying the large clay pot and set it on the table. He paused for a moment to ladle out soup into everyone's bowls. We bowed and said, "Itadakimasu," together.

"What's your idea, Yasahiro?" Mom sat forward as I filled up her cup with saké and we toasted again with her.

"After our trip to Izakaya Jūshi on Friday, I did a little research into that brewery Etsuko mentioned, and you're not going to like what I found out." He sighed, pushing his glasses up on his nose. "It turns out that if I had asked a few questions right up front, I would have known immediately, but anyway, it looks like the *yakuza* have a large stake in the brewery and several others in a few chains across the country."

"What? What's going on?" Mom glanced between us, her face blanking in fear.

"It's okay, Mom. We're just doing some research. Etsuko mentioned that Tama has become friends with a brewery owner in Chiba. I wonder..." I stopped to slurp up noodles. "I wonder if Tama has gotten mixed up with organized crime. That would explain why he wants to sell the family house so badly. Maybe he needs the money?"

Yasahiro gestured to me. "That's exactly what I was thinking."

"No, not Tama." Mom shook her head. "He couldn't be. And the police cleared him. They said he was at school the day of the attack."

"Maybe he hired someone to do it?" Yasahiro asked, snapping up some salmon with his chopsticks.

"No. There was no sign of a struggle." I pushed my empty bowl away. Wow, I ate that fast. "I feel like we're on the right track, though. I should do some more internet searching."

"Hasn't that gotten you in enough trouble already?" He smiled at me, and I kicked him under the table. He laughed and rubbed his shin, and Mom spooned out more soup for everyone.

After lunch, Yasahiro invited me outside to go for a walk. We ambled along the property line slowly, our hands stuffed down in our pockets and faces turned up to the sun.

"Did you, um, tell your mother about us?" he asked, knocking his shoulder into mine.

I smiled at the ground, unable to look at him. I said I wasn't coy, but I could barely make eye contact with him half the time. The way he looked at me, like he could read my thoughts, melted me. I had a hard time handling it. "I did. I told her you were a gentleman and asked to date me. I did *not* tell her I kissed you."

"Smart move. I want to stay in her good graces, so whatever you suggest for... the future is fine with me."

I got to call the shots? Okay by me.

"Did you tell Goro when you went out yesterday?"

"No!" I tripped on a rock and he caught me by my elbow. "No, I did not. He didn't ask or anything. I thought I'd keep it quiet for a while."

"Really?" His face fell in disappointment and he let go of my elbow. "Are you ashamed of me?"

"Me?" I laughed and the disappointment did not fade from his face. It deepened. "No. Of course I'm not. I thought I wouldn't say anything because..." I gestured between us. "Because I'm afraid... No, I'm sure you'll change your mind."

"Mei —"

"You'll see. You may think I'm funny and charming and direct now, but I'm sure that'll fade with time and you'll miss the red carpets and the traveling and the shopping in Venice and cafés in Paris..."

He groaned and stopped walking.

"You really did find everything, didn't you?"

"My google-fu is unprecedented. I saw the intimate dinners in Amsterdam, too. You kissed her hand and looked into her eyes, and

I felt the love, just like everyone else did. I even saw the ring. It was gorgeous. You have exceedingly good taste." His face fell, so sad, as he ran his hand through his hair and turned to look out at the rows of dirt, freshly tilled and ready for winter. "I wish I hadn't seen it, but I did. I would have seen it eventually anyway, though, so maybe it's better that it happened now, before we got too far in, too hurt."

"You're right. I've been dreading this, meeting someone new and having to explain Amanda and that life because I can't. I can't go back and undo any of it. I can only move on."

I debated how I felt as I looked at him. I wanted him, but I wanted him to go away. I liked him, but I couldn't stand him for loving her. I wanted to fall in love and erase the last years of solitude, but staying single may have been safer.

Cold tingles washed down my body as a cloud covered the sun, and I shivered. Yasahiro stepped over to me and hesitantly put his arm around my shoulder.

Instead of pushing him away, I sank into his warmth. The scales tipped in favor of being with him, trusting him, wanting him and a relationship. I turned my body to his and wrapped my arms around his waist, resting my head on his chest. He squeezed me to him and kissed the top of my head.

He wanted to move on, and so did I.

"I'm sorry you saw all of that. I really am," he whispered into my hair, breathing in deeply through his nose. "Someday, I'll tell you more about why things were never going to work out between us. Amanda and I, we weren't good for each other. We weren't on the same path."

A well of hope bubbled up in my chest.

"And we are?"

"I *think* so. It's hard to tell just yet. So don't count me out, Mei. Don't think I'm going to dump you before we even start. I accepted the challenge to woo, and I never back down from a challenge."

He smiled down at me, so I hugged him tight again.

"Hey," I said, pulling away from him so I could gauge his reaction, "did you... ask my mom to set us up?" I'd suspected this for the last few days, and I was ready to outright ask for the information.

He tried to hide a smile, but I still saw it. "Whatever gave you that idea?"

"Hmmm, okay then." Liar. But at least the last few weeks made more sense. "Where do we start?" I released my grip on his waist, grasped his hand, and continued our walk by pulling him along with me.

"Well, I started the wooing today with saké."

"A good choice," I said, laughing.

"And I thought maybe you would show me your studio?"

I hesitated, wondering what he'd think of my workspace, but if this was to go forward, I would have to open up, way up.

"Okay."

The happiness on his face said it all. I was making the right choice.

Inside the barn, I pointed out the stores of sweet potatoes, squash, and other root vegetables we'd keep for ourselves and to sell at the market through the winter to help pay our bills. The tractor sat idle as usual and the tools we used were hung up on the wall. Taking our shoes off at the bottom, we ascended the stairs. I flipped on the space heater, cracked open the window, and waited as he walked around and looked at my supplies.

"I kind of expected a lot more paintings," he said, glancing at the few unused canvases stacked against the wall.

"Chiyo bought the one painting that was left. It sat right here for a long time." I pointed to the wall, and then gathered up a few of the canvases that had something on them. "These two I started but never finished."

He stroked his chin as he looked between my easel, the tackle boxes of paint, and the couch. "What about all the paintings you made as a kid?"

"Destroyed them." I shrugged my shoulders as he gasped. "I was done. It was all crap and everyone hated them." I shrugged my shoulders again, resigned. "So I slashed the canvases and pulled them apart then trashed them. About six years ago? Yeah, I think I was twenty at the time."

"How could you do that?" His eyes were wide, so I tried to soften things by smiling warmly.

"It's okay, Yasahiro. I don't regret it."

He shook his head. "You're a stronger person than I am."

"Either that or I'm just stupid," I said, laughing, but he grasped my hand and squeezed.

"Don't say that about yourself."

His kindness shocked me. "Okay," I whispered.

He gestured at the dark canvas on my easel. "What's this?"

"My current work-in-progress." I released my hand from his and pointed with all five fingers at the center. "A fire here, the bonfire that nearly killed me..." I dragged my hand up. "Smoke and stars." I stepped back and folded my arms across my chest. "Wheat fields in the background, but everything will be dark." I closed my eyes and remembered the scene, the way the air smelled, the laughter of the kids running around, how happy I was right before it happened.

Yasahiro blew out a slow, hissing breath. "You *are* stronger than me. I could never face my fears like this."

"What kind of fears do you have?" I asked as I bumped my shoulder into his.

"The standard ones. Fear of failure, fear I'll lose it all in one big mistake, so I just plow ahead."

I nodded in agreement, turning from my painting. "There's not much you can do about those."

Yasahiro patted his pockets a few times. "Hmmm, I don't

have my phone on me. Do you know the time? I'm always misplacing my phone."

I pulled mine from my jacket. "It's 14:50 already."

"I have to go," he said, disappointment evident in his voice.

"I'll walk you out," I offered, but he waved me off.

"Stay and work on your painting."

We stood close to each other, and the memory of our kiss the other night flashed across my vision. I bit my lip to stop a sharp intake of air. He tilted his head and reached up to play with a curl of my hair that came free during our walk.

"Will you be at the bathhouse opening on Wednesday?" he asked.

"Yes." My answer came out breathy and light. "Chiyo is a treasured friend. I wouldn't miss it."

"I'm looking forward to seeing you. Will you call me tomorrow?"

I nodded and he stepped away, not turning his back to me. "I'll miss you at the restaurant this week. I was thinking you should come by at our time anyway. What do you say?"

"Okay."

He waved and headed down the stairs, and I waited until the door closed to dance a victory jig. Wow. I was the luckiest girl on the planet, which seemed impossible. I went from my constant bad luck of the last five years to turning it around in just three weeks! And I did it at home, the one place I'd been avoiding. Ah, Yasahiro... Spending time with him made me excited and happy and fearful and amazed. My body buzzed wondering when we were going to kiss again.

Turning to the painting and staring at it, I peeled off my coat and threw it onto the couch. I needed to add in the base for the reds of the flames next. I flipped open my tackle boxes and pulled out the reds I had set aside the last time I painted. Grabbing my palette, I dispensed out a dollop of each onto the surface in order of hue. Yeah, that was perfect.

Movement in the corner of my eye startled me. I whirled around and Tama stood at the top of the stairs.

"Oh my god!" I yelled, clutching my chest and nearly sandwiching the palette to my shirt. "Tama, what are you doing here? I didn't even hear you come in."

"You were humming. I'm sure I wasn't that quiet with the door." Tama kept his distance from me, his hands pushed into the pockets of his jeans. "I waited until that Yasahiro left."

Danger detectors blared in my head. Yasahiro was gone, and Mom was in the house. I was all alone here.

"So I guess you guys *are* dating? That's so strange."

"Why?" Anger peaked, running my blood hot.

"Well, why would anyone date *you* after dating Amanda Cheung?"

My face began to heat. "What do you want, Tama? It's not like you have any reason to be here."

He paced to the window and back, eyeing my current work-in-progress and stepping around the space heater a few times. "I came by to tell you that Akiko's been cleared of our father's death, and you don't have to worry about it anymore."

"Really? How did Goro clear her?" I set my palette down and approached him, but he wove away from me, heading back to the window.

"It's not important. He called today to say she's free and clear, and I can go on with the family business plans. She *does* get a portion of the estate. I'm going to make sure of it."

"A portion?" I didn't like that term at all.

"Twenty percent. It's more than generous."

My heart beat twice as fast. "Twenty percent? That's outrageously small!"

He sighed, looking around the barn, as if he was unable or unwilling to make eye contact with me. If I could rewind time, I would find the younger Tama here with wildflowers in his hands

and a swagger in his step as he unbuttoned his pants, but this? I
didn't know this guy at all.

"It is what it is, Mei. I think Dad killed himself. He smothered himself. It's the only explanation. And now we're fortunate
because the police are done, and Akiko and I can sell and
move on."

Who smothered themselves if they wanted to die? Knife to
the gut, slit the wrists, drown in a pool, sure. But smother themselves? No. "That's crazy."

He shrugged his shoulders. "Believe what you will." He
leaned towards me, finally making eye contact. "Just back off and
give Akiko some peace." He nodded once, satisfied he'd delivered
his message, and I heard it loud and clear. Back off or I was next.

"That's a fascinating painting you have going there. A fire?"

"Yeah," I whispered, my head light as a balloon.

He pursed his lips as he looked at it again. "Interesting
choice, considering."

When he turned to leave, my knees began to shake.

"Take care, Mei."

He descended the stairs and walked out the door, and I
moved to the window to watch him walk away from the barn to
Akiko's house across the street.

I was convinced he'd killed his own father.

I just needed evidence to prove it.

CHAPTER
TWENTY-SEVEN

"Mom! I'm back inside!" I yelled into the house as I shucked off my shoes in the genkan. In the kitchen, Mom washed dishes and listened to Rachmaninoff, her favorite composer. She'd always wanted to learn to play the piano, but it never happened.

"I'm going to my room to do some internet research." I filled up a glass with water and grabbed an apple from the kitchen counter.

"Mei, wait." She turned off the sink and lowered the volume on the stereo. "I'm worried about what's going on with Tama, this brewery, and the yakuza." Mom wrung her hands together. The very mention of yakuza, Japan's very own organized crime syndicate, had set her on edge. "You know that we do our best around here to keep them away from our land and our businesses, so I don't want to do anything that would call attention to us."

"It's okay," I said, patting her hand. "I'm not going to do anything to call attention to us. *I* don't have that kind of power. But if Tama is in with the mob, then they already know where he's from, who his friends are, how much money he makes, et cetera et cetera. Besides, it's only a guess. I only have a gut feeling about this."

"You *and* Yasahiro."

"Still," I said, shrugging my shoulders. "We're probably wrong. I've been wrong about many things before, and I would love to be wrong about this too, so I'll continue to search until I'm sure."

Tama's face popped into my head. *"Just back off and give Akiko some peace,"* he'd said, trying to make this all about Akiko. But I knew, I felt it deep down in my toes, that this was about him. Otherwise, he'd be willing to help, right? If he were innocent, he would do everything to help the police track down the murderer. Instead, Akiko was the one under house arrest and voluntarily giving herself over to the police, and Tama was the one pretending like nothing happened. That in itself told me a lot. If he killed his own father, he was as dumb as a rock to do everything he was doing. I used to think he was pretty smart, being a teacher and all that, but now I questioned his sanity.

"Okay, Mei, but I'm still worried."

"It'll be fine," I said, smiling at her as I left the kitchen. She turned up her Rachmaninoff and the water began to flow in the sink again by the time I reached my room. I stepped over two piles of clothes on the floor and edged around a tower of boxes to get to my bed. Pushing away a pile of books, I set my glass of water on a napkin on the tatami mats and sat cross-legged on the bed, pulling my computer onto my lap. I needed to take the time to clean up, but I wanted to find out more about the brewery.

I'd always loved alcohol, I'd admit. Growing up in a household where alcohol flowed free, like many other Japanese houses, there had never been any stigmas attached to what we drank and when. The legal drinking age was twenty, but I would drink at home with Mom once I was eighteen. She was great like that. She didn't want me to learn about life without her help, and that's probably why we were good friends now. My brother wanted nothing to do with us as he got older, which was fine. It was his job to get good grades, a college education, and marry into a good family, all of which he did. My mom had left everything optional for me, and even though I shot for the stars with excellent grades and a decent city job, she'd never expected those things of me. She was proud of me for what I did, no matter what I did. I loved that about her.

I bit into the apple and held it in my mouth as I opened my browser. Unfortunately, the last search I had open was for Yasahiro and Amanda. I allowed myself to look at the photos again, the two-carat diamond and platinum engagement ring, them together on a sail boat, and her applauding him as he won some award in Paris.

"It's over," I said aloud as I closed the window. I said it, but it'd be a while before I believed it.

Opening a new browser, I got to work. I couldn't remember the name of the brewery but I searched for new breweries in Chiba until I found a name that sounded familiar. Cruising their website, everything up front appeared legitimate. They'd been open for three years and they distributed to all of central Japan. The place was owned by a team of brothers, and their family had been brewing beer since 1926. I closed my eyes and remembered the taste of the beer. It'd been pretty good. Served ice cold, it went down easy. They must have invested a lot of money into high-quality wheat and hops.

I plugged the names of the brothers into Google and hit the jackpot. Where were they from? Kobe, of course, the city of yakuza, as far as everyone was concerned. Mom was worried, but I was not. I grew up in the age of yakuza in the media, yakuza handing out Halloween candy, yakuza holding annual meetings, yakuza showing up for the local festivals. No big deal, especially if you're not related to them. But these men were, tangentially. They were distant cousins to a few of the less prominent families, and seeing how the brewery had grown and prospered since they opened only three years ago, it had to be a front of some kind. And if I could figure that out from a simple Google search, the police already knew.

I picked up my phone to call Goro and hesitated. Maybe I was overreacting? Whatever. I dialed his number anyway.

"Hello, Mei. How are you?"

"I'm good, Goro, and you?"

"Good. Good." In the background, I heard a high-pitched voice. "Kumi says hello and wants to know why you didn't return her texts the last few days."

"I just got back my phone on Friday. It took a bath in a puddle. Tell her I'll write her back later." I smiled down at my jeans as I played with a thread on the seam. Kumi was awesome. I hoped we were going to be best buddies soon enough. "Anyway, I have some new information for you, and I was wondering if you could check up on it?"

"Sure. Let me grab my notepad." He fumbled around on the other end. "Okay, go."

"Etsuko, the waitress at Izakaya Jūshi, told Yasahiro and I that Tama has made friends with a brewer in Chiba. After doing some digging, it looks like the brewer is connected to the yakuza."

"What? What are you saying?"

My right hand began to shake so I switched to my left hand. "I'm saying I suspect Tama is involved in his father's death."

"But we cleared him. He was at school the whole day."

I sat in silence for a moment. "Please understand. I don't *want* him to be involved, but the more I look at what's going on, the more I see his hand in everything. Shinzo Kano was killed before he could will the estate to Akiko. Tama wants to sell even though it would put his sister out, and now he's involved in some new business? Plus..."

I stopped talking because I had absolutely no evidence to back up my ideas.

"What, Mei?"

"It's just a feeling." I chewed on the skin around my nails and then dropped my hand in disgust. I missed my long nails and nail polish.

"Well, you better tell me because, in my line of business, we act on gut feelings until we know they're wrong."

"Really?"

"I do." I imagined him shrugging on the other end of the line. "More of my gut feelings have ended up true than not."

"Okay. Well, he came here to the house and snuck into the barn while I was working on a painting. He threatened me and told me to back off."

Goro groaned. "No one else was there?"

"Nope. Yasahiro was here today, but Tama waited until he was gone."

Goro stayed quiet for a moment, but Kumi in the background asked, "What is it? What's wrong?"

"I'll tell you in a minute," he said to her before coming back to me. "Mei, you need to be careful."

"No. What I need to do is figure this out before anyone else gets hurt. Did you call Tama and tell him that you cleared Akiko?"

"Uh, no. Why would I do that?"

Another lie. "He said you had." I rubbed my eyes, suddenly tired from the stress of this day.

"I'm sure she didn't commit the murder, but I haven't officially cleared her. Hey, I want you to call Akiko and check on her, then..."

"Then what?"

"Then I want you to go by Tama's school tomorrow and ask the principal and other teachers about his work there. But you'll need to be discreet and keep it from him, okay? I'll call the principal now and text you back in a little bit."

I stood up from the bed and tried to pace, but I had no available floor space for that.

"Shouldn't you go? You're the police and all that."

He laughed. "I thought you were determined to win our bet!"

"I thought the bet was off!"

He laughed again. "It is. I just wanted to see how riled up I could get you. Look, I thought you wanted to solve the crime?"

"I do. I want to help Akiko."

"Then help me out by going to the school. I'll be dealing with the video footage tomorrow. We have four officers working on that, so I'll need your help."

"Okay, fine. Sure. I'll go." My forehead immediately broke into a sweat though. Tama told me to stay out of it. If he saw me there, I was dead for sure.

"I'll text you in a little bit. Call Akiko and check up on her."

We hung up, and I dialed Akiko.

"Mei, hi. How are you?" She sounded tired, worn out.

"I'm good. I wanted to check up on you. It's been ages since I last saw you."

"You saw me on Thursday."

"Well, it's not like we sat down and spent time together or anything."

"Right, right." She sighed, the tiredness in her voice magnified by ten. "It's been a hellish week, and now I need to look for a place to live. Tama stopped by earlier to tell me he's selling the land." She swore under her breath. "It's probably for the best. I'm thinking I may find a place in town."

I perked up. "That sounds nice. You'd be within walking distance of most of your patients."

"I could sell the car and get a bicycle."

I laughed. "You hate bikes."

She chuckled and my heart grew a whole size. I'd missed my best friend. "Yep. I should buy one of those motor-assist ones." I heard a door open and then close. "Anyway, it's nice that you called, but I was about to get into a bath. I need a hot bath and some whiskey. Then tomorrow I go back to work."

"That's fantastic! I'm happy to hear things are getting settled down."

"Me too. Hey, are you going to Chiyo's bathhouse opening on Wednesday?"

"Absolutely. I'm so looking forward to it."

"Great. I'll see you then. Later, Mei."

"Bye." I hung up, realizing I forgot to tell her about Yasahiro. Where would I have even begun with that anyway?

I flopped down on my bed and stared at the ceiling. My life was confusing. A few weeks ago, I was living in Tokyo, single, alone, my own job, and my own life. It wasn't much, but I was independent and trying to make my way in the world. Now, I lived at home, getting my "salary" from my mother, but dating a new guy and trying my hand at being both a detective and an artist. How did that happen?

My phone buzzed with a text from Goro. *"You're all set. Meet with the principal at 10:00. Come by the station after and we'll debrief."*

Well, that settled that. I was off to sleuth tomorrow!

CHAPTER
TWENTY-EIGHT

I sat in the car and stared at the school, my high school, the place I'd spent many glorious years of studying and keeping out of the path of bullies. I hadn't been a popular kid, but I wasn't unpopular either. My family had done well, and my brother had graduated with high marks from the same school four years ahead of me. I had a good clique of friends that never got into trouble. In any respect, my high school years were pretty boring, nothing like the manga and drama series on TV. I'd studied hard to pass the entrance exam even though it was a long drive from home. Akiko made it in, too, and we were inseparable for most of high school. Ironically, Tama had never attended this high school. He went to another one farther away.

Walking up the steps to the front door, I transported back ten years to the conversations on the sidewalks, across the soccer field, and out to the pick up area.

"Mei Yamagawa?" I paused on the steps but continued when I saw the young woman holding open the door for me. "The principal sent me to retrieve you from the front door." She probably worked in the office during school hours. I had done this once or twice when I was in my third year. I would deliver notes to teachers or students, clean up after meetings, and greet people who came to visit.

"Thank you," I said, following her in and through the halls, past the classrooms, auditorium, gym, and cafeteria. I glanced left and right to make sure no one saw me (well, make sure Tama didn't see me) but the hall was empty.

In the administrative office, I smiled at the familiar surroundings. You never forgot your high school, no matter how hard you tried. A few people said hello and bowed, but I didn't recognize any of the faces. Ten years was a long time, and many teachers and administrative people came and went in that time.

"Mei Yamagawa, I'm the principal, Ms. Aizawa." A small, old woman approached me, and I jumped to attention. The principal we had when I went to school here was a man in his forties, so I wasn't expecting a little old lady. She smiled and we bowed before she beckoned me into her office.

"I was surprised to get a call from the Chikata police department yesterday, especially at home. But Goro Hokichi is an old friend, and I'm always happy to help him in any way I can."

"Thank you for seeing me." I sat in a chair opposite her desk. "How do you know Goro?"

"His mother and I are old friends, and he comes to the school twice a year to talk to the students about preventing sexual harassment and cyber bullying. He's been very convincing." Her smile lifted and eyes narrowed to slits.

"I didn't know he did that. I'll have to ask him about it."

"Now, how can I help you today? Goro mentioned you may need to question some students?"

"It's possible," I replied, pulling my own notebook from my purse. I flipped past my pages on the different suspects I'd considered in this case and started a new page. "You heard that Mr. Kano's father passed away recently?" I made sure to switch to Tama's last name. I didn't want to appear rude to Aizawa.

"Yes. We were all saddened by his loss."

I nodded my head in agreement. "We wanted to get a whole picture of Mr. Kano's schedule that day, so we can be sure of everyone's whereabouts during the time of his father's death."

Aizawa sat back in her chair. "Is Mr. Kano in some kind of trouble? Goro told me you'd be asking questions about an open investigation, but I had no idea Mr. Kano was involved in anything."

"Oh, don't worry, please," I said, assuring her. "This is standard procedure." At least, I hoped it was. That seemed like the right thing to say. "There are some questions about the nature of his father's death, and we need to be sure of everyone's whereabouts should the case go to trial."

"Very well," she said, turning to her computer and hitting the space bar. "Let me look at the schedule."

"The day in question is Friday, October the second." I leaned forward, placing my notebook on her desk and readying my pen to take notes.

"Hmmm. On Fridays, Mr. Kano has two periods he teaches and then two periods where he gives individual students help."

"What does he teach here again?"

"Chemistry. It's a specialized science so he doesn't teach a class for every period." She returned to the schedule. "Let's see. He was supposed to be tutoring two students during that time period. Let me find out where they are right now, and I'll have them brought in." She stood up from her desk but paused as she straightened out her skirt. "I'm assuming you already asked Mr. Kano about where he was that Friday?"

I nodded and smiled, trying to look as unworried and amiable as possible. "He says he was here, and when someone called from the police department to verify the information, your office said he was here and didn't leave all day."

"We use a time card system that's automated. You check in at the beginning of the day and check out at the end. It's mainly used to help track sick or vacation days, and the amount of time a teacher spends in the school. These things are necessary when we negotiate contracts."

"But it's not mandatory? You don't use it to check in and out of buildings so you can't track movement in the school?"

"No. Not for teachers. We've experimented with student tracking because of parents' worries, but that's it. Excuse me a moment, please."

I remembered lots of schools experimenting with RFID tracking chips ten years ago, but they were only implemented in elementary schools. Once kids were in high school, it wasn't needed anymore.

I took out my phone and scrolled through my texts while I waited for Aizawa to return. Mom texted that she finished pulling out the kabocha squash, and Yasahiro wrote, *"It was so cold this morning it took twice as long for the restaurant to heat up. Come by for lunch later?"*

My body tingled, thinking about our walk around the property yesterday. *"Sure. I'll be there around 13:00. Okay?"*

I slipped my phone into my purse as the door reopened, and Aizawa entered with two young men. I rose up from my chair and we bowed. One boy was tall and skinny with mop hair that hung over his eyes. The other had the build of a rugby player with spiked hair and tortoiseshell glasses. Was I ever this young? It felt like ages ago.

Aizawa hovered while we introduced ourselves, but then turned for the door. "I need to go speak with the office staff. I'll be back in a few minutes."

"I don't know if Ms. Aizawa told you but I'm here to double check Mr. Kano's schedule on Friday, October the second."

I stopped to glance up from my notebook and found the boys eyeing one another.

"The schedule says that he was with you that day during the morning. Is that correct?" I poised my pen and waited, but they didn't say anything. I raised my eyebrows at them, and they eyed each other again.

"It's not correct?" My hearing rang, my scalp prickling. I expected them to jump on this and not hesitate.

"Well, that day was three Fridays ago, right?" The boy with the glasses asked.

"It was," I said, sitting forward in my chair.

"Mr. Kano said he was feeling ill that day and needed to lie down in the infirmary. He canceled on us, but then I saw him later that day during yearbook club. He said he took some medicine and felt better. I thought it was his stomach, so I didn't ask."

"Did he have health problems all the time?"

The other student shook his head. "This was the first time he ever looked ill. That's why I didn't say anything. We studied in the library that day, and he made up for the absence by giving us study guides."

"I see." My stomach shrank and twisted. I wanted to find no evidence against Tama, but instead my worst fears were coming true. "Thank you both."

The tall boy headed out but the shorter one with glasses turned to me. "Mr. Kano is a good teacher. This won't get him in trouble, will it?"

I shook my head and patted his shoulder. "Don't worry. I'm sure he was sick, just like he said."

Aizawa returned as the boys left the office.

"Can I help you with anything else?" she asked with a smile and a bow.

"One more thing. I need to talk with whomever works in the infirmary."

———

I PULLED THE CAR INTO AN OPEN SPOT IN THE MUNICIPAL

parking lot across from Sawayaka, turned off the engine, and stared into space until my phone rang. It was Goro.

"Mei, I wanted to check in and see how your visit went."

I put pressure on the bridge of my nose, an impending headache barreling down on me. "How it went?" I chuckled before slapping my hand over my mouth. "He wasn't there. He just wasn't there."

"Speak some sense, Mei, or I'm going to call someone to come get you."

"I'm fine. So, I went to the school, and the morning of the murder, Tama was supposed to be tutoring a few kids but he faked an illness and took off."

"Really? Did the principal know about this?"

"No. The kids thought he went to the infirmary, but the nurse who runs it said no one came in that day except some girls faking a cough." I rolled my eyes. I had a friend in high school that faked an illness every week. She was under a lot of stress and spent half her senior year in the infirmary.

"So he was missing in action then."

"Yeah, that's my best guess. Any chance there are video cameras around there you could access?"

He laughed. "I'm just now getting the footage from the bank and convenience store. At least it's only one day's worth of video to watch at high speed." He sighed, and I heard him drink something. "I need more coffee. Anyway, I'll call you later when I get more information, and I'll let the others know what you found out. Tama didn't see you, did he?"

"No. I was in and out in an hour and both times class was in session." That was my only lucky break this morning.

"If you don't hear from me, you can always stop by the station later."

"Okay. See you then."

I hung up and stared at the gathering of people at Sawayaka. It was nearing 13:00, and the lunch hour was still going strong. I rubbed my thumbs up and down the side of the phone before chewing on the skin around my index fingernail. More evidence my high school boyfriend was a killer, and the new guy I was dating was more popular than I would ever be. I'd been thinking a lot about what it would be like to date him. Would I attend restaurant openings? Would he open more restaurants? What if he traveled? I wouldn't be able to travel with him on my flimsy budget. He'd have to go alone. Would he meet with famous people while he was there and go on dates with other women?

I breathed in slowly and let it out until my stomach collapsed against my spine. I was in for a world of hurt with this guy, wasn't I? I could never keep up with him. I closed my eyes and pressed my head to the steering wheel. Doubt raced through my blood like adrenaline.

I picked up my phone to text him. *"Hey, I'm in the parking lot but the restaurant looks really busy and I don't want to bother you. Should I come back some other day?"*

I sent the text and waited, but then after a few minutes of watching the crowd outside Sawayaka, I figured he was probably too busy to text me back. I started up the car and turned on the radio. Oh well. I'd get food from the convenience store and head home for a while.

A sharp knock on the window scared me, and I yelped and jumped, turning down the radio. I hit the window down button and Yasahiro's face poked in the car.

"What are you doing sitting out here? Come inside."

"I, um, I saw how busy the place is, and I thought I'd go get a sandwich from the convenience store."

"Nonsense, Mei. You'll always have a seat in my restaurant. If all the tables are taken, you can come eat in the kitchen."

"Oh. No. I could never do that." Freeloading guilt blanketed me from head to toe. "And I feel weird about taking the free food. I should pay when I come and wait in line with everyone else."

"Turn off the car and come inside." His voice was stern and

his face unforgiving as I rolled up the window. I counted to five to pull myself together, turned off the car, and opened the door.

Yasahiro backed away as I came out. "I don't own a restaurant so that I can turn you away and make you wait with regular customers." He took my elbow gently and turned me towards Sawayaka. "I *know* you don't have the money for food from the convenience store—"

"Not true. Mom paid me yesterday."

"All the more reason to hold on to it for something better than food I am happy to give you for free."

"I'm not a charity case, Yasahiro." I pulled my arm from his and stopped. "If that's what this is going to be, you feeling pity for me and giving me things because of some misplaced guilt, then it's not going to work between us."

I was going to cry. I whirled around to head back to the car.

"Stop stop stop..." He came after me, grabbing my shoulder. I jerked it away from him and reached for the car handle, but before I could open the door, he wrapped his arms around my shoulders. "You think I pity you?" he whispered into my ear. I nodded my head, unable to talk because the tears were coming.

"Mei..." He pressed his cheek against mine. "You've been so down to earth about it, I didn't think you cared all that much."

"About being poor?" I lived way below the poverty line, and the only thing I'd spent money on in the last three weeks was a few convenience store lunches and the art supplies, of which Mom paid for half.

"Yeah. I know a lot of people who struggle and it really bothers them, but you've acted okay with it."

I sighed and stepped out of his embrace. "I'm trying to be. Really trying. But it's hard when I see how much everyone else has." I swiped the tears from my face. "And that sounds horrible too because I have a roof over my head, a computer and mobile phone, and I'm not going hungry. I'm just..." I threw my hands up and let them fall back down again. I didn't know what I was.

"Do you get a headache when your blood sugar is low?" he asked, and I jerked in surprise. "My sister was like that. I can see it on your face." He stepped closer to me, running his hand down my arm. "The space between your eyes is scrunched. You're hungry?" I nodded, stunned into silence. He was more perceptive than I gave him credit for. "You've been out all morning and you need a break."

What did I have for breakfast that morning? A cup of coffee and a slice of toast. Mom had left, off to run errands, and she ate noodles she cooked up and forgot to leave some for me.

"Yeah. I'm hungry, and I do have a headache." It's times like these I felt like a liar because he could see the truth before I could.

He put his arm around my shoulders and directed me towards Sawayaka. "Let me see if I can get you a table. You will always eat for free in my restaurant. Always. Even if you dump me."

I laughed as I smoothed out my face and wiped my eyes. "If I dump you, I doubt I'd come back to your restaurant. Just to save face, you know?"

"I know, but you could."

We walked straight past the people waiting, stopping to hug Ana and chat for a minute, and Yasahiro craned his neck to look around. Several people caught his attention, and he stepped to them to chat, smile, clasp hands, or bow. I watched him navigate the waters of his success, both envious and slightly proud of this guy who came out of nowhere to woo me.

He circled around to me, leaning over to take my hand and whisper in my ear, "The place is packed. Come back to the kitchen."

"Oh my god," a hoarse voice uttered from my right. Haruka stood up from her table, noticing my blush at how close Yasahiro was to me. I tried to back away from him, but he was good about detecting my instinct for flight, and pulled me closer by my waist. "Wow, Mei. You certainly work fast around here."

"Haruka, hi." The blood drained from my face when her ring flashed in front of me. She was engaged to Tama, remember? And I was investigating him for the death of his father.

Despite our past history of antagonism, I was tempted to tell her what was going on. Maybe she could remove herself from Tama before it was too late. But I couldn't. Letting her know would let Tama know he was being watched. And if he was the killer, I couldn't let him get away.

"So, you and Yasahiro? How does that even happen?"

I glanced at Yasahiro, and his face fell from a smile. *Here we go, Mei.* He was about to find out how unpopular it was to date the local farm girl.

"Haruka," he said, returning the smile to his face, "I hope you enjoyed your lunch."

She smiled, cocking her head to the side. "Sawayaka is the talk of the town. You must be proud."

"I am," he said, squeezing me before letting go and leaning close to Haruka's ear. I couldn't tell what he said, but her face flattened and her skin whitened. She nodded once as he pulled away. "Have a great afternoon. Your meal is on me, ladies," he said to the entire table behind Haruka.

They all smiled and bowed and thanked him over and over, as he took my hand and pulled me to the kitchen. We side-stepped a waitress exiting and entered into the controlled chaos of plates clinking, ovens whirring, and pans sizzling.

"What did you say to Haruka?"

"Doesn't matter." He pulled out a stool at the island and sat me in it. "I know you had udon yesterday, but how about some noodles with sesame sauce, and I have fish or eggs, too?"

"Sure. Sesame noodles sound good, and eggs."

I looked out at the restaurant as the door swung open, and

everyone at Haruka's table was gone. I didn't think I wanted to know what he said to her. It was probably better I didn't.

A plate of egg sushi appeared in front of me with a glass of water, and Yasahiro returned to work, his jacket off and chef's whites back on. I popped the egg and rice in my mouth and chewed as I watched them work together. One washed plates. Another stacked them. Two people worked the stove while Yasahiro chopped and called out orders. He was at ease in his kitchen, like it was part of his own body, not some foreign place he had to struggle to work in. The man and woman cooking at the stove talked about their weekends and laughed over some inside joke, and Yasahiro dropped by each to dip a spoon in, taste, and nod or instruct. He was so good at this.

My phone rang in my bag at my feet. I bent over to dig it out, and when I straightened up, he was behind me with a bowl of noodles. I could've sworn he was checking out my ass.

I raised my eyebrows at him as I answered my phone, and he set the bowl down next to the sushi.

"Hello?"

"It's Goro. I decided to call instead of waiting for you to come here." I set down my chopsticks and braced myself. "No luck, Mei. We found nothing on the surveillance cameras." He sighed, sounding more than exhausted. "It's a dead lead. I guess we'll have to go back and question the second woman again. Maybe, with some prompting she'll talk to us."

"Oh no. I'm sorry. I really thought you'd find something."

"It's okay. It was a good idea and worth a shot. Back to the beginning for now."

"Yeah. I guess so."

"See you Wednesday, if not before."

"Okay. Bye." I hung my head in defeat. All of that work for nothing, and my eternal bad luck had resurfaced.

Now what?

CHAPTER
TWENTY-NINE

I woke up on Tuesday morning, warm in bed, the alarm beeping incessantly at 7:00. Right. I wanted to wake up early and go for a run before harvest time. Today, we had pumpkins that needed to be brought in, and some of them were so large, we'd hired one of the local workers to come and help out. He'd be here at 9:30, so I had enough time to run and eat some breakfast.

I stared at the ceiling for a little while, willing myself to emerge from the warm cocoon of blankets to the chill of the morning. Mom turned on the space heater in the main room when she worked between there and the kitchen, and the kotatsu could be turned on at a moment's notice, but that didn't stop my room from being ice cold each morning. It wasn't even winter yet! Winter would be brutal.

I threw off the covers quickly and jumped into my warm terrycloth robe, one of my favorite belongings. Opening the shades on my window, weak morning light filtered in and highlighted the complete disaster I called my room. Okay, I'd had it. I had to clean it *right now* or else I'd hate myself. Plus, my clean running gear was in there somewhere and it would take a bull-dozer to find it.

First thing, I opened my closet and prepared it to accept my clothes. I threw open the doors and cleared out the old stuff from high school — papers, folders, and notebooks. I could recycle or burn those later if I needed to. I opened a cardboard box, pulled out my clothes still on hangers, and hung them in the closet. When I was a teen, I had this closet converted from all shelves to one for clothes as well. It used to be a place to put a futon, but I wanted something modern and easy. I emptied two large boxes of clothes onto the rod in the closet and then looked them over. I wondered if I should keep these? I could sell most of them to a second-hand clothing shop and make a few yen. It wasn't like I was going to find a new job any time soon, and I'd shrunk a whole size in the last four weeks.

With those boxes emptied, I opened my door and threw them into the main area.

"Mei, you're up?" Mom called from the kitchen.

"Yes! I'm finally cleaning my room." I turned back to the disaster and sighed.

"Coffee?" Mom called again.

"Sure!"

I picked through my pile of clean laundry and started to fold clothes, actually putting said folded clothes into my empty dresser.

"Wow," Mom said, handing me a cup of steaming hot coffee with milk and sugar. "I'm beginning to see the tatami."

"I'd had enough." I sipped the coffee, set it on my dresser, and kept folding.

"I'm heading outside soon. Let me know if you need anything."

I nodded before she left, speed folding and sorting. Way at the bottom of the pile, I found my workout clothes and set them aside. I went through two more boxes, finding things like knickknacks and photos and placing them on my dresser and windowsill. There was a stack of bills, all paid now, I could add to the burnables. I gathered up my dirty clothes and threw them in the hamper, but at the foot of the bed, I found a pink and orange furoshiki bundle. Oh no! The package Chiyo gave me when I arrived in Chikata!

I set the bundle on my bed and opened it hesitantly. If I remembered correctly, she gifted me a whole bunch of newspaper clippings and her homemade sweets, and they were probably pretty gross by now. Why hadn't I eaten them when they were fresh? The sweets, wrapped in wax paper, were growing mold, so I placed them in my pile of burnable trash, then I withdrew the newspaper clippings she gave me. I almost threw them in the pile as well, but stopped, familiar names and faces swimming out of the random text.

Sitting down on the bed, I began to read through them. The top article detailed Midori Sankaku's plans for the town, their partnership, and projections heading into 2018. In the accompanying photo, Shin Tajima and Fujita Takahara shook hands and walked around the town. I wondered where Takahara was now and if he was angry with me for turning him down.

The next article was from the business section showing Chiyo outside of her new bathhouse. The article stated that she hoped to open before the end of October and that the whole community looked forward to the new ownership.

I flipped through a few more articles about my old high school athletic teams doing well today and the shake up in town as new places of business opened. I paused on an article about Yasahiro and Sawayaka. He garnered an entire half page on his time spent in Paris, the breakup with Amanda, the restaurant he worked at in Tokyo, and now his success at Sawayaka. I set that one aside. I wanted to put it on my dresser so I could see him every day.

I read through more of them becoming bored by the second. Chiyo had always been the town gossip, and her newspaper collection was legendary, though Goro started her on clipping them and recycling anything older than five years. Otherwise her home would have been a fire hazard. It was just like her to find out I was returning to town and try to catch me up on everything Chikata related.

The second to last article made me stop and pay attention. Another news story about my old high school, the one where Tama currently taught, boasted about the after school clubs' successes. In a photo of Tama with teenage kids in the woods, he pointed at plants and the kids examined them. The caption read, *"Tama Kano, chemistry teacher and head of the survival skills club, uses his love and knowledge of botany to instruct students on edible wild plants."* Another inset photo showed him posing in his home garden.

Home garden. Botany. Survival skills. Edible and *non-edible* wild plants. Poisonous plants.

I jerked my hand out and reached for my computer, powering it on and heading straight for my browser. I googled, "Japanese poisonous plants" and clicked on the top link entitled "Three Major Poisonous Plants in Japan." Aconitum, or Wolfsbane, was the top number one plant on the list. I'd seen these purple flowers all around the area, and I'd always known they should never be picked, but I didn't know they were *this* poisonous. Wikipedia said, "If ingested, the initial signs of poisoning are gastrointestinal including nausea, vomiting, and diarrhea. This is followed by a sensation of burning, tingling, and numbness in the mouth and face, and burning in the abdomen."

Senahara said Kano had stomach problems for a few months until one day he suddenly got better. Is it possible that...? No. I examined the photo of Tama again, smiling in his garden and with the kids he taught. But I knew he was capable of menace.

He practically threatened me in my studio. He had seemed cold and aloof, not warm and paternal like he did in these photos.

Had he used his knowledge of poisonous plants to try to kill his own father? And when that didn't work, he smothered him?

A wave of chills traveled up my spine and made all the hair on my head stand up. I felt sick imagining this. How did Tama do it? Slip it in Kano's food? He would have had to be at the house every day and put it in food his father ate regularly. That seemed impractical. Maybe he made a liquid of it? Put it in his saké? But then Tama may have accidentally poisoned Akiko as well, and Akiko had never complained of being sick.

I closed my computer and imagined every possibility. I walked through their house in my head and tried to remember everything I last saw when I was there — the kotatsu, the pile of tins next to the TV, the stack of blankets. Nothing jumped out at me. It had to be something!

I picked up the phone and dialed Akiko. It was almost 8:00, and she must have been getting ready for work or on her way out.

"Morning, Mei. How are you?"

"I'm good," I said, playing cool. "I was just cleaning my room before heading out for a run."

She laughed. "Won't that take a solid week?"

"Ha, ha. Funny. Yes, it was super messy but I couldn't find my running clothes. Hey, I was wondering about something..."

"What's that?"

"Remember when your dad was sick over the summer?"

"Yeah," she said, sighing. "He was sick every day for a few months. Lost a lot of weight."

"What was wrong with him?"

She hesitated, and it sounded like she was opening a car door. "They thought it was a parasite or something. So we put him on a restricted diet and gave him antibiotics and he felt better after that."

"And that was it?"

"Yep. Sad that he had to be sick so long before he died of something totally unrelated. Tama says the police think he killed himself. I don't know..." Her voice fell off. "Anyway, it's over now, and I can't bring him back."

Over now? That was a weird choice of words.

"Akiko, maybe he was poisoned all those months he was sick?"

Silence for a few heartbeats. "Poisoned? Mei, what's gotten into you?" Her voice sounded angry, so I began to backpedal.

"Nothing, nothing. I was just thinking—"

"Please. Poisoned? That's ridiculous. Look, I'm on my way to my first patient of the day, so I have to go. Just..." She sighed again, sounding as worn out and tired as she did a few days ago. "Just let this go. I know you want to help, but continually dredging this back up again is too much. I need to move on."

"Okay. I'm sorry. Really. I just wanted to help."

"Don't."

"Okay."

"I've gotta go. I'll see you tomorrow night at the Kutsuro Matsu opening. Let's put this all behind us."

"Okay. Sure. I'll see you tomorrow."

We hung up and I looked between the phone and the clippings of Tama. I couldn't help feeling that this was the missing piece of the puzzle. It set off every warning bell in my head. Didn't Goro tell me to go with my gut?

I dialed him, thinking that if anyone was going to take me seriously, he would.

"Poisoned? Are you kidding me?" Goro's voice raised almost an entire octave. "Whatever gave you that idea?"

Refusing to work properly, my voice cracked and my lips bumbled. "He was sick for a long time with stomach problems. What if Tama had tried to poison him and it didn't work? So he moved on to smothering his father when he didn't get results."

"You realize you're describing a cold-blooded killer, right? Do you really think Tama is capable of that?"

I didn't know! I held two very distinct images in my head of Tama and neither of them seemed real anymore.

"No." In my heart, I hoped Tama wasn't capable of that. If he was, I was in deep trouble.

"We're running out of ideas, and the prosecutor is close to moving on since we have no real suspects. You know they only ever go to court if the evidence is rock solid. Tama hasn't complained about the death of his father, and Akiko is the only other person mentioned in the will. With no one throwing an uproar and no evidence, this will die out and be done with in no time."

I nodded at the phone, a tear leaking out of my eye, down my nose, and falling onto my robe. The poor man. He never had a chance.

"I'll see you tomorrow, Mei. You've done good work here. Don't forget that."

"Thanks."

I hung up the phone and glanced over at my running shoes. I should've gotten dressed and headed on out. I should've put this behind me. No one cared enough about Kano's death to do anything about it. Tama was untouchable. Akiko was resigned. And now the police were ready to move on, too. Mom still cared, but who else could I persuade to my side?

I scrolled through my address book until I saw Yasahiro's full name.

"Morning, Mei. How'd you sleep?" His voice sounded tired but not depressed. Nothing like Akiko's.

"Did I wake you?"

"No, but I'm still in bed." I imagined him warm in his apartment, tucked into bed, maybe reading something on his phone when I called. I wondered what he wore to sleep in. "Mei?"

"Sorry. I was just, uh, cleaning my room." Nope. I was daydreaming about being in bed with him and what that would be like. My brain was all over the place. "And I found these old newspaper clippings about Tama."

"What were they about?" he asked, yawning again.

"He's the head of a survival skills club at his school."

"Oh, I did that for a year. I was a pro at the wild vegetables. I've been picking those things since I was a kid."

"I'm not surprised, considering."

He laughed. "I still go out and pick them in the summer. I miss that. Winter is not my favorite season."

"Me neither." Despite the fact I was going to go out for a run, I lied down in bed and pretended I was next to him. "I wanted to ask you about something. Because I called Akiko and Goro, and they both think I'm nuts."

"I doubt that, though I think you're crazy to always be running away from me. Come on. I'm not that scary."

I couldn't believe he could make me blush over the phone. "Sorry."

"Anyway, what's up?"

I told him my theory about Tama and the poison, and he hummed on the other end.

"Maybe the problem here is that you're all too close to him to see him for who he is now." I sat up in bed and stared out the window. Huh? "You've known him his whole life, so your vision is colored by what you already know."

"Hmmm, maybe so."

"I barely know Tama. I've seen him around town a lot, heard about him through Chiyo or Haruka, and then I've talked to him a few times at Izakaya Jūshi. If you told me he was arrested because he poisoned his father to death, I'd believe it."

"Really?"

"Absolutely. You know what I don't like about him? He looks

straight through you. When he talks to me, it's like he isn't looking at me, he's looking at someone right behind me. He's distant, like he's here but not. It's hard to explain. It reminds me of some of the books I read. He's out of phase with reality, living in an alternate universe."

I imagined Tama, fading out from the world, slowly, his form becoming indistinct and hazy.

"It's the look of a psychopath, I swear," he said, yawning.

"Why didn't you say anything before?"

"Before? When?"

"Before we went to Izakaya Jūshi." It was Yasahiro's idea to go and find Tama there, to hopefully ask him questions and find out more about what he was up to.

"Ah. Well, I wanted to go on a date with you. It didn't turn out the way I planned. I thought he wouldn't show up and we'd spend the evening talking and drinking, and I'd take you home and kiss you."

I laughed at the sincerity of his confession. "You got the ending you wanted."

"I hope to get the whole package next time. Remember, I said I'd woo you. Speaking of which, any chance you're available on Thursday night? We could go to the city for the evening. I know a great rooftop place to have drinks and then we can head to my friend's restaurant. I'd take you on a Friday or Saturday, but Sawayaka is booked solid for Friday and Saturday night through the end of January, and I have to be there."

"I understand. I'm fine with Thursday night. It's not like I have to be at work the next day."

"Exactly. And I'll see you tomorrow night. I'm catering so I have to be there early with the van and everything."

"Okay. I'll see you then. Have a good day, Yasahiro."

"You too, Mei."

I hung up and stared out the window. I hadn't been seeing my world with fresh eyes. All of my daydreams and thoughts were based on two decades of seeing the same faces, the same buildings, the same relationships.

Yasahiro had seen everyone here for the first time in the last year, and if he thought Tama had the look of a psychopath, then I had no reason to doubt him.

I had every reason to doubt everything else.

CHAPTER
THIRTY

Chiyo's bathhouse, Kutsuro Matsu, was bright and cheery when Mom and I entered the following evening. Mom decided to wear a kimono, but I knew the inside would be hot, so I opted for one of my lighter black dresses under a wool coat. Most of the town would be in and out all evening, and the place was prepped and ready to go. Kumi smiled and bowed when we slid open the front door.

"Welcome, welcome!" She launched towards me with a big hug and I squeezed her back. "I've missed you this last week! I wish you had come by for a visit, but I know how hard it is to plan anything without a phone."

That, and I tried to save money on gas and not drive everywhere, plus the weather had been very spotty for October so walking had been out of the question.

"I promise to come often and use the bath now that it's open, as long as there's a family discount." I winked at her and she nodded eagerly.

"Chiyo says you're on the VIP list, which means you pay nothing, of course."

I pumped my fist and Mom laughed. "It's good to know

people in high places. Between free hot baths here and free food at Sawayaka, I'll be clean and fed through the winter."

"Speaking of which," Kumi said, taking my arm and leading me to Chiyo's office. "Your man is in there."

"Stop," I hissed at her, smacking her arm. "He's not 'my man.'"

"Oh yes he is. Supposedly, he can't stop talking about you. All the kitchen staff at Sawayaka know you're dating." She lowered her voice. "Why didn't you tell me?"

"I... I didn't believe it was true." Honesty was my policy tonight, especially if I'd be drinking.

"Of course it's true! I could tell right away you'd be a good couple."

Inside the office, coats hung on temporary coat racks, and Chiyo gathered leaflets designed for the new customers.

"Are we talking about Mei and Mr. Suga?" Chiyo asked, her face lighting up like Akihabara at night.

My jaw tightened in response. Everyone always in my business!

"We are indeed. Aren't we happy, Mom?"

"Ecstatic. What a catch for our Mei."

I cleared my throat. "Yasahiro is not a dog or a bear you catch. He's a man with his own ideas." I lifted my chin, trying to be haughty and possibly diffuse some of this embarrassment, but both women laughed and clutched each other's arms.

"Did you hear that? She called him by his first name!" Kumi melted into a puddle. I backed away slowly. "No one calls him that around here."

"I've gotta go." I turned on my eight centimeter heels and sprinted from the office before they could grill me anymore.

The front entryway was packed with people, my mom nowhere in sight. Both doors to the men's and women's side of the bathhouse were open and people came and went from each. I was closer to the women's side, and people left there with glasses of champagne and small plates of food, so I chose that direction.

I should have prepared myself ahead of time. Standing inside the room, several groups of people I knew turned to watch me enter. It was a good thing I worked hard all afternoon on my appearance. I tamed my hair and found my favorite red lipstick to go with the black dress and high heels. I painted my stubby nails with dark gray nail polish and buffed every bit of skin I could reach. But even though I stood tall, clean and presentable, the dirt of the farm weighed heavily on my shoulders.

Music played in the room, soft enough to be heard but not too loud because the tiled room bounced noise everywhere. In a corner, Haruka, Tama, and their friends whispered and jerked their heads in my direction, then looked at my painting on the wall. My stomach sank as I focused on Yasahiro standing and staring at it. Great. I thought he would never see it because it was on the women's side of the bathhouse. I didn't think about today.

I wanted to walk out of the room and never go back. I'd learned a lot about myself these past few weeks, especially that I would avoid conflict at all costs. *Go, Mei!*

"Hey, Mei," Haruka called to me, my cover blown. "That's an... interesting painting."

"It was never my favorite," Tama said to her. "But then, I didn't like anything she painted." Tama stared in my direction, but his gaze was as Yasahiro described, cold and vacant. I tried to glance at Yasahiro to see if he was witnessing this. "Did Chiyo really pay you for this?"

My entire body grew hot with rage. I wanted to yell at him that, of course, I was paid for that painting. The supplies alone cost 10,000 yen! Not to mention the hours that went into it. But Haruka and her friends snickered, and I lost my confidence.

A glass of champagne and a plate of food slid in front of my face along with the smile of Yasahiro.

"There you are. I was wondering when you'd get here. For

you." He handed me the glass and plate, and then leaned forward and kissed my cheek, a slow press of his lips to my jaw line near my ear, my skin burning on contact.

"You look lovely." He rested his hand on my back between my shoulder blades, and his face changed to shock as his fingers dipped into the ripples of my burn scars down the entirety of my rib cage to my waist. I knew this black dress was light, but I didn't think he'd touch me. Why don't I ever think? I should have worn a sweater.

"I... I..." His voice tapered off, his skin whitening. His lips tightened in a line as he dropped his hand away. I felt as if my soul was trying to crawl out of my mouth and limp away. I couldn't fix this so I leaned into his ear.

"It's okay if you're disgusted. I totally understand." And I did. I expected it. No one wanted to date someone physically damaged. I was lucky I could keep the mottled and snarled skin covered most of the time. I didn't go to beaches or bathe in pools with strangers. When I went to the onsen, I went with my family or close friends who wouldn't be freaked out because I had been kicked out of an onsen when I was a teen. The owner thought I had a disease and made a huge deal out of it. I was happy Chiyo owned this bathhouse because I'd be welcomed here.

Yasahiro did his best to pretend like nothing happened. He stood next to me, silent, his eyes searching the room. A distance widened between us, from a fissure to a canyon. I had to give myself credit for being as positive as I had been about our relationship. If he had been any other guy, I probably would've ignored him and pushed him far away at first flirt. But I let it get to this point, and it was good while it lasted.

I resigned myself and kissed him in the exact same place he kissed me, feeling like it might be a good moment to savor his closeness before he bolted. If his skin were any colder, he'd be dead.

I kept my eyes on the floor as I made my way from the room

with my alcohol and food, but as I reached the door, Yasahiro's voice rose above everyone else's. "It's the most beautiful painting I've ever seen, Mei. I'm lucky to be dating such a talented woman."

My knees weakened, but I managed to look over my shoulder to him and nod with a smile.

"I'm the lucky one."

I SAT IN A CORNER OF THE MEN'S WASHROOM, SURROUNDED by Mom's friends, and drank until my face flushed and the world around me turned fuzzy. If only Kumi hadn't been busy. I would've much rather chatted with her, but she was floating around, her head in the clouds and a giant smile on her face. I wished I had something awesome to be happy about like her. This bathhouse was the perfect opportunity, to work with her family and run a real establishment. She deserved all this happiness.

I texted Akiko an hour ago, asking where she was, and she wrote back that she got held up with a patient she had to escort to the hospital. I hoped that wasn't too stressful for her. She'd just gotten back to work. I doubted she'd be able to handle another death right now.

Yasahiro came by a few times, mostly working the crowd, talking about business or the food or the drinks, and conferring with Chiyo about what she wanted or needed. His work would be done soon and then maybe we could sit and talk, try to overcome what happened earlier. I didn't know if that was possible, but I had to reach him, make him understand that my scars didn't, shouldn't, matter. That was never an easy conversation to have, and I'd had it with previous boyfriends, all of which left me because of it. I didn't expect this to be any different, but I would try, nonetheless. I remembered how he recovered from the shock gracefully. Perhaps with time, he would accept all of my flaws.

I gulped down the last of my champagne as another glass was handed to me.

"That Yasahiro is a fine looking young man," one of Mom's friends crooned at me.

I couldn't tell any of them how sick I was of hearing this. I betted no one complimented him on dating me.

I raised my glass to her. "He has a nice ass, for sure."

"Mei," Mom admonished me. She turned and Yasahiro stood right behind her. He laughed at me, raising his eyebrows.

"It's true," I said, shrugging my shoulders. The truth in champagne form was very flattering.

My phone buzzed in my bag as the women pursed their lips and returned to gossiping. It was Akiko. *"I'll be there in five minutes tops. I'm walking up the street now. Going to talk to Tama first and then I'll find you."*

"Great!" I texted back. I'd have someone I could talk to until Yasahiro was free, and it'd been ages since Akiko and I drank together. I missed hanging out with her.

"Mei." Goro appeared at the door and headed straight for me. He was still dressed in his uniform and seemed too serious to be at this fine party. "Can I speak with you for a moment?" He jerked his head in the direction of the front entry.

"Sure," I said, excusing myself from the circle of ladies. I caught Yasahiro's eye, and we smiled and waved to each other. Goro glanced between Yasahiro and me, his keen eyes detecting everything in our little gestures.

Activity had died down in the front entry, the open space vacant since the party moved into the two main rooms. Funny that tomorrow, the baths would be filled and each room would be populated with naked people.

"Hey, so, Kumi tells me you and Yasahiro are dating. She's just joking around, right?"

I glanced around the room a few times and sighed. "Is that really what you called me out here for?"

"No. Sorry. I was just surprised, that's all."

I threw my hands up. "Why? Why is *that* surprising? Of all the things lately to be surprising, you think Yasahiro dating me is worth lumping into that group?"

His face grew pale. "Kumi is going to kill me. Sorry, Mei. That's not why I pulled you out here. We got a call at the station an hour ago and I went to follow up on it, which is why I wasn't here. That second patient of Akiko's that we tried to interview confessed. She said Akiko did come to examine her that day, but she had taken money from a young man the day after to report to the nursing agency that Akiko was missing from her duties."

"What?" I grabbed his arms and shook my head.

"That's why she didn't want to speak with us. She was lying about Akiko. Akiko *had* been there but someone paid this woman to say she hadn't."

"Who?" My ears rang. I already knew the answer.

"It had to have been Tama. I have her waiting down at the station now, and I'm going to bring him in for a line-up. I thought I would show her a picture of him, but that would have tainted the whole case. She described him pretty perfectly though."

I made sure no one was listening and turned back to Goro. "You're way out of place in your uniform. You should take off your coat, at least. Look like you're here to stay. Tama is in the women's area with Haruka and their friends. Do you have backup coming?"

He shook his head. "They're at least fifteen minutes from coming. There was a meeting in the next town over, and I wanted to make this as low profile as possible."

Right. Because if the woman didn't identify Tama, then we'd have to let him go, and we didn't want everyone in town to think he was a suspect. We headed into the office, and he left his coat while I grabbed mine. "Akiko is on her way here. I'm going outside and I'll meet her so she doesn't get in the middle of this."

Throwing on my coat and leaving Goro in the office, I slid open the front door and headed out into the cold. If she parked in the town lot, she'd be coming from the left, so I started to walk in that direction, reaching into my coat for my phone and finding nothing. Damn. My phone was in my purse in the bathhouse where I just left it.

I didn't walk farther than the side alley when her voice came from the area at the back of the bathhouse.

"But you didn't do anything! Why is it all taken care of?... Hey, don't. Stop!" Her voice echoed off the brick pavers and hardened clay walls. I froze, terrified, my skin prickling all over. She sounded scared right before she stopped talking. The click of a car door opening and shuffling of metal objects bounced towards me. Someone was still out in the back of the bathhouse. I unstuck my feet and started a slow creep down the alley, hastening my steps since I didn't hear anything anymore. Maybe she went inside through the back door?

A van came into view, its back doors both open and no one around. As I got closer, I found a pair of high heeled shoes discarded on the ground outside the van.

"Hello? Akiko?" My heart pumped so hard I could hear my own heartbeat in my ears. It was deafening, and I couldn't breathe. I nudged open the van's doors further and Akiko was passed out inside next to aluminum chafer pans, food trays, and serving utensils.

A strong arm wrapped around me from behind, clasping my arms down. "Hey!" I screamed, but the sound cut off as I was hit upside my head. I struggled to free myself as another hand came to my face, smothering me in a sickly sweet scent, before a wall of black descended upon me.

CHAPTER
THIRTY-ONE

"Oh my god, wake up, Mei. *Wake up!*"

Something hit my leg as my brain slowly unfolded from unconsciousness. One layer of blackness peeled away from another and light faded into my eyes as I tried to come to grips with my surroundings. I was just at the bathhouse, but I wasn't there anymore. Coldness from a hard surface seeped up through my hind end, my hands in pain behind my back. An ether-like cotton-stuffed sensation, sweet, with an aftertaste of champagne filled my mouth.

"Why isn't she waking up? Wake up, Mei!"

Akiko? That sounded like Akiko. Oh no. The last thing I remembered was Akiko passed out in Yasahiro's van. A wave of sickness flowed up my body. Was Yasahiro the killer? Had I fallen for a monster? I never suspected him!

"It doesn't matter why she's not waking up. It would be better if she slept through it all."

All the blood in my body cooled, and I began to shiver as I opened my eyes and found Tama standing over me with a gas can. He was still dressed in his fancy dress shirt and pants from the party, but his sleeves were rolled up. He examined me and his sister with clinical detachment before shrugging his shoulders.

"There. She's awake. Happy?" he asked Akiko, also next to me on the floor. He turned from us and walked around. I was in my own barn, tied to the pole next to the tractor, my artist loft space above me.

My head throbbed so hard I had to close my eyes against the pain.

"Don't go back to sleep. We have to get out of here," Akiko whispered to me, but I couldn't speak. The room around me washed back and forth, like a boat out to sea in rough waters.

"He chloroformed us. You were drinking at the party, right?"

I swallowed a few times and found my voice. "Yeah. I can't move."

But I could smell, and I smelled the sharp scent of gasoline. It was so strong I gagged and Akiko retched. This was not good. Not good at all.

I breathed through my mouth and tried to take stock of the situation. My brain was slow, so I kicked it into gear by blinking and tapping the back of my head against the pole I was tied to.

Tama must have been waiting in the shadows once he heard me coming around the corner at the bathhouse, knocked me out, threw me in Yasahiro's catering van, and took off. How did he have keys to the van? Didn't matter. He got them somehow — picked them from Yasahiro's jacket in the office or maybe he left them in the van. I had no idea.

Tama with a gas can in his hand could mean only one thing. He'd been inspired by my painting and wanted to sacrifice me by fire. Yasahiro thought he might be a psychopath. He was right.

My barn was the worst possible place to be. It had been built on a concrete slab but the structure was made of wood and gypsum board, not clay like most Japanese storehouses. When we knocked down the old horse barn and put up this one, we had to finance it and got the bare minimum. Admittedly, it'd been the perfect barn the last ten years but it wasn't looking so great a choice right now.

The floor above us creaked as Tama walked around my studio, knocking things to the floor, and I heard the distinct sound of canvas ripping. He'd gone mad, destroying everything he could get his hands on. The fact that he was destroying my stuff and brought us here told me he hated me more than he'd let on.

Akiko burst into tears next to me. "I'm sorry, Mei. So so sorry."

"What? Shhh, it's not your fault. Can you undo my hands?" I tried to turn and show her my hands, but they were definitely tied to the pole, and I couldn't budge them.

"It *is* my fault," she whispered at me. "I knew he was poisoning Dad. I figured it out after a couple of months. Dad was drinking this tea Tama bought for him, and he was always sick afterward. I saw a piece of dried purple flower in it and figured it out." She dissolved into a sob, and I shrank away from her. "I knew, and I didn't tell anyone. I couldn't turn in my own brother. I replaced the tea, and Dad got better. I thought Tama would give up—"

"I didn't," he said, hopping down the stairs, the gas can splashing along with him. Something wet fell on me from above. I looked up and gas was dripping down through the slats of the loft. Drip, drip, drip on my head.

Panic stopped all thought, pushing everything into a tiny box in my brain. I couldn't breathe. I sucked in air and nothing happened.

"If you had just let Dad drink the tea, we wouldn't be here today." He pulled a pack of matches from his pocket. "It's time to end it. I'm ready to move on."

"Move on where?" Akiko screamed at him. "You think people aren't going to know you did this?" Her voice squeaked and raised an octave. "Help!" she shouted, tilting her head back.

I struggled with whatever he used to bind me, but I did nothing but injure myself more.

"No one will rescue you, and no one will figure it out. I've covered my tracks. Mei wanted to show you her new paintings, so she borrowed Yasahiro's van and drove out here. She was careless with her space heater and set the place on fire. I'll untie you once you pass out." He gestured to a bottle of chloroform on the table. "After your funerals, I'll sell the house and land, and I'll persuade Haruka to move to Chiba. Everything will be easier with you both gone."

"You're crazy."

"Maybe so." He lit a match, calmly walked over to the stairs, and threw the match onto the first step. It whooshed up into flames, and the panic ran down my body, grabbed hold of my chest, and squeezed until I hyperventilated. All of those books I read when I was a teen about amateur sleuths catching the killer and getting themselves out of sticky situations were beginning to look a whole lot like fiction.

Tama turned to us, and everything inside me died. His expression was exactly as Yasahiro described, cold and calculating, like he didn't actually see us, didn't feel anything as his sister and former girlfriend sat in a barn erupting into flames. The young man I once loved was gone, obliterated. Why? Why had this happened to him?

Flames traveled up the stairs one by one, lighting and dancing. Fire evoked a deep fear in me, the kind of fear that seized my mind and threatened to take me under once more.

Tama put on his coat and zipped up. "I always knew fire would be your undoing, Mei. You should have died all those years ago. You had a second chance, and look what you did with it. Nothing." He laughed without humor, his voice bitter deep. "Your mother loved you so much, always bragging about you to everyone. On and on and on about your talent and how successful you'd be. It made me sick. Then Akiko told me how

you kept losing your jobs and had a string of terrible boyfriends."
The small smile on his lips gutted me. "You deserved that. I've
wanted to destroy you for years, and now's my chance."

I wanted to shout at him that I was already a failure,
destroyed in heart, mind, and body, and that he didn't have to do
this, but the heated air swirling around me told me it was too late.
I thought I'd have a chance to change things with a new life at
home, with Yasahiro, but now I had nothing.

"Tama!" Akiko's hoarse voice squeaked. Smoke filled the
space. "Don't do this!"

The door to the barn flew open, and I thought for a moment,
"It's the police! Come to rescue us!" But no. It was Senahara, the
only neighbor left in the area.

He may have been old, but he was spry and fast. He yelled a
high-pitched battle cry, a samurai sword lifted above his head,
and charged at Tama. Tama, unprepared for an attack, shrieked
and crouched low, raising his arms up to shield himself. Senahara
hesitated, realization spreading across his features. Here was his
best friend's son and he was charging in to kill him? Tama took
advantage of the pause and swept his leg to knock Senahara over.

"We're tied up," Akiko shouted. "Kill him!"

"Stop!" I yelled at her, watching Senahara roll to the side.

"I'm sorry, Mei," she said, sobbing. "So sorry. Please forgive
me. Please."

Senahara jumped up into a crouch position in time to stop
Tama from running for the door. Tama dodged right and Senahara lunged forward, stabbing him in the leg. I closed my eyes
briefly and opened them to Tama screaming and rolling around
on the ground, clutching his leg.

I swore loudly, trying to process the confrontation, the barn
burning, and Akiko and me prisoners. "I forgive you," I said to
Akiko. I didn't know if I did, but it seemed like the right thing
to say.

Senahara stood over Tama, his chest heaving. "I knew it was

you." He raised the sword high and brought it down into Tama's shoulder. I cringed and screamed, closing my eyes against his pain. But thank god for Senahara! I always thought that sword was just decorative, but he could use it.

While Akiko screamed, I tried to lengthen my body and reach the wall of tools next to the tractor. Even with my legs fully extended though, I was at least a half a meter away and I couldn't make myself longer. Smoke detectors blared and shrieked, and the loft popped, shooting sparks down on us.

We were dead if we didn't get out quick. I couldn't reach anything, and I had nothing on me I could use to cut my hands free before Senahara had dealt with Tama.

A loud pop exploded above us, and I dipped my head down in time for a rain of sparks and wood to come down on me. My jacket sleeve lit on fire, my mouth opened, and I screamed, the most terrifying feeling of hatred and dread washing over me.

Senahara, satisfied that Tama was incapacitated, jumped around the fiery debris, threw off his coat, and put out the fire on my arm. I burbled thanks at him, pain searing through my arm and shoulder, as he grabbed a pair of gardening shears. A fit of coughs overtook us as more debris fell down from above, but this time it hit the tractor. We had moments left before it all came down.

Reaching for my hands, Senahara's eyes were watering, and he hesitated over my bindings.

"Cut me loose! I don't care if you hurt me."

Akiko had passed out, probably from smoke inhalation. Suddenly, my hands were free, and I still had all my fingers.

"Grab her legs," I called out as I took the shears and freed Akiko's hands. I bent over and grabbed her shoulders, another piece of the loft falling and hitting me on my back, knocking me to the side. I groaned as I struggled to my feet again and dragged her to the door with Senahara's help. We jolted past Tama as he tried to grab at my legs, but I kicked him in the face and he let go.

I didn't care if he died in the barn. He could go to hell as far as I was concerned.

"You're on fire!" Senahara screamed, and I felt my back heating and smelled singed hair. Adrenaline spiked through my legs and arms, and I threw Akiko through the doorway and fell to the ground, rolling side to side to put the fire out, pain shooting from my back and my arm.

Lights approached the house, police lights atop a speeding car, but I couldn't stand up, so I rolled over a few more times to put distance between me and the barn. In through the door, Tama struggled to get out, making it past the threshold and limping away. I watched helplessly as Mom's store of sweet potatoes and winter squash caught fire and began to smoke. Flames crawled up the wall, shooting through to the outside and climbing to the roof, already half engulfed in fire from the loft.

A short period of silence preceded a deafening crack. The loft inside the barn gave way and crashed down inside, sending an explosion out both doors and breaking the windows. I covered my head and cried. I cried and screamed, terror leaking out through my eyes and mouth. Fire. I hated fire! Fear paralyzed me and I couldn't move.

A pair of hands came down roughly on my shoulders and legs, and thinking it must be Tama back to finish the job, I kicked and screamed.

"Mei!" Goro and Yasahiro leaned into my face so I could see them.

My body went limp with exhaustion and relief. Goro leaned over and picked me up, running me farther away from the barn. "Is anyone else inside?"

"No." I coughed and hacked, trying to breathe in, but my lungs hurt and felt like they were the size of a bean. "Tama. Getting away."

"We got him. Don't worry."

Goro hoisted me into the backseat of his car and took out his flashlight to shine on me. He examined my face and down my torso once, then stepped out of the way to let Yasahiro in.

"We need two fire trucks and ambulances at the Yamagawa estate on route 53, San-dōri, now!" Goro screamed into his radio.

My eyes focused on the barn, completely engulfed in flames. Yasahiro snapped his fingers in my face.

"Mei, look at me," he demanded. I turned my face to him, and his cheeks were covered in sooty tears. "What happened?"

"I... I was looking for Akiko. Tama knocked us out and drove us here. He tried to kill us."

Senahara appeared over Yasahiro's shoulder, his katana sheathed and tucked into his waistband. "I was out drinking on the porch. I like when it's cold and I can see the stars." He directed his eyes up at the night sky, obscured by smoke. "I heard screams and thought it was people getting drunk and arguing. Then I saw the barn catch fire, so I grabbed my sword and ran. I didn't see anyone else around and sped up when I heard Akiko scream for help. I'm afraid I hurt Tama pretty badly."

Next to the police car, Tama laid on the ground, handcuffed, and Goro's partner was putting pressure on his wounds.

"Serves him right," Yasahiro mumbled. Senahara nodded at him.

I rested my head against the seat of the car, wincing at my shoulder, the skin hot and painful.

Yasahiro grabbed my hands and squeezed. "I came out to get my phone from the van and the van was gone." He hung his head. "I'm always losing my phone, leaving it places I can't find it. Always. So I turned on that Find My Phone feature ages ago. I had Goro access the GPS data for it, and we saw the van had been driven here. We wouldn't have made it in time if Senahara hadn't found you."

The two men embraced quickly, in an uncharacteristic fashion. "Thank you," Yasahiro said to him. Senahara nodded and walked away.

"I just met you and I almost lost you. My heart..." He touched my face and kissed my forehead as I wheezed and tried to breathe. "My heart would never have recovered."

An ambulance drove up the long driveway and came to a screeching, gravel-throwing stop next to Goro's car.

"Come on. You need help." Yasahiro helped me up and walked me to the waiting paramedics. I closed my eyes and turned my face away from the fire-consumed barn.

"You had a second chance, and look what you did with it. Nothing." Tama's words echoed in my aching head.

Looks like I get a third chance, Tama.

And I was going to make it count.

CHAPTER
THIRTY-TWO

The air was crisp and cold, my breath fogging in front of my face, as I tightened my scarf around my neck. The streets around the starting line were packed with people, so I walked through the crowd slowly, edging around spectators and runners as Mom and I got closer to our destination.

"Kumi said they'd be over on the northeast corner," Mom said, pointing in the direction of a colorful banner held up by balloon arches.

I kept my eyes alert for danger, though there may have been no need. Tama was in jail, and I hoped I'd never see him again, but I couldn't let my guard down. He confessed to dozens of crimes in a plea for leniency. He admitted to poisoning and killing his father because he wanted to sell the land to pay his debts. He had made friends in the mob, blew his savings gambling with them, and owed them money. Akiko and I didn't die in the fire like Tama intended, and now we would be in danger for the rest of our lives. I imagined hitmen around every corner, lying in wait for me in the house every time I came home, tracking me down to collect on Tama's debt.

In my head, I replayed Tama's words over and over, *"Your*

mother loved you so much, always bragging about you to everyone. On and on and on about your talent and how successful you'd be. It made me sick." I thought long and hard while recovering about how he slashed and destroyed my paintings before he set fire to the barn, making my destruction deep and personal. Jealousy had driven him mad. His desire to hurt me made me fold in on myself, like a broken origami crane, and I became worried about how I was perceived by others and wanted to be as small and insignificant as possible. I had to fight the urge to become a hermit every day.

But now, my eyes fell on Kumi and Chiyo gathered around Goro, who was running today's race, thankfully fully clothed. He was decked out from head to toe in winter running gear, looking fit and smiling.

"There you are!" Chiyo called to us as we approached. "I was worried you wouldn't make it."

We all leaned in to hug, and everyone took care not to squeeze me too hard. The burn on my shoulder was a second degree whopper and still smarted. The ones on my back were only first degree burns, but the skin was already damaged. This new back burn would take longer to heal.

"I'm sorry we're late!" I said, as Goro leaned in to give me a kiss on the cheek. We were closer than we ever were. He and Kumi came to visit me and Akiko often in the hospital as we recovered from the smoke inhalation. Akiko had had it worse than I did. She was on oxygen for a long time, but she didn't sustain any burns. She had already returned to work. "And I'm sorry again that I'm not running the race with you, Goro. I really wanted to."

"It's fine," he said, jumping in place and pumping his knees to his chest. "I've been running every day since the fire. I'm ready."

Kumi's eyes widened and sparkled. "I'm so proud of him. He's been working hard to get ready for this."

"I'm going to train for the marathon here next year," he said, smiling. "So, thank you, Mei, for giving me a reason to do this. I needed the kick in the pants."

"Any time."

I laughed and punched him on the shoulder.

"Hey," he said, stopping to stretch his quads, "I have a proposition for you, if you're willing to hear me out."

"Oh, oh, yes, Mei!" Chiyo danced back and forth and Kumi squealed and grabbed her arm. "You must hear this idea. I think it's fabulous."

Goro rolled his eyes and Mom laughed. It must have been complete agony to always deal with Kumi and Chiyo and their effervescent personalities. Really, though, he was one lucky guy.

"I'm hoping that you'll always help on any criminal investigations, just like this past one. I think you have the knack for it."

"Really?" My chest filled with pride. "Would it be a job?"

"No," he said, disappointed. "We couldn't hire you, unless you went through the formal training. But our captain loves you and would like your help, if you can give it."

I understood it wasn't a job that would pay, so I tried to control my excitement, though it leaked out to my face. A few months ago, I would have given anything to return to the city and not come back to Chikata. Now, both Mom and Akiko needed my help, the police needed my help, and I didn't want to leave Yasahiro either. He'd been the best boyfriend ever the last few weeks, bringing me food in the hospital, sitting with me, watching TV, holding my hand and talking about his time in Paris. I loved hearing those stories. He even fell asleep there several times, wanting to be close to me while I healed. I was falling for him, hard, and I hoped we could continue without any more crazy interruptions.

"Wow, that sounds like a great opportunity. I'd love to help out."

I still needed to find a real job, though. A real job in Chikata would be a huge turning point for me. It would be that third

chance I needed to make my life worth living. Tama thought he
was going to destroy all of this. He would have *loved* to destroy
my life and my happiness, but I couldn't let him. Even if I
succeeded in a small and quiet way, it would be enough.

Kumi pumped her fist by her side. "See? I told you she'd be
into it."

"You did," Goro deadpanned. "I'll let my boss know you're
interested. Okay?"

"Okay." I just had to make it through the winter with Mom.
She was certain the insurance money for the barn would come
soon and we could continue on with our lives. We had very little
budgetary leeway since we lost our vegetable stores and my
painting supplies in the fire, plus her extra money was tied up in
investments. All in all, the fire would cost us a whole lot in both
money and comfort.

The crowd surged to the starting line, racers gathering into a
pack of people as spectators moved to the sidelines. Goro waved
to us from the crowd, and we waved back.

This race was supposed to be something completely different. It was supposed to signify my win of the challenge to find out
who killed Kano. Instead, Goro was running in my place, and I
was lucky to be alive. My phone buzzed in my pocket with a text
from Yasahiro. *"Let me know how the race goes. I can't wait to see
you later."* I smiled down at his words and took a deep breath as
the starting horn blasted and the runners took off.

My life in Chikata wasn't over. It was just beginning.

THANK YOU!

Thank you so much for reading *The Daydreamer Detective*. I hope you enjoyed your time in Chikata! This is certainly not the end for Mei and her adventures, so please stay tuned!

If you want the next book in the series... *The Daydreamer Detective Braves The Winter* is now available!

Please leave a review of *The Daydreamer Detective* wherever you purchased it. I welcome all reviews positive or negative. Reviews are so important to both authors and readers.

Want news of upcoming books, events, or free stuff? Subscribe to Steph's mailing list at https://www.stephgennaro.com/subscribe/

If you want more books like this one, you can check for more books on my website at http://www.stephgennaro.com/books/

A NOTE ABOUT CHANGES TO
THIS BOOK

In Japanese, the most common way of showing respect to another person's social standing is with the use of honorific suffixes that are appended on the end of either first or last names. The most common, -san, means either Mr., Ms., or Mrs.

In earlier versions of this book, and in the whole series, I did use these honorific suffixes. But for 2019 and onward, I have switched to the English way in order to make this series more accessible to English speakers. I hope you enjoy this version!

The town in this novel, Chikata, is completely fictional, though the area I put it in is not. Saitama prefecture is located to the west of Tokyo, and many of the eastern areas are considered to be suburbs of the city. Chikata is located farther out west, nearer to the prefectures of Nagano and Gunma.

ACKNOWLEDGMENTS

It's always hard for me to end a novel with the acknowledgments! I feel like the writing is truly done and over with when I get to this point, and I never want it to end!

Biggest thanks goes to my critique partner, Tracy Krimmer. She continues to be my sounding board and best writing buddy. I heart her.

To Amy Evans and EJ Wesley, both of whom gave me great ideas and helped me brainstorm even better ones for further books in this series. I can't wait to show you how Mei grows!

To Cori Wilbur and Christina Adcock-Azbill. They both read and gave me their best impressions of how this book did with both the character development and the mystery.

And thanks to TK Toppin for beta reading!

Thank you to my entire ARC team! You all know who you are. They get the books before anyone else, read them, and then jump at the chance to review. Reviews are so important, and this team helps me get the lead on such a daunting task. I love them!

Big thanks to Lola Verroen of Lola's Blog Tours who helped me promote this book and get some new eyes on my work.

Thanks also to Germaine Fletcher who has helped immensely with the entire series and most of my books. She is a true fan, friend, and eagle-eyed proofreader.

To my new cozy mystery writing friends, Nikki Haverstock, Rachel Blalock Bateman, Kristy Price Douglas, and the other ladies of the Cozy & Traditional Writers Facebook Group. Thanks for all your advice and general happy natures.

I continue to be grateful for my family especially my mother and father, Claire and Ray Bush, my sibling, B, and his family, my extended side of the family, Vic and Karen, all of my husband's brothers and sisters. Thanks to my girls, C and D, again for letting mommy work in the afternoons and evenings after homework was done! My husband, Keith, still thinks I'm nuts but that's okay. I still love him.

Once again, thank you Japan for continuing to be an inspiring place that makes me happy to have met your people, traveled your lands, and eaten your awesome food. You're the best.

ABOUT THE AUTHOR

Steph Gennaro is a long-time Japanophile, and she's been studying Japanese culture and language for over 20 years. She loves dreaming of far-off places, going for walks with her dog, Lulu Ninja Assassin, hanging out with her family, and reading outside in the summertime. There is no better season than summer. She's a Capricorn, mother, knitter, and web developer, and pasta is her favorite meal. Steph Gennaro is her pen name for cozy mysteries, but she also writes science fiction romance and many other genres.

Find her online at...
www.stephgennaro.com

facebook.com/StephGennaroAuthor
bookbub.com/authors/steph-gennaro

www.ingramcontent.com/pod-product-compliance
Lightning Source LLC
Chambersburg PA
CBHW031707170626
46808CB00005B/1647